Death by Séance

A Sadie Snow Historical Cozy Mystery: Book 2

Marsha Whitney

Copyright

Table of Contents

Séance Circle Seating Plan

AROUND THE CIRCLE CLOCKWISE ARE SEATED 13 FICTITIOUS CHARACTERS:

Authors Note: Between 1862 and 1865, at least four and possibly as many as eight séances were held at the Lincoln White House.

HEAD OF THE TABLE 1. Sadie, age 24, playing the part of séance medium "Belle," nearest to the entry door

2. Mary Merritt Menendez, age 47, co-owner *of Cypress Pointe Plantation*, seated on Belle's left

3. Celeste Menendez, age 22, Mary's niece, visiting New York journalist

4. Phoebe Graves Crews, age 24, blonde wife of Benjamin Crews

5. Benjamin 'Ben' Crews, age 23, recently released prisoner of war

6. Jane Marsh, age 20?, at the foot of the table, Belle's friend and housemate

7. An empty chair ___________________

FOOT OF TABLE 8. Philippe Cooper, age 35, in front of the window, half brother of Martha and Mary

9. Nanny, age 59?, dark wizened family retainer

10. Virginia Crews, age 45, perfumed, bejeweled wife of John III,

11. John Crews III, age 52, owner of neighboring plantation, *The Landing*

12. Terra Graves, age 22, botanist, Phoebe's younger sister visiting *The Landing*

13. Albert Cooper, age 14, Philippe's son

14. Martha Merritt, age 48, co-owner of *Cypress Pointe Plantation*, seated on Belle's right.

CHAPTER ONE

June 1, 1865 Early Evening at Cypress Pointe Plantation, Eau Gallie, Florida

Beneath a chandelier with its candle flames doused, a violent crash of thunder shook the plantation house dining room.

BOOM!

The lone candle in the middle of the polished mahogany table flickered and died, leaving the strong smell of candle wax in the stuffy room.

Out of the darkness came a moan.

A flash of lightning illuminated the room momentarily, and the cameo at 'Belle's' throat glinted. She said, "It's all right. Keep your hands on the tabletop around the circle. A spirit has come into our midst. Charles Merritt, father of Martha, Mary, and Philippe, if that's you, ring the bell."

"I don't like this, Sister," said Mary Merritt, a bespectacled white-haired lady, who, with her sister Martha, owned Cypress Pointe Plantation.

Playing the role of séance medium 'Belle', soberly dressed and in her brown wig, now a cascade of shoulder-length ringlets, sat Sadie Snow at the head of the table. Next to her was Mary Merritt. Sadie put a comforting hand atop Mary's wrinkled one.

On the other side of Mary was her very erect, no-frills niece Celeste, a journalist visiting from New York. Her big gray eyes assessed their situation and gave Mary's other hand a reassuring squeeze. "It'll be fun, Aunt Mary. Don't worry."

"If it's good enough for the Lincolns, it's good enough for us," said the self-assured Martha, seated across from Mary.

Belle reached for the jar of matches.

Ding!

"Oh. Unngh."

Thump!

Outside the storm raged.

Crash!

Rain lashed the window, and loose palm fronds, propelled by the gale, smacked the window glass. Thunder roared-*boooom!* Lightning flashed-*crack-* white-bright.

They all jumped

Boooo-ooom!

'Belle' said in full theatrical voice, "I feel the spirit of Master Charles, who created this plantation. Your family is gathered here, Charles. Do you have a message for us?"

Near the foot of the table, Old Nanny, a dark shrunken woman, whose bright white crocheted cap seemed to float above her, interrupted sharply. "Philippe, sit up, you rude man." With her bony elbow she reached over and poked Philippe in the side. "Will you ever grow up? Don't go ruinin' our séance with none of your shenanigans."

An assassin, a form darker than the shadows, skulked in the room. *I must watch how I go. She always did have eyes in the back of her head. And in the dark...*

The killer moved close to the walls by the furniture. *Looking for Martha. Where is Martha? I should have found her before he blew out the candle.*

"Eeeeeeeek," shrilled Mary, her voice high with fright in the dark room, which no longer felt friendly. "Something bumped me."

Celeste held her hand a bit tighter. "It's probably just the cat," she said.

"I say. Who's there?" said the deep gruff voice of John Crews III, the Merritts' neighbor here with his son on business. The pompous man, who smelled of cigars, shook his hands free and swatted the air all around him. "Did somebody put trick wires in here?"

On his right, engulfed in a cloud of floral perfume, sat his formidable wife Virginia, a striking middle-aged brunette. Her pale fingers, ablaze with sparkling rings, grabbed his hand and placed it on the table. "Of course not, dear. Put your other hand on the table next to Terra's and be still."

Rumbling continued, rattling the building.

Calm, petite, blonde botanist Terra Graves was visiting her older sister Phoebe, also blonde, who was married to Ben Crews and lived nearby at the Crews' family plantation with John and Virginia. Terra said, "I can assure you sir, I checked earlier and found no wires or hiding places."

"It's just a hoax, Father," said the gaunt, disabled, recently released prisoner of war Ben, from across the table. With his right hand he kept a firm grasp on Phoebe.

"By Jove. This isn't half a lark. Ha, ha, ha," exclaimed Philippe's 14-year-old son, Albert, from his seat between Martha and Terra. The youngster's loud raucous laugh set off a storm of noisy comments around the table.

"Be quiet, boy. I want to hear from Master Charles," said Nanny.

The candle stand scraped heavily across the table as Belle pulled it toward her.

Scratch. Scritch, scratch. She struck a match, which failed to light.

Oh, no. Better get out. Forget Martha for now.

Over the hubbub of shouting, Martha said, "Yes, Daddy? What do you want to tell us?"

With her most ghostly voice, Belle intoned, "Deleila's spirit is here. She is happy and at rest. Now, my children, I want our name Merritt to stand for the very BEST. But without modern equipment Cypress Pointe will always be a small unknown producer of rum. You must invest in new boilers..."

Kaboom!

"... improved storage, and new..."

Crash!

"EEeee."

Knock, KNOCK.

"Has the storm caused you trouble IN THERE? I heard SCREAMING. Are you ALL RIGHT?" came plantation overseer Tom's worried shout, over the noise from outside and chaos around the table. "Do you need HELP?"

Knock, Knock, KNOCK! The door burst open. The bulky form of Tom, dimly backlit by the candle in the hall sconce, stood dripping in the doorway. "Who screamed? Why is everybody in an uproar?"

Boom! The storm continued to crash around them.

Martha said, "We are fine, Tom."

Close behind him came the butler Winston, a tall, dignified dark man with a sparse black goatee beard and well-trimmed fuzzy caterpillar mustache.

"Winston, please send the footmen in here to reignite the chandelier. Meanwhile give us some light, Belle," said Martha.

After more scratching the candle flared and faintly illuminated a small area at the head of the table.

At the foot of the table, Jane Marsh, the quiet pragmatic Cuban housemate and friend of Sadie Snow said, "Philippe? Are you ill?" She rose from her seat behind the table and pointed at the man slumped near her. "I saw his hand drop from the table just after the bell rang."

They passed the candle toward Philippe and all looked. Philippe sagged forward over the table, where his handsome face lay in a dark pool.

"AAaaaaah." Phoebe screamed. "The spirit is angry. We are all in danger."

Tom, a broad-shouldered, black man of medium height, with close cropped hair, black eyes, and deep frown lines, squelched across the polished parquet floor in the semi-darkness and stopped behind his half brother. He said, "Philippe?" He pulled the limp body to a sitting position. "What is this?" he said, looking down at his hands. The overseer wiped his hands on his britches. "He isn't answering."

"I knew it. He is being punished for his past wrongs," said Nanny.

Mary said, "Nonsense. What has happened to him? 'Belle,' do something."

"Philippe, talk to us," said Martha.

Crash!

Boom!

He didn't move.

Jane stepped in front of Tom. She picked up Philippe's dangling limp hand. Her other hand she put in front of Philippe's mouth. She shook her head, looking toward 'Belle' at the other end of the table. "He isn't breathing. I think... he's dead."

'Belle' jumped up, knocking her chair back. "You're not serious, Jane?"

"Dead? He can't be," said Martha.

"Look at the three gaping holes in the back of his vest. He's been stabbed," said Jane.

"How is that possible? Our hands were on the table next to someone else's all the time. Nobody could get in. The window was locked. And we'd have seen anyone coming in through the door," said Martha.

"The spirit of Master Charles done killed Philippe," said Nanny.

As 'Belle' rushed around the table to examine Philippe, she thought, *Oh folly, fudge, and flummediddle. When I agreed to play the part of Belle at this séance for Martha and Mary, murder wasn't part of the deal.*

Nanny said, "It's a warnin' to the rest of us that he wants this plantation to change. We best be gettin' up-to-date real soon. Don't want to mess with no more vexed spirits."

I'm the stranger here. These people will think I'm Philippe's killer. Am I going to be involved in a murder investigation? Again?

I did nothing wrong, but this puts me in the spotlight... again. Police are still looking for John Booth's friends. I could find myself back in Washington – or hanging at the end of a rope.

Two weeks earlier, May 19 and 20, 1865 at Cypress Pointe Plantation in Eau Gallie, Florida

Martha and Mary cut short their vacation trip to the St. John's River and the beauties of Enterprise, Florida. They arrived home at Cypress Pointe Plantation on the Indian River at dusk of May 19, 1865. Martha said, "It's good to be home. I really love this last part of the journey. Everything feels familiar and welcoming."

"After four days of rolling around in steamers on the St. John's and the Atlantic, it was a relief to be at the helm of our own cat boat. The sail down from Saint Augustine was perfect. A perfect day for the perfect homecoming."

"We're lucky the wind cooperated, so we could manage a broad reach most of the way. But I'm tired and ready to be home," Martha said.

Mary took a deep breath. "Smell that sweet jasmine. *Mmm.* Just look at our tall canopy of oaks and queen palms swaying in the wind. Silhouetted against the riot of purple and orange in the sky, they look like they are lined up to cheer our return."

"Good heavens, Mary. You are hopelessly poetic."

"I suppose so. This is beautiful. But I wasn't ready to come home," Mary said.

"You're never ready to come home," said Martha, with a little laugh. "But Brock House was in such an uproar after all the business with the murder. And before you say it, I know we paid for a whole month, but it just wasn't restful any more. Here we are and I, for one, am looking forward to sleeping in my own bed." She turned and said, "While I'm making everything fast here, will you please go up and tell Winston that we need the footmen to come get our things?"

"Yes, Sister." Mary stood, grabbed the painter, focused intently on the rise and fall of the 26-foot sailboat. *Up. Down. Up. Down. Up.* She timed her step onto the dock just right. After tying the painter to a cleat on the dock, she caught the stern line tossed by Martha, and drew the agile boat alongside the dock.

Martha went in search of the butler. Soon she returned with a greeting party of two footmen, one very dignified butler, and their gray tabby cat Fredrika. The feline, named after Swedish journalist, writer, and feminist reformer Fredrika Bremer, trotted along to supervise operations.

The next morning the ladies rose early and dressed in riding clothes. Mary's maid Petunia, a tall, angular dark woman with a love of hats, helped the sisters pull on shiny boots, while the cat wove in and out around their feet.

"Yes, we missed you too, Fredrika," said Mary, as she bent to stroke the affectionate animal. "Come on. Let's get something to eat."

Downstairs Flora, their short petite parlor maid with big brown eyes and a pleasant smile, served breakfast, which included fresh pineapple. Chafing dishes were set out in a long row on the sideboard in the cheery morning room, full of slanting rays of sunshine on wicker, chintz, and china.

Fredrika trotted to her full dish in the corner and sat, waiting expectantly, as if desperately hoping for a plate of ham and eggs, instead of her gruel laced with drippings.

"Will you ask the groom to saddle our horses? I am ready to ride this whole plantation," said Martha to the girl.

"Yes'm. Right away."

Half an hour later the sisters aimed their small, agile, Spanish-bred Florida cracker horses toward the old disused storage barn and dilapidated sheds. Mary said, "I am curious to see the progress they've made in our absence."

"Me, too. They've had ample time to dismantle those crumbling old buildings."

As they rounded a curve in the road they caught sight in the distance of their half brother Philippe, whom their planter father Charles had fathered by his then-slave Deleila. Of medium height, Philippe was a wiry mulatto, with brown eyes and brown hair, held back at the nape of his neck. He was considered by many to be a handsome ladies' man.

"Oh, no, Mary. Our decrepit, tumbledown old barn is still standing there."

Philippe's angry deep voice floated to them from that direction. He said, "Albert, why aren't you at the cooper's shed learning your trade? I should beat the tar out of you. You're just a lazy good-for-nothing. Why I didn't leave you in France, I'll never know."

"Philippe is yelling at his son again... and scaring all the birds," Martha said.

"Poor skinny boy. Philippe's always shouting at him."

Albert said angrily, "I hate you. I hate you. I wish you were dead."

Mary said, "My goodness. He has a stormy disposition."

With a frown, Martha said, "They both do. Is there no end to their arguing? And the barn. If that doesn't beat all. That blasted old thing is still there, leaning to the right. We trusted Philippe to manage renovations while we were gone. He said he would take charge of the project. It looks just as bad as it did when we left."

"Yes. It's a mess." After a moment she said, "Martha, I don't entirely trust Philippe. When Daddy sent him abroad to school -- what? 15 years ago? -- I never dreamed that he'd up and disappear from our lives. He could have been dead...nary a word from him. Where was he and what was he doing all that time?"

"He said he was learning things. He's been really vague about that. But he's only been back three months, Mary. He'll improve."

"Well, you mark my words. Albert's going to be trouble. He's 14 and you know what a rebellious age that can be. I see in him that same bullying attitude as his father. I heard him yelling at Flora for nothing at all. I rather wish our long lost brother hadn't returned. I don't think he's a very effective manager. Remember when he first got back? He was fully expecting, just because he's a man, that he would take over as the new master of Cypress Pointe."

"True, but what can we do? We pretty much had to hire him. He has a son to look after."

"I guess he thought we mere women would hand over the reins and just sit on the porch and knit. We dissuaded him of that notion in a hurry," said Mary with a chuckle.

"Yes, but we had to give him a job to keep the peace. And it was the right thing to do."

"Daddy *did* leave Cypress Pointe to us. I'd say that for two old women we've done a top-notch job of running this place for the three years since he died."

"Look. There's Tom coming around the corner with a fierce look on his face. What are they up to?"

Tom said in a thunderous voice, "How many times do I have to tell you, Albert? This whole area is off-limits. It's unsafe. I'm not going to tell you again. And I don't want to see you around the molasses shed, either. We can't have you ruining our rum. Now clear off, before I box your ears. And don't come back."

Albert turned tail and fled.

The Merritts' tall, husky overseer Tom was also Deleila's son. He was fathered by another of Charles' former slaves, Chombo, and was a year older than Philippe.

The ladies slowed their mounts to a walk and approached the barn. Martha said, "Philippe, Tom. Good morning. Why are these old buildings still standing? Before we left, we gave distinct instructions for you to tear down the rickety old things."

Tom said, "Good morning, Ma'am. I'm sorry. We tried. But the workers are superstitious about this place. Not a one of them will come near it. They were afraid of old Deleila's fits. When my mother died shaking, rolling her eyes, and gagging on the ground in front of that barn, the stories grew until now everyone is scared stiff to be near it. Why can't we build the new barn somewhere else?"

Martha said, "No. That increases our transportation time and costs. And besides I can't stand to look at the old buildings anymore. Eyesores they are. And as you said yourself, they're unsafe, just waiting to fall down on us."

"Ma'am, you could pay the workers double and it would do no good. They would rather be whipped than set foot in there. There's nothing we can do." With his perpetual frown still in place, he walked away and Philippe followed him, signaling an end to the conversation.

After the men had gone, the sisters continued their tour of the plantation, where they had ridden their ponies as children. Martha said, "Huh. They work for us. I suppose we could replace them."

"That would cause a lot of bad feelings and might slow production. I noticed that Philippe didn't say much. It looks like he has joined with our overseer to stall the renovation plans." After a moment, Mary said, "I think we could easily do without Philippe. But what about Tom?"

"I suppose we could find someone as qualified. He's very popular, for an overseer, and smart. He was an excellent cooper before Daddy elevated him to overseer. And this is the only home he has ever known. I imagine he would be bitter and might cause us trouble. As for Philippe, we can't get rid of our own brother... well, half brother."

Mary said, "He hasn't acted like a brother for a long time. And he still thinks he should be master here. Remember, he said, 'How can our father have left the running of this large plantation to two women?' He acts like we are an inferior species."

They stopped in the shade of a towering oak. "Ouch. Blast it all. Blacky has sandspurs all over his legs and now I have them stuck in the legs of my riding pants. I thought we got rid of those spiky weeds." A blue jay scolded them from a high branch.

"We did, everywhere except that old barn. I'll be so glad when that thing's gone... Those two think the case is closed. I don't see any way we can convince them to stand up to the workers and persuade them to do the job. We are stymied by superstitions," said Martha.

"Should we just abandon our plans to expand? We've been doing very well this past three years with our old equipment."

"No. We have already allocated money for the new boilers and timber for the buildings. If the cane workers won't do the work because of superstition, let's figure out a way to eliminate the superstitions," said Martha.

"Brilliant, Sister. But how?"

"What comes to mind when you think of superstition?"

"Fear. Maybe fear of dead people coming back to hurt us."

"Haunting. Dead people talking to us in ghostly voices. Séances, where people can summon spirits -- can talk to them and get answers to questions."

"You mean like rap once for yes and twice for no? Or ring the bell if you are such-and-such a person?"

"Why not? I read about Mary Todd Lincoln's séances at the White House. A séance just might work. If we could find a séance medium to contact the spirit of Daddy, he could say that Deleila's spirit is fine. Then he could order us to take down the old buildings and put up a new large storage barn for aging the rum. I can hear it now. He says, 'I want you to make Merritt Rum famous... the best in the world.'"

"It would be perfect if we could use their own superstition to convince Philippe, Tom, and the workers to do the work. But where are we going to find a medium? Especially a tame one, who will say what we want. Maybe we should just dismiss those two and hire somebody else."

"No. The fears of the workers are the main problem. We can't dismiss all those people. I think, rather than force our hand as owners, we should go back to Enterprise and seek help from our friends. Lots of urbane people visit Enterprise. We should be able to find a spiritualist there, someone who can recommend a séance medium. Or we may be able to recruit someone to play the part. It shouldn't take long. It would also allow us to take advantage of our unused, already-paid accommodations at Brock House."

"Oh, yes. That sounds pleasant. When can we go?"

"Let's finish our survey of what needs to be done here. We'll deal with any business matters that have come up in our absence. And the day after tomorrow we'll take the stagecoach route from Saint Augustine over to the river."

"The stagecoach route... do we have to? It's so dusty and cramped. I always end up with bruises when we knock around in one of those coaches. Even in first class, though we don't have to get out and push when they get stuck, they jostle and bump us so much that my delicate stomach often rebels and I lose my lunch. I like steamboats much better."

"Mary, it'll take four days or more to get there by steamer, whereas it's only 14 miles by stagecoach from the depot near Saint Augustine to Piccolata on the Saint John's River. I know it's tedious, but it only takes three or four hours to the Piccolata landing, where the *Darlington* will pick us up and take us on down to Palatka for the night, and then to Enterprise."

"All right. But don't blame me if we get ambushed by Indians."

"Don't be silly. You know there are no Indians there anymore."

"Are you sure?"

CHAPTER THREE

May 22, Stagecoach from Saint Augustine to Piccolata

The sky was still sunrise-pink on the morning of May 22, when Martha, Mary, and Petunia climbed into another of their fleet of cat boats in front of their home, Cypress Pointe Plantation.

"Thank you, Zack," Mary said to the bespectacled footman with slicked-back, wavy, dark hair, as he stowed her bags in the small, light craft.

Winston, who was overseeing the loading of luggage, said, "You have a nice day for it, Ma'am. Mind the shell banks. You know they can be powerful dangerous. Master Charles would not like to see you going all the way up to Saint Augustine on your own."

"Yes. He was overprotective, but he's not here now. Relax. I've been sailing since I was a girl. I have good skills and I'm careful. We'll be fine. Martin will take good care of the boat while it's moored in Saint Augustine, until we need it again."

The ladies and their maid had a pleasant morning sail to the most antique city of America. "I hope the crêpe myrtle trees are in bloom," said Mary.

From Saint Augustine they transferred their luggage to a hired carriage and traveled another mile south to the stagecoach depot. They passed through an avenue lined on either side with great Queen's crêpe myrtle trees. "You got your wish, Mary. Their branches are forming a perfect archway. Smell those huge pink blossoms," said Martha, breathing in deeply.

"I see a bridge ahead," said Petunia, whose eyes were wide with excitement.

"Yes, we cross the long bridge and the causeway next."

"Ohh, look at the big birds swooping down over the water," said Petunia.

They tossed and bounced over the old pavement. Martha said, "This road is in dire need of repair."

Arriving at the station, Martha said, "Mary, if you two will stay by the coach and see to our luggage, I will go purchase our tickets."

"Yes, gladly," said Mary, as they all descended to the parking area behind a stagecoach with four mules.

Petunia, who had never been here before, stood wide-eyed, staring at the signs posted all around. A very tall man in a red plaid shirt approached them and read the signs out loud:

""First class ticketed passengers may sit and ride all the way.

"Second class passengers must walk at bad places.

"Third class passengers must walk at bad places, as well as occasionally having to help push the stage coach.

"Rules: abstinence from liquor is requested, but if you must drink, share the bottle. To do otherwise makes you appear selfish and unneighborly.

"Chewing tobacco is permitted, but spit with the wind, not against it.

"Don't snore loudly while sleeping or use your fellow passenger's shoulder for a pillow. He or she may not understand and friction may result.

"Gents guilty of unchivalrous behavior toward lady passengers will be put off the stage. It's a long walk back.

"In the event of runaway mules, remain calm. Leaping from the coach in panic will leave you injured, and at the mercy of the elements, hungry bears, and coyotes."

He said, "Hmph. Looks like I might be a pushin'. Hi. I'm Jeremiah. "

Petunia stood wringing her hands. "Runaway mules? Hungry bears and coyotes? No, no. I'll...uhh...I cain't go.."

"Don't be squeamish. It will be fine. Here, watch that our luggage gets placed aboard properly," said Mary.

"Oh, Lord a mercy," said Petunia, who looked faint.

"You want to see the St. John's River, don't you? And all the beautiful birds?" said Mary. "This is the fastest way to get there. We'll be all right. Here comes Martha with our tickets."

At that moment they were joined, at the door to the stagecoach by another passenger. The short, bespectacled, expensively-dressed young man introduced himself as William.

Martha joined them and introductions were made. "Pleased to meet you, gentlemen," said the ladies quietly.

A tall, brawny, tanned fellow, wearing a big black felt hat with a three-inch brim, strode up. He tipped his hat. "Howdy. I'm Cracker Joe, your reinsman, or stagecoach driver, as some say. I'm responsible for gettin' you to Piccolata. Your coach is pulled by four very reliable mules.

"These two heavy pole mules are 'War Haas' and 'Donkey Hotay.' The smaller leaders are 'Side Kick' and 'Jester.' Stand well clear. They kick fast and hard. The distance is 14 miles and it takes three to four hours, barring trouble. The weather looks good and I'm not expecting any difficulties." He handed up to his driver's seat a shiny shotgun.

He pulled a boarding step from the luggage area and placed it in front of the door. Mary went first. "Here, Petunia. Sit on this side." Mary patted the seat next to her.

When his five passengers had boarded, Cracker Joe removed the step and checked that all the luggage was tightly strapped.

Petunia covered her face with her gloved hands when they heard, "Git up."

They all rolled and bumped against one another as they passed palm and cypress thickets, with now and then a group of handsome palmettos. Martha bounced between the hard side of the coach and Petunia.

The road curved and Petunia said, "Lookit Cracker Joe ridin' near the pole mule. He's got a rein in one hand and that 'black snake' leather whip in t' other."

"That rein connects with the bit in the mouth of the near lead mule. He pulls it when he wants to direct them to the right. If he wants them to go left he jerks a time or two and yells at them in mule, gibberish that sounds like an unearthly screech and groan," said William. "The bits of the lead mules are connected by an iron bar. Whatever movements are made by the near one directs the movements of the off one."

"Do the pole mules always follow the leaders?" Petunia said.

"They usually do and are also controlled by their own short reins, which hang over their necks. The driver flicks his whip near their ears to get their attention," William said.

Midway through their trip, the coach slowed, rocked forward once, and then stopped. On either side of the coach Spanish bayonet plants reached up to the sky from bare sandy soil and the hot sun beat down.

Jeremiah opened the door and hopped out. "Looks like deep sand here. William, get out and help me put some dried palmetto leaves in front of the wheels. Then we'll get behind and give 'er a push."

William said, "I'll help with the leaves, but I bought a second class ticket. I don't have to push."

"All right. You walk a piece and I'll push."

Cracker Joe, now standing up on his perch atop the coach, said, "That ought to do it, Jeremiah. And y'all keep a look out for bandits. This would be a mighty good place for an ambush."

After they placed the leaves for traction, the reinsman cracked his whip and hollered, "Gee-up." They lurched forward, then rolled back.

They repeated this maneuver twice more.

As they were readying for another go at it, Jeremiah said, "Somebody's coming. We're about to have company."

A tall person, whose face was hidden by an enormous hat and long flowing blond beard, appeared in ragged clothes on a short, black-and-white, Florida cracker horse atop the hill in the distance behind them. Martha stuck her head out the window to watch.

"What's happening?" Mary said.

Martha said, "That rider has stopped. He's watching us. Cracker Joe is up high... gun aimed. He's swiveling all around."

"Ladies, keep low."

Martha hunched down. "Mary, Petunia. On the floor. Now."

"We need to get this coach moving," Cracker Joe shouted. "William, help Jeremiah push the next time I give the signal to the mules."

"I'm in second class. I don't have to push," William said petulantly.

"You won't be any class at all, son, if we get ambushed out here. Now, push. 'Side Kick. Jester. War Haas' and 'Donkey Hotay,' GIT-UP."

They rocked forward, then back again.

"No good. Gents, quickly. More leaves in front of those wheels. Good. Now, HEAVE for all you're worth. GIT-UP.'"

"Jumpin' Jehoshaphat. That rider. He's galloping right for us, rifle aimed. William. Get down. What do we do now?" Jeremiah hollered.

Boom!

Cracker Joe fired a warning blast. He reloaded.

Two bear cubs burst from behind a palmetto thicket and gamboled across the track midway up the hill, followed closely by their startled and angry mother. The rider veered to his left. He shouted, pulled off his hat, and waved it wildly, heading the bears off into the bush away from the coach.

When the three bears were fuzzy brown specks in the distance, the rider returned. "Lawrence Nielsen, at your service. Didn't think you could see those critters from down here. Do y'all need some assistance?"

Cracker Joe stayed up top, gun at ready and said, "Thank you kindly. We could use someone to push."

Lawrence added his muscle to the next attempt and they finally freed the wheels from the loose sand. Jeremiah shook hands with the tall horseman, climbed to the top, and sat lookout next to Cracker Joe. William, hot, sweaty, and looking vexed, scrambled in next to Petunia.

When they resumed, they still jounced and knocked against one another. "At least your stomach had an opportunity to settle while we were stopped," said Martha to her sister.

"Until we saw that bandit, then my stomach clinched again. I'll be glad when we get there."

"Was he? A bandit? He helped us," said Petunia, who seemed both afraid and thrilled at seeing a possible bandit. "Do you think that Lawrence has friends with him? Mightn't they be following us?"

"Just keep that kind of thinking to yourself, my girl. Look out at the scenery," Mary said.

In a disappointed and somewhat sulky voice, Petunia said, "Everything looks the same. Sand and more sand. There's a few pines and bayonets. Where are the animals?"

"We probably scared them all away with our rattling noises, and the loud roar of the shotgun," Martha said. "Just think, Petunia. In a few minutes you will get your first view of the St. John's River."

"Is it very beautiful?"

"Yes, indeed. There's nothing like it."

An hour later they disembarked at the Piccolata station. Passengers flocked to the wharf, while their luggage was being offloaded and readied to be loaded onto the *Darlington*.

"Look at them fish leaping out of the deep," Petunia said. "They wiggle around a bit, up in the air, and then disappear again."

Several strangers with fowling pieces now elbowed her out of the way. A discreet and dignified pelican sat calmly on the water. A rifle ball went by just over its back -*whiz!* Carefully unfolding its huge pinions, the sober bird gathered itself up and winged away to a more hospitable part of its native element.

"I say. That was a pelican. You cannot eat it. Why were you shooting at it?" said Martha to the shooter.

The stout gray-bearded man shrugged. "They eat all our fish."

"Our fish? I should think the fish are theirs, as they need them for survival." Martha said. "And these waters have an abundance of fish. You find all kinds, at all hours, in all places."

In a huff, the man moved to a different spot and continued to shoot at birds. Luckily, he was a terrible shot.

Within an hour they were aboard the *Darlington*. That evening they had a hearty dinner and enjoyed a red and purple tropical Florida sunset over the river, while moored at Palatka.

Mary said, "Tonight we'll be rocked in our bunks by the rhythm of the river. That should be soothing to our bruises."

"Yes, and tomorrow evening we will be in Enterprise," said Martha. "I'll be glad to see Sadie and Mac."

"And we'll get to meet new guests. I wonder who will be there?"

CHAPTER FOUR

May 23, at Brock House in Enterprise, Florida

On the evening of May 23 Martha and Mary, with maid Petunia walked down the *Darlington* gangplank in sunny Enterprise, Florida. Mac sat in his usual chair on the front veranda of Brock House talking with Sadie.

Sadie said, "Oh, look. The Merritts are back. They just left, during all the kerfuffle with catching the killer. How wonderful." She stood and went to greet her friends. "Hello, you two. It is so good to see you again so soon."

Mary clasped her in a hug and said, "It's good to be back, my dear."

"Mmm. I've missed you."

"Sadie, you are absolutely a sight for sore eyes," said Martha, who sank into a chair next to Mac. "And you, too, Mac. Jacob asked me to give this to you." She handed him the *Savannah Daily Herald*, dated May 19. He unfolded it and the headline read, "Serratt Family All Spies-Weichmann.

He said, "Thanks, Martha. Here's news." He read aloud, "Louis J. Weichmann, a lodger at Mary Surratt's boarding house in Washington, D.C. and friend of her son John Surratt, Jr., who is still sought by authorities, testified about the Surratt family's ties to a Confederate spy and courier ring operating in the area. He established an intimate relationship between Mrs. Surratt and the other conspirators."

Sadie's heart beat so fast that she felt it might escape. *Don't faint. Yes, you were there. Deep breathing. Yes, you know John Booth. But you did nothing wrong.*

Martha said, "That's bad news for her. I wouldn't want to be in her shoes. If she were a man, they would probably hang her. But politics aside, we came in hopes that you two could help us with a problem at our plantation. Do you have time before dinner to listen to our tale?"

"Yes, of course, Martha," said Mac.

Sadie took a slow deep breath and forced herself to smile. "You know we'll do what we can," she said, with as much grace as she could muster.

Hovering nearby was a tall dark woman in a pretty, wide-brimmed straw hat with a blue ribbon. By way of introduction, Mary said, "We brought Petunia, our maid. Petunia, please go tell the manager, Mr. Lavigne, that the Merritts are back, and we want his best room. Then go to the kitchen out back and ask Mrs. Flowers or Jane for water for washing. We'll find you in ten minutes."

"Yes, ma'am."

Mary lowered herself into a nearby lounge chair with a sigh.

"Mac, we are being held at the mercy of superstitious workers," Martha said. "They refuse to go near our old barn, which we need to tear down before we can build a new one on the site."

"They fear that the place is haunted by the ghost of a woman who died there 15 years ago," Mary said. "We have an idea about how to get them to do the work, but we'd like to hear your thoughts. How would you get them to cooperate?"

"That depends on why they are afraid," Mac said.

Sadie said, "What is your manager doing about it?"

"Nothing."

"Is your manager delaying the renovations for other reasons?" said Mac.

"All good questions," Martha said. "Give us a few minutes to wash off our travel dust and we will give you answers. Maybe the four of us together can come up with a solution. Let's go, Mary, and see which room Lavigne gave us."

Sadie said, "Meanwhile, I'll go tell Jane you are back...and get us a pitcher of lemonade and plate of cookies."

"Mmm," said Mac. "You're not afraid that will kill our appetites?"

"I'll get small ones, so they won't ruin our dinner," Sadie said with a wry smile, knowing that it would take many, many cookies to destroy Mac's appetite.

In 20 minutes, they all sat with Jane's mouthwatering almond drops and glasses of lemonade. "Our half-brother Philippe, who is our new manager, along with Tom, who has been our overseer for five years, have joined forces to oppose our renovations."

"Are they actually being obstructive?" Sadie said.

"Yes. We told them to have the workers demolish the barn and old sheds while we were gone. When we returned nothing had been done. All they would say is that the workers refused to go near the barn. In their view, that was the end of it."

"Have they ever before refused to follow your orders? Is there ill will between you?" asked Mac.

"No," said Mary.

"We didn't think so, until this happened," said Martha.

"Would they have personal reasons to go against your directions?" said Mac.

"Philippe is probably jealous because our father left the plantation to us and not to him. As for Tom, I can't think of any reason for him to oppose us," Martha said. "I might add that they have the same mother, a slave named Deleila, but Philippe's father is our father, Charles."

Mary said, "Tom has been bitter since his wife ran off with a peddler years ago."

"But he is fair to the workers and an excellent overseer. Everyone stayed since emancipation," Martha said.

"We paid our workers long before emancipation and they all have signed contracts with us," Mary said.

Mac said, "What exactly do the workers fear?"

Martha said, "Superstitions run long and deep around here. They fear epilepsy, which they call hysteria or insanity. Tom and Phillipe's mother Deleila died in the middle of a fit, rolling on the ground in front of the old barn. Her angry ghost is said to roam the area threatening anyone who comes close."

Sadie said, "It's no wonder they won't go near it. Can we change the superstition?"

Martha said, "We thought of that, too. We were wondering if a séance might be the answer. Since we're fighting against superstition, perhaps someone is willing to lead a séance in which they could guarantee that our dead daddy, Charles, would speak. He would need to assure everyone that the spirit of Deleila is happy in paradise and that his living children need to modernize to bring good fortune to the Merritt family."

Mac said, "That might work, but it would be hard to find a séance medium on short notice. Don't most of them live in New York?"

"That's what we thought, too," said Martha. "I don't want a trip to New York."

Sadie said, "Well, if all you need is someone to dress up and play the part of the medium, I could do that for you."

"Oh, could you really?"

Sadie looked at Mac, whose eyebrows shot up.

"We would be delighted to have you as a guest at Cypress Pointe Plantation," said Mary, her face brightening at the prospect.

"And we'll pay you twice what you are earning here for your time," said the ever-practical Martha.

"Would it be all right for me to bring Jane? She's good company and very clever."

"Of course," said the ladies in unison.

"We'll pay her, too," Martha said. "How long will it take you to get ready to go to Cypress Pointe with us?"

"I'll check with Jane tonight and we'll tell Mr. Levine in the morning. But I'm sure it won't take long. We can probably catch the *Darlington* tomorrow."

"Very good. Then it's settled. We'll plan to take the *Darlington*, unless we hear from you. That will put us home on the 24th, taking the overland route."

"Starting the 25th we can plan the séance. We'll invite the neighbors," said Mary with glee.

"The overland route? That sounds interesting."

"Not so much interesting as...practical. It takes only two days to get home, versus four days on the steamers."

"Oh, a big difference. I'll enjoy exploring new territory," Sadie said.

The screen door at the front of Brock House opened and two vivacious ladies, Southern belles by their clothing and the sound of their vowels, emerged.

"I will continue my reading, Mac, and write my assignments in my notebook while I'm gone," said Sadie. "I should be back within a week."

Mac said, "All right, Sadie. Martha, you and Mary left before Alan Pinkerton offered Sadie a position as a Pinkerton agent. Some of her studies are addressing that work."

Mary said, "Eeee, you are a Pinkerton agent, like Kate? Oh, Sister, imagine that. Congratulations, Sadie. I know you'll be wonderful."

Everyone on the veranda looked their direction.

Sadie said, "I haven't said I'll do it. I'm just looking into it."

"Why, they law! Look who's here. If it isn't the Merritt sisters," said a willowy brunette. Her black chignon, eyebrows and world-wise dark eyes contrasted with her very fair skin. She rushed across the veranda to Martha, bent, and wrapped her in a tight embrace.

"Helen Jones. It's lovely to see you," Martha said, when Helen let her go.

The lady hugged Mary, too, then said, "I don't believe you've met my sister Christine Sheldon, from Georgia. Christine, these are my dear friends, Martha and Mary Merritt, who own Cypress Pointe Plantation. They produce sugar and rum. Martha was formerly a journalist for the *New York World* and was married to an explorer who died in Alaska. Mary is the widow of a prominent physician, Dr. Menendez."

Martha introduced Sadie and Mac. "It's time for dinner. Shall we all go in?"

As they entered the dining room they heard, from a corner table, raucous laughter and an enthusiastic young voice saying, "Tell us another one, Cump."

"Who is that grizzled, red-headed braggart holding court?" said Mary."

Helen, steering them away from the noisy table, said, "That, my dear friend, is General William Tecumseh Sherman, who is responsible for burning half of the south."

"...including my plantation, High Gaite, in Griswoldville," said Christine, through gritted teeth.

The ladies chose six seats situated on the far side of the room. After they were seated, Christine said, "They say he suffers from depression and is here for a rest, but I think he must be here to gloat."

"I did see him looking downcast in the parlor yesterday, Chris. He was by himself and scowling, with his head in his hands," Helen said.

"I don't care. He is responsible for the total destruction of Georgia's railroads, houses, and businesses. Nobody and nothing was safe from them. Ernest, that's my husband, said that by the end of the war 5000 horses, 4000 mules, 13,000 head of cattle, and millions of pounds of corn and fodder had been seized by Sherman's foragers."

Mary said, "I had no idea it was that drastic."

"At least, he didn't burn Savannah," Helen said.

Christine said, "...only because Savannah is a prized port, which he presented to President Lincoln."

Fluffy, the resident mouser, sprang onto Mac's lap and waged a silent war of her own against his string tie. *Bap, bap.* She sent the dangling cord flying. Mac fished out a treat from one of his many pockets and pacified the frisky cat. "Sorry. You were saying?"

"He doesn't much care about his personal appearance, does he?" said Martha, sneaking another look at the blue-uniformed tall man with haphazardly trimmed hair and beard. His high forehead, brightest-of-red hair, hawkish dark eyes, frowning brows, beakish nose, and thin lips made him look fierce, even though he seemed to be telling funny war stories to a rapt audience.

"He looks like a devil to me. You've heard about his 'Field Order 15,' which allows the Union to seize a strip of Confederate coastal lands and property for 30 miles inland? They are confiscating land from Charleston, through Georgia, and down to Florida, on the St. John's River," Helen said.

Mac said, "We heard that he issued 'Order 15' in mid-January, but we are not affected by it yet. Sherman is quoted as saying that his appointees are presently doling out Savannah area property in 40-acre plots to some 40,000 area freedmen and their families."

"They haven't taken your lovely Tidewater Plantation near Savannah?" said Mary.

"Oh yes, they have. And Union troops, who are living in our plantation home, have distributed all our land. It's only a matter of time before they get to the Saint John's."

Mary said, "Our Cypress Pointe Plantation is coastal land, though it is a little bit south of the St. John's. They wouldn't take our plantation and give it to freedmen? I've read about this, but it seems so far removed from us. What can we do, Martha?"

"I don't think there's anything we can do. If the Union needs more land, they could extend the area of confiscation. I've read that General Sherman and Secretary of War Stanton worked together on 'Field Order 15' and had the approval of Lincoln. It's supposed to be a punishment to us Confederate planters and a solution to the Union's problem of what to do with four million freed slaves."

Sadie's eyes grew huge. It was Secretary Stanton who interviewed her, just hours after Lincoln's assassination, when she was known as actress Evangeline Bright. Standing behind the plush curtain at Ford's Theatre waiting to go onstage, she had heard the shot that killed president Lincoln. Like many other actors and actresses, she had been hired by John Booth's brother Edwin. Still fearing that she could be pulled into the investigation of John Booth's plot, she remained mute.

Helen said, "We escaped with our clothes and what little we could carry. Our husbands are in Washington trying to get our land back. They are talking to politicians, especially President Andrew Johnson, who isn't particularly an abolitionist. He can rescind 'Order 15' and return our property. I don't know what we will do if he won't."

After a delicious dinner of roast venison with vegetables, Christine said, in a quiet voice, "Martha, will you and Mary come to our room? There's something special you should see."

Martha looked questioningly at her sister, who nodded, and said, "All right, but just for a few minutes. We've been traveling and are quite tired."

"And I need to go find Jane, especially if we are planning an early departure in the morning," Sadie said.

"I'll have some assignments ready for you in the morning, Sadie," said Mac.

The ladies excused themselves and left the dining room. As they followed Helen, Sadie stole a glance at the celebratory group led by the famous general, whose dark red mustache dripped with Madeira wine, before his rough hand swiped a white napkin across it. He said, "... no truth to the rumor that Johnson will proclaim my 'Field Order 15' void. Even he wouldn't return confiscated land along the coast to the very people who declared war on us."

During their fifteen-minute walk home to Snow Bird Cottage, Sadie and Jane decided that the proposed trip to Eau Gallie sounded like an interesting break from their routine work. "I'm going to read my lessons and then pack, so I won't be rushed in the morning. And I have to do a little preparation for my role as séance medium," said Sadie.

Jane said, "Mmm. I'll wear long skirts, as usual, so I'll fit in. But I'm going to take my knee length skirt and trousers, which go underneath. You will make a feminist of me yet," she said with a quiet laugh. "And we mustn't forget to ask Percy to feed the chickens while we're gone."

A few minutes later Jane was drawn to their back porch by the sounds of hammering. "What on earth are you doing, Sadie?"

"I'm trying one of your flamenco dances on these dratted walnut hulls, but I need harder shoes. I have to crush these shells, not just bruise them. Will you put on some water to boil in our smallest pot, please? "

"All right. Then I'm going to sleep. I'll see you in the morning."

Well, I hope you see somebody else.

In their room, Christine said, "We've been living as refugees, Martha. In Griswoldville and surrounding farms, including our plantation, northern foragers stole all that could be of use to them. Then they burned everything else to the ground. Our workers had become increasingly disobedient and we didn't trust them. With all our men folk gone, we had few options. The night I saw wild flames on the horizon I quietly loaded a farm wagon and abandoned our home.

"Neighboring planters' wives joined the mass exodus, sticking together for safety. Hundreds of women and children walked in the dark, some bareheaded, and in all kinds of clothes. Women searched for their babies along the road, where they had been lost, others sat in the dust crying and wringing their hands."

Mary said, "How dreadful. How did you get here?"

"I made it to Helen's in Savannah. Then the enemy followed and took everything. She fled with me. We trudged with my wagon through mud and bivouacked in open fields, despite rain. We traded furniture and household goods for food and fodder along the way. Finally, we traveled by boat through swamps, rowing for miles and enduring terrible storms." She turned to her sister. "Go ahead and show them, Helen."

Helen looked at the floor and then said, "We've no income. I'm ashamed to say we've been selling our mother's jewelry to provide for basic needs." She opened a small jewelry box. "Would you like to buy this beautiful ruby brooch?" She named a modest price.

Mary removed the clump of sparkling jewels. "Oh, it is magnificent, but we couldn't possibly deprive you of it."

Christine said, "Don't think of it like that. You would be helping us get by, until our land can be returned to us."

A look of agreement passed between the Merritt sisters. "Well then, we carry some emergency cash. We will purchase it, but for a more fair price and with the provision that you may buy it back at the same price any time," said Martha.

"It will be like borrowing it for a while," said Mary.

Helen heaved a great sigh and, with tears in her eyes, hugged her two friends. "Thank you. That's a splendid way to look at the whole thing. And we won't forget this kindness."

"Now you and Christine must come to our room, so we can finish this business. Mary and I need to get some sleep," said Martha, with a yawn.

When all was complete and the Merritt sisters were alone again, Mary said, "We are lucky that all this confiscating and distributing hasn't gotten as far as Eau Gallie."

"Yes, I'm thankful for that. But it still could happen. Union troops, full of rum taken from our plantation, could do much damage to persons and property. What will we have left, if we have to flee? And where are displaced owners supposed to go?"

CHAPTER FIVE

May 24, Snow Bird Cottage; Darlington to Palatka

The next morning Sadie removed the walnut shells from the dark liquid in the now-cold cooking pot and swabbed the dye onto her eyebrows until they were properly brown. She put on her brown wig.

Upon seeing her housemate, Jane said, "Oh, my stars. You look foreign. Your eyebrows are an ugly brown."

Sadie said, "Yes. Thank you. Black walnuts are useful in that way. I'm traveling as 'Belle' today. You must call me Belle. And you'll have to talk to Lavigne to tell him we'll be gone for a week or so. He can't see me like this. It would just give him more reason to dislike me."

"You know I hate having him look down his nose at me."

"You can conquer your shyness. Just march in there and say it."

A few minutes later, Jane knocked on the door of Guillaume Lavigne, manager of Brock House. "Come," he said.

She entered his office, where the judgmental hotel manager sat, feet propped on his desk, blowing smoke rings with acrid pipe smoke. *Just like the caterpillar in that new book "Alice's Adventures in Wonderland"* she thought, with an inner chuckle that relaxed her. *I remember Daisy mailed it back to the guest who left it, but not before we all read it.* Lavigne's combed and curled dark brown handlebar mustache and fastidiously trimmed beard pointed at the ceiling.

"Sadie and I are going to help the Merritts in Eau Gallie, but we'll be back in about a week," Jane said in a rush.

He frowned. "This is highly irregular." He paused for effect. "But, as it's the Merritts, we will employ temporary staff until you return. Close the door on your way out."

Outside in the hall, Jane said to Sadie, "That went well." She grimaced and rolled her eyes. "I'll go talk to Percy while you finish with Mac."

Within a few minutes they joined the Merritt sisters on the *Darlington*. Martha said, "Oh, my, Sadie. It's hard to credit how different you look with the brown wig and dark eyebrows. And I've never seen you wear black."

"Please call me 'Belle' from now on," said Sadie.

Under a long black shawl, she wore a white blouse and a long black skirt. 'Belle' tied on a broad-brimmed, black-fabric hat, then took her book bag and climbed to the hurricane deck for some early morning reading.

Later that afternoon, she descended to the promenade deck, where she found Jane and Mary at the rail. Holding up her big textbook *Anatomy: Descriptive and Surgical, Anatomy of the Human Body* by Henry Gray, she said, "Did you know that the adult human skeleton has 206 bones?"

A whole cloud of gold and black butterflies rose from a tree as the steamer clattered past. One fluttering monarch with a ragged wing landed on Belle's hand, which rested on the rail.

Jane said, "Oh, how pretty. In answer to your question, No, I never heard that. How does anyone know the exact number?"

"The author is a lecturer on anatomy at Saint George's Hospital Medical School in London. Mac said that Gray and his illustrator spent a year and a half dissecting unclaimed bodies. They included woodcuts of many bones. Want to see?"

"Oh. Ugg. Our insides? A dreadful topic," Mary said. "Move over. My stomach…" She leaned over the rail and, in a very unladylike manner, lost her breakfast.

Belle passed her a handkerchief. "I am sorry. I forgot about your delicate stomach. Do you want some help back to your cabin?"

"Thank you. No. I'm better now. I like the soft breeze. It smells like flowers." They traveled past a stand of magnificent magnolia trees and remained quiet, listening to the splash of water from the wheel. The butterfly abandoned Belle's hand and flew up to perch atop her hat.

"I'm curious." Jane said. "May I look?"

Belle opened the book to the page she had been studying and said, "This woodcut of a hand is very practical."

The monarch crept to the underside of Belle's hat brim.

"That tickles. Don't shoo him. He'll go on his own. He looks like he needs to rest his wings. I can't begin to imagine all the places this lovely little insect has been. But about the bones -- look how they fit together."

Jane shivered. "Now, every time I look at a hand, I'll think about this."

Mary said, "Don't you have some other books that have more pleasant topics?"

Belle said, "We could discuss my Philosophy lesson. Socrates was sentenced by a jury of 501 Athenians to drink hemlock." She grinned at her friend, who wrinkled her nose in retaliation.

Jane said, "What? Why?"

"He didn't accept their gods and he taught the youth to think for themselves. The Sophists, teachers of the day, charged money to fill peoples' heads. Socrates taught for free and challenged pupils to question accepted ideas. He said, 'Wonder is the beginning of wisdom. To find yourself, think for yourself.'"

"Is that your lesson? "Mary said. "Question the powers of the land... and get sentenced to death? He might better have made friends with the powerful people, ignoring what they stood for."

"No!" Jane said.

Mary said, "I suppose he didn't have to make friends, exactly. He could just not oppose them."

"People have been arguing about this issue for centuries. I read in Proverbs 24 that 'If you do nothing in a difficult time, your strength is limited,'" Belle said.

"I learned that for myself in Cuba. History is full of leaders lusting after conquest and willing to do anything to get what they want. That's evil," said the Cuban lady. "And they will win if we stand by and do nothing."

"One could oppose them in secret, behind their backs," Mary said.

"That's only a half measure. If we don't take a public stand against evil-doers, then they get stronger," Belle said.

"It takes courage," said Mary.

"Aunt Cora always said we should stand up for what we know is right. And we are stronger if we stand together. Mac is big on debating these issues. Like Socrates, Mac said education makes us think, or look down inside ourselves..."

"Or get a really bad headache," Mary said, with a chuckle and another wrinkle of her nose.

The *Darlington,* which was headed north, docked at Palatka beside the southbound *Katie Asbell,* the other steamer providing regular service on the river. Belle breathed in deeply. "Mmm, datura. That sweet smell is the perfume of purple datura flowers."

Belle and Jane went to find *Katie Asbell's* handsome captain, Noah.

Adam, who was fond of Sadie, stood working on the deck when they approached. He glanced at them without interest, then went back to his work.

Jane said, "Hi. We are looking for Noah."

"I reckon you'll find him in his office dealing with records and licenses. Go on up."

Belle said quietly, "Good. He didn't recognize me. Careful on this ladder. Gather your long skirt with one hand and hold it tight up to your knees. Use the other to hold the ladder. Always have one hand on the ladder."

With some lurching and bouncing, they ascended unharmed and knocked on Noah's door. Belle's heart beat fast.

When the tall, lean, and commanding sternwheeler captain opened his door, the brows over his dark eyes shot up in surprise. He looked hard at Belle and then addressed Jane. "Jane. What are you doing here? And who is this?"

Belle said, "Hi, Noah. We came to let you know that we are going with Martha and Mary to Cypress Pointe Plantation for a week or so."

His mouth dropped open. "What in the Sam Hill? Sadie, is that you under all that brown and black?"

"Yes. I'm going to give a séance."

"A séance?! Is that why you look like that? It's been only a week and a half since you caught a murderer and sent him to jail in chains. Isn't that enough excitement to last you for a while? And you have your studies with Mac."

"Yes, I know. But it's only for a week or so. And the Merritts need our help. I'm going to pretend to be their long departed daddy."

"Great Caesar's ghost."

"No. Charles Merritt's ghost... his voice, to be precise."

Not for the first time, Noah thought, *Just about the time I think I have this woman figured out, she goes off in another direction. I'm perpetually off kilter. It's like squeezing a watermelon seed — you never know which way it's going to fly.* Then he let out his breath with a whoosh. "Is that entirely safe?"

"Of course. I just wanted you to know we won't be home. That's all."

Now is your chance to show her you care, he thought. His face brightened. "You haven't put in your new locks yet, have you?"

"No. It didn't seem so pressing, since we caught the killer."

After a killer put a monster alligator in Sadie's dining room, Kate, a visiting lady-Pinkerton-agent, was concerned about Sadie's safety. Kate sent five shiny new locks from Linus Yale in New York. Linus' son, Linus junior, made some important improvements and let it be known that he planned to patent the new lock in June. He sent the newest version, with cylinders and pin-tumblers, to Sadie.

"Tomorrow evening, as soon as I get into Enterprise, I'll install them for you. Linus Yale's package with your locks is in Guillaume Lavigne's office, and I have a brace and bit, chisel, file, and screw driver here aboard the *Katie Asbell.*"

"You don't have to do that. I'm perfectly capable..."

"But I *want* to. Who knows what could happen at Snow Bird Cottage while you're gone? You don't want to return home to another scary alligator. You have little spare time and your safety matters to me."

"All right. Make yourself at home there. Any key will unlock the doors." She gave a rueful laugh. "It should be quiet, now that we've caught Neville."

"I might get a couple of my deck hands to help me. They have free time of an evening. And while I'm at it, where do you ladies want your henhouse?" He looked at Jane and smiled broadly.

They stared at him. "Just because Jane said she bought chickens and needs a coop, that doesn't mean you have to make one."

"I know, but I used to be a fair carpenter and I need to keep my hand in. All I need is some lumber. I have tools."

"In that case, I think the south side of the garden would be a good place for it. What do you think, Jane?"

"Yes. Not too far from the back door," Jane said.

"And how many nesting boxes do you want?"

Jane said, "Two?"

"Hmm. Better make it four. If Jane is as good at raising chickens as she is at everything else, we'll have a flock before you can blink." Belle paused. "Do you hear that? It sounds like Fiona from the general store."

"I hear a fiddle and people are singing *Amazing Grace,*" Jane said.

They stepped outside his door and the tune changed to the lively dance tune *Well Hall*. "Let's go find that splendid instrumentalist," Belle said. "Are you coming, Noah?"

Intrigued by the happy-sounding music, he said, "Yes. Give me five minutes. I am almost finished with these ledgers."

By the time they made their way down the gangplank of the *Katie Asbell,* the fiddler was playing a tune Belle recognized as a gigue by George Frederick Handel.

"There he is," said Jane, pointing to an area in front of the Palatka general store, where passengers from the two steamers were dancing in the light of the moon and oil lamps suspended from the eaves.

A short, wiry, dark man in a top hat stood poised with one shiny black boot propped up on a tree stump. He smiled, swayed, and played. His costume of white shirt, red bowtie, black pants with a shiny red stripe up each side, and red suspenders set him apart.

The general store proprietress Fiona, a sturdy 30-year-old, raven-haired beauty with a bun at the nape of her neck and a long red and white checked dress covering her ample figure, stood next to him and called dance moves. Her charming, popular husband Curly danced spiritedly with all the ladies.

"I think everyone within hearing distance has come," said Jane. "Look. Martha and Mary are already here." She moved to join them

As the music transitioned to *Red Haired Boy,* Noah said, "Shall we join the dance?"

"With pleasure," Belle said, and they lined up with the other couples.

I really don't want to release her hand and let her dance with someone else, thought Noah, as the music stopped. *But it's my social duty to mingle and to make sure that everyone has a pleasant time. Confound it.* Noah danced with all the ladies that evening, though he had feelings for only one.

During a break, Martha made a deal with the musician, Happy Dan, to go with them and play for a barn dance at Cypress Pointe Plantation.

After a full day of work and three hours of dancing, many dancers were leaving. The fiddler ended the evening with *Galopede,* a fast contradance that showcased his technique and left everyone breathless, but contented.

Noah thought, *What a day. What a woman. I can't let her get away.*

At daybreak the next morning, when the steamers departed from Palatka in opposite directions, the four séance ladies stumbled, amidst the sounds of noisy paddlewheel churning and splashing, to the stern of the *Darlington* and waved to the departing figure of Noah, high up in the wheelhouse of the *Katie Asbell.*

I'm going to miss that man. Belle felt her heart beating faster. *And I'm a little nervous about the séance. But what could go wrong?*

On the seat she spied a newspaper abandoned by a fellow traveler. "WILL U.S. FEDS HANG MARY SURRATT? Conspiracy Trial of Boarding House Owner Mary Surratt, Arrested April 17 in Connection with Lincoln's Assassination, Could End in Hanging."

Her heart raced. She casually scooped up the paper and held it under a fold of her full skirt as she made her way back to her cabin.

It felt hot, as if its flaming words could burn her flesh. In the dim morning light, she sat and read, "The federal government initially tried to find legal counsel for her, but almost no attorneys were willing to take the job, for fear they would be accused of disloyalty to the Union. One of her lawyers, John Wesley Clampitt took the job, but did little for her. Another, Frederick Aiken, said all evidence against Mary was circumstantial. An unnamed source said the public is demanding that anyone connected to the conspiracy must hang."

The poor woman. It's just as well I'm being 'Belle,' the séance medium for a while. The public is angry, demanding justice for a slain president.

They wouldn't really hang Mary. Would they?

CHAPTER SIX

May 25. Evening aboard the Katie Asbell; Brock House; Snow Bird Cottage

Noah thought, *I know that several of my sailors are fond of Sadie. It won't hurt to ask for help with those locks.*

As soon as they made fast at the wharf next to Brock House at Enterprise and his men were at liberty, Noah climbed down from the wheelhouse and addressed Shorty, Abel, and Adam. "Thought I'd go install those five new locks at Sadie's house before the sun goes down. Anyone want to lend a hand?"

All three of his trusted men agreed without asking questions. They headed for Lavigne's office to get the package of locks and see if perhaps they could borrow more tools.

The man, surrounded by a fog of smoke, was just leaving his office for the evening. Noah walked in through the open office door and said to the hotel manager, "I'm glad I caught you before you finished for the day. Do you have some simple tools, like a brace and bit that we could borrow for the evening?" He pointed to his sailors, who waited out of earshot in the hallway.

Lavigne removed his pipe from his mouth and said, "Only tradesmen have those things. This is a high-class hotel, not some village smithy."

"I see," Noah said. "Well, give us the Yale package with Sadie's locks and we'll be going."

Lavigne puffed a fat smoke ring from his pipe and said, "Well, now. I can give those only to Sadie."

"We are going to put them in for her this evening and we are burning daylight here. I would appreciate it if you would give us the locks now. Otherwise you will stay here while we search your office. We may not be very neat."

"You are a hard man, Noah Asbell. Here. Take them and go." He pulled open a deep drawer and produced a large heavy package.

Noah opened one end a little and found the edge of a shiny lock. "Thanks very much, Mr. Lavigne."

"Let's go, fellas."

"What took so long, Noah? Didn't you tell him that we are racing the sun?" said Shorty.

"Lavigne wasn't best pleased to give me the heavy package for Sadie. But I convinced him."

Noah and Shorty, who was over 6 feet tall, found that their long legs made it easy to travel the distance from Brock House to Snow Bird Cottage. Abel and Adam struggled to keep pace.

This stretch of road has a beautiful view of the lake, Noah thought, as he breathed in the fresh evening breeze coming off the sparkling water.

At the cottage, Noah produced his toolbox. "Use these to start taking off the old locks," he said. "I'll try to find us some more tools."

He searched in all the logical places. Finally, he found in the boat house an old screwdriver, with a handle that felt rough in his hand.

Well, look at that. They're hidden from view in the drawer of the workbench. Ahha. Brace and bits. A chisel. A file and a mallet. We're in business.

He removed a pretty ward key with an ornate heart-shaped handle. *Let's see if that will open the doors.*

He grabbed the screwdriver and headed for the kitchen door. *Open, sesame.*

Success. Now to unscrew the plates from the door and frame.

They came right off. *And that's that.*

He said in a loud voice, "I found some more tools. Come help yourselves."

When he opened the package from Linus Yale, he found, in addition to the five locks, an adjustable drill bit for drilling large-radius holes. *They thought of everything. That will make it much easier to make the big hole for the cylinder.*

Sharing Noah's and Aunt Cora's tools, they removed all the ward locks and replaced them with the new Yale cylinder type. Drilling the large holes for the cylinders was the most time-consuming part of the job.

Almost done. It took a little under two hours. Good thing there are four of us. "Whew." Perspiration dripped down his forehead and off the tip of his nose.

Shorty and Abel came around the corner of the house. "All done, Noah. And Adam is coming down the home stretch. By the way, he said he found a letter for Sadie just inside the front door. Percy must've brought it when he came to feed the chickens."

"He didn't bother it any?"

"Nope. It came by US post. He said he left it right there, so she'll find it soon as she gets home."

"What letter would be so important that Percy would bring it here?"

"It's from the Pinkerton agency, if that's what you're wondering."

"No, I...uh. I just, that is..."

"We made it before we lost daylight," his good first mate said, coming to his rescue.

Noah blotted a perspiration droplet off his nose onto his upper sleeve, and then shook hands with his men. "Thanks."

"You bet. That ought to keep your lady safe," said Shorty, with a glint in his eye.

My lady. I like that, but she isn't. Not yet.

CHAPTER SEVEN

June 1, Immediately After Séance at Cypress Pointe Plantation, Eau Gallie, Florida

'Belle' thought, *If these people disperse, we'll never find out what happened.* Quietly she said, "Martha, how long before we can expect to get a doctor here to examine him?"

"The storm is still lashing down out there. And when it's over, we'll have a lot of cleanup before anyone can get through by boat or on horseback. I expect it will be three or four days, maybe more, before we can fetch Doctor Grove from Saint Augustine. Don't hold your breath."

"Could you summon the footmen to remove Philippe to a more suitable place?"

Flash!

Rrrrruuummble!

"We can use the small bedroom in the back. I'll ring for our housekeeper."

"Thanks." Belle turned to her quiet friend, Jane. "When they come, go with them, please. Find his regular bedroom. Make sure it's locked. And see if you can find us an argand lamp."

"Of course."

In her most commanding voice Belle said, "Quiet, please. Will everybody take a seat in exactly the place you were during the séance. Martha, may we use some of your writing materials?"

Lightning momentarily lit the room.

"Of course. I'll get them."

"Let's stay calm. While she's doing that, each of you close your eyes, take a deep breath, and think back." She sighed deeply. "Imagine how you felt the moment you sat down. What happened during the séance?"

Albert said, in a wild agitated manner, "What happened? My father was killed. That's what happened. And we are shut in a dark room with a dead man and a murderer."

"That's not helping, Albert," said Martha. She thought, *The poor boy,* as she took his hand. "It's hard, I know."

Belle continued. "Yes. Now, everyone I need for you to write those feelings down. Were you nervous at first? Excited? Skeptical? Whose hands were next to yours on the table? Did that stop at any time? Don't consult your neighbors. Just write what you remember. Write about your actions, the actions of others, what you saw, heard, and felt. Put down where you were and what you were doing before you arrived here.

"Tom, that goes for you, too. Please remove your oil skin and hang it on that hook on the wall back there. Then have a seat in the extra chair."

"Why should we listen to a séance medium?" said John Crews III. "How do we know you didn't do this?"

"No, she didn't. The spirit did it," said Nanny.

He rolled his eyes.

"I feel faint," said Phoebe in a plaintive voice, to her husband. "I want to go home." She began to weep great wet sobs. "I would not have come, except Celeste said this would be a fun surprise to help celebrate my birthday, which is tomorrow. This was my birthday surprise." Through hiccups and gasps for air, she said, "This is the worst birthday EVER."

Rumble! Rumble!

"Hush, you people and do as Belle says. She's a Pinkerton agent," said Mary.

Well, not yet, thought Belle. But I am the most qualified investigator here.

John III said, "Don't be daft."

"Really, John. You mustn't speak to our hostess like that." His wife put a restraining hand on his arm. Under her breath she said, "That is a silly notion, indeed, but it doesn't matter, dear. It won't hurt to write our account of events. Please don't make a fuss."

Flash!

The footman Paul, a tall lanky mustachioed lad with close-cropped brown hair, carried in a ladder, which he set under the chandelier. He used flame from a very long match to relight the candles. He finished and, accompanied by a long low rumble of thunder, warily hoisted his ladder and made his way out.

Martha returned and passed out paper and a handful of pencils. "These were a gift from a New York visitor, friendly with Eberhard Faber. He's a German whose family made the pencils with red cedar from Cedar Key, Florida. I've been saving them for a special occasion. I think this qualifies."

"Ahh. Thank you, Martha. Everyone may begin writing. No detail is too small. And when you're finished, sign your name."

While they were busy, Belle moved to Philippe's body and quietly searched his pockets. The search revealed a pocket knife, a pouch of cut tobacco, a rum cask label stenciled *Black Ball*, two cigars, a clean white handkerchief, some scraps of paper, and... a small drawstring bag. *And here is another bag.*

She turned toward the window to avoid being observed and found that the first bag contained a whole pocket full of Spanish silver 8-reale pieces.

Great Caesars ghost. She counted 40 Spanish coins. And in the second were more coins. *These are écus, French five-franc silver coins.* She counted 50 French coins. *Where did he get all of this silver?* She put the coins back in the bags and tucked them through the slits in her skirt and into the tied-on pockets underneath. *Oh folly, fudge, and flummediddle. I don't want to carry this around. I'd better turn it over to Martha right away.*

Next, she checked the window. *Locked. But, why are these puddles by the floral curtains?* She looked up at the ceiling. *Dry.* She made a circuit of the perimeter of the room, looking for anything out of place. *Nowhere to hide. Except for all these puddles, it looks much as it did when I checked everything before the séance.*

"All right. Here is my account. I'm finished," Celeste said.

"And here is mine," said Virginia, as she signed hers with a flourish. Are we finished?"

"Not quite."

Both ladies resumed their seats.

In a petulant voice, Phoebe said, "This is all I can write. I want to go home." She pushed the paper away from her on the table, then stamped her foot. Her pretty face was peaches and cream, with big brown eyes, upturned small nose, and a scowl. She tugged on one of her blonde ringlets, radiating anger and fright.

Belle said, "Thank you, Mrs. Crews. I appreciate how hard this is for you -- for all of us. I think it best that everyone take advantage of the Merritts' hospitality tonight, and see where we are in the morning after the storm has gone."

Benjamin said, "Excellent idea, madame." He shoved his written account at Sadie. "Here, for what it's worth." He helped his wife to her feet. "Let's go to our safe comfortable room, Phoebe."

"Phoebe, before you go, will you hold open your balloon skirt and do a slow pirouette, as if in a ballroom dance. You look to be a wonderful dancer," said Belle, adding a gentle smile to the compliment.

With a questioning look the woman complied. Belle said, "Thank you. And Ben, I'm going to be looking at the jackets of all the gentlemen here. Will you please remove yours and put it at the head of the table?"

"You're joking?"

Belle shook her head, her small smile still in place. "No, it really must be done. Thank you for your help. I'll return it to you in the morning."

"Here. Take it." Phoebe looked away as he unpinned the jacket sleeve that covered his damaged arm, and removed the dinner jacket. "I'm just too tired to argue," he said with ill grace. "Come, Phoebe."

Belle gathered all the statements. She looked at each person for knife hiding places or signs of blood on hands or clothing as they exited by ones and twos to the safety and comfort of their rooms. The gentlemen removed their jackets, and the ladies twirled before leaving. Belle received varied reactions to these requests --a little bit of resistance from some, but Albert, who was not wearing a jacket, twirled and chortled like it was great fun.

The room was empty when Jane returned and placed a bright argand lamp on the table near Philippe's body. Suddenly the room looked very red, reflection from the red walls.

"Thank you. That gives the light of six or eight candles," said Belle.

Jane took paper and pencil. She started sketching.

"What are you drawing?"

"I am making a sketch of him, as he looks now. And I think we need a floor plan of furniture and carpets, to show water and blood puddles, plus paths of wet foot prints and blood droplets. I can add the guests, too, in their places around the table, if you like."

"Thank you, Jane. That will be very helpful. I found a few drops of blood on the bottom of Nanny's dress. She was sitting right next to Philippe. Could she have done this?"

"That little wisp of a thing? I don't think so. She looks like a light breeze would blow her away. And I would have seen her bright white cap bobbing around above him. I guess she could have given him food or drink laced with a sedative before the séance. We can't rule her out."

"Tom was bloody, too, but he would be, wouldn't he? He handled the body. Everyone else was clean. This puddle of water next to the window is still a mystery, though. The window was closed and does not seem to be leaking, but the curtains are damp. And I can't account for the heavy trail of water on the floor from the door to the window on the West side of the room. Tom didn't go that way. He came in, wet from the storm, and went around the east side of the table. Understandably, he left a trail from the door to Philippe's chair."

Belle lifted the lamp and inspected behind the large mahogany china cabinet, the matching buffet, and the hutch. *Red walls and a little dust. No knife.* She opened drawers and cabinet doors, prodded and poked. *Nothing.*

Martha returned with Paul and Zack, a bespectacled dark man whose wavy black hair was slicked back. He carried a light plank. "May we move him now?"

"Yes. All right. But take him directly there. No one is to disturb the body until the doctor arrives to examine him," said Belle. She looked at Martha. "Be sure to lock the bedroom door and guard the key. And may I speak to you, Martha?"

"Of course," said Martha, with a sigh. "Take him to the small green room, Zack. I'll be along in a moment." With Martha and Belle looking on, the footmen removed the body.

Martha said to Belle, "I'm terribly sorry to get you mixed up in all of this."

"It must be dreadful for you, Martha, to have your half-brother killed. In the circumstances, I'm glad I could be here to help. Do you want me to keep on with this charade about being a medium?"

"Yes, I think that's best. We've done what we can to dispel the superstitions surrounding the old barn. Now maybe the workers will get rid of that death trap."

"All right. And I found these silver coins in Philippe's pockets." Belle fished the heavy bags from her pockets and handed them to her hostess. "Do you know why he carried this much silver?"

"Will wonders never cease?" said Martha. She shook her head. "I have no idea. I'm too tired to think about where he got them or what to do with them. I'll deal with it tomorrow. Good night ladies." She discreetly covered her yawn, took charge of the bags, then exited gracefully.

Trees outside of the windows continued to thrash in the stormy wind. Jane offered her drawings for Belle's approval. "These are better than photographs," said Belle.

Knock, knock!

From the hallway came the voice of the housekeeper Bertha, a stout, matronly, buxom woman, who bore a large red birthmark on her chin and neck. "Mrs. Merritt wants me to ask if I can clean them blood stains from the floor and rug before they set, permanent like."

"Yes. Come in, Bertha."

The bucket and string mop entered first, followed by the head of the housekeeper, whose hair, escaping from her mob cap, closely resembled her string mop.

Belle said, "I understand the need to remove the carpet stains as soon as possible. But it's important for you to leave everything else undisturbed. Can you do that?"

"Yes, ma'am. I won't touch nothing else."

As soon as Bertha finished and bustled away, the temporary boost of energy, that had propelled Belle thus far, left her. She sank onto a chair at the table.

"Oh, Jane. I've never felt so inadequate. I really wish Mac were here. We need a real investigator. What do I do now?"

"Lock the door and let's write down what we know and what questions we have so far," said Jane.

"Yes, we do have some evidence." Belle locked the dining room, then took paper and pencil. They sat at the table and she wrote as they conferred.

"On the Evidence Page, I'll put those things you have already included on your drawing: puddles of water on the floor by the window; water puddles by Philippe's chair; blood puddle on the floor by Philippe and on the table where his head rested; water on the floor at the doorway leading around both sides of the room to Philippe's chair. One was from Tom's entry, but the other is a mystery. You drew blood droplets on the carpet near the door forming a trail around the west side of the room to Philippe's chair. Was that a mistake?"

"No mistake. There was a clear blood path from the door to the window."

"Hmm. Yes. I remember. How can that be, if everyone was seated, with hands on the table top?"

"That goes on the Questions Page. Also, some evidence I couldn't include in my drawing. For instance, the curtains at the window are damp, while the window is locked."

"Mmhmm. And I noticed candlewax drips appear to have been blown with a hard gust from Philippe's end of the table, the window end, toward the direction of the door, where Martha, and Mary sat by me. That means someone on that end of the table blew out the candle. If the window had been open, I'd think it was a wind gust, but it was closed and locked."

Jane said, "So, another one for the Questions Page. Who blew out the candle?"

"I walked all around this room and did not feel a draft - Especially one strong enough to blow out that candle. Jane, I am not up to making a list of suspects tonight. I really don't know who could've done this."

"You don't suspect Martha or Mary?"

Belle said, "Hmm. I'll consider that after my fact-finding missions." She closed her tired eyes and felt exhaustion creeping up on her.

A week ago I was happily dancing in Noah's arms. Noah, where are you tonight? I hope all our friends on the Saint John's River are safe.

Aunt Cora, I'm in up to my neck this time. "Sorry, Jane. It looks like I've gotten both of us involved in murder this time."

I thought it would be an easy way to earn some cash.

"We can't go home any time soon."

CHAPTER EIGHT

June 2, Two a.m., After Séance at Cypress Pointe Plantation, Eau Gallie, Florida

The upsetting events of the evening kept marching around and around inside Belle's head. She lay gazing up at the white muslin canopy above her bed, that showed during the now infrequent flashes of lightning that still illuminated the night sky. She thought, *I hope everybody in East Florida is safe from the storm — Noah and the Katie Asbell crew as well as the residents up and down the river.*

Noah's probably sleeping soundly in his berth on the Katie Asbell. It's been a little over a week since I've seen him. I could write him a letter and tell him... what? We are all safe here, but we are up to our eyebrows in murder. That does not sound romantic.

Her room was perfectly comfortable, elegant even, though sparsely furnished compared with the usual cluttered style. Pale yellow silk-covered walls, polished marble around the fireplace, a marble-topped washstand, an expensive cherry wardrobe, and tasteful ornaments all showed in the occasional flash from her window. The storm was winding itself down.

Oh folly, fudge, and flummediddle. I might as well get up and do something useful. She got out of bed, wrapped herself in a blanket, and lit a candle. At the cherry writing desk, she completed her lessons. Then she sat thinking. *I wonder if the murdered man was really related to Martha and Mary? Maybe he was an imposter. They said Philippe was a youth when he left and they hadn't seen him in years.*

He seemed to be a wanderer, who only recently returned to his birth place. Whoever he was, he wanted to be master at Cypress Pointe Plantation.

If it really was Philippe, it must have been hard for him, as the only male heir, to find that 'his' plantation is now being capably run by his two highly intelligent sisters. Martha has a gift for logical thinking. Men don't expect that... or like it especially, in women.

Belle opened a drawer and retrieved the statements from those at the séance.

Albert, you are a mysterious youngster. What is this? In the upper right-hand corner of his paper, the boy had drawn a skull and crossbones.

With a soft laugh, Belle said, "O folly, fudge, and flummediddle." She read:

I am happy to have some thing intersting at last. Terra hold my hand...

"Aaa. Help. Help."

Above the sounds of the last drips and puffs of air from the storm, a muffled cry came from the room next door.

That sounds like Martha.

Belle wrapped her dressing gown around her, picked up her candlestick, and rushed out to the empty hallway. She turned to rap on Martha's door.

Knock, knock.

After a short pause, she pounded loudly on the door. "Martha. Martha? Did you call for help? Are you all right?"

Celeste stuck her head out of a nearby door. "What's happening?"

Jane appeared at Belle's side. "What on earth is going on?"

Belle handed the candle to Jane, then tried the knob. She pushed abruptly, and fell forward into the room. *Empty? But I just heard her call out.*

"Martha? Martha, where are you?"

"Belle? Thank God." To the amazement of Belle, Jane, and Celeste, the trim, night-gowned matron log-rolled from under the bed, sedately stood, and strode around to the side of the bed.

She sat staring down at a scrap of brown-dotted muslin. The window was open and the light, wedgewood blue curtains were dancing in gusts of storm-damp wind.

Mary joined the small group in Martha's bedroom. "Why is everyone up at this time of night?"

Belle said, "What happened? I heard you cry out."

The older woman said, "It's a good thing you came when you did. Somebody just tried to stab me."

"What?" Mary reached out and held her sister in a tight embrace. She said in amazement, "I can't believe this is happening. Our séance was a huge mistake. We have unleashed a deadly spirit."

"Nonsense, Mary. This was no ghost," Martha said.

"What happened?" Belle said.

"Luckily, I was upset by the events of the evening and still awake. I heard my door hinges squeak and, the next thing I knew, a shadow was coming at me with a big shiny knife. I rolled out of reach and onto the floor. I screamed and scrambled under the bed --not dignified, I know."

"Dignified, be hanged. You're alive, and that's what counts. And thank God for insomnia, at least tonight," Belle said.

"I'm thankful for your actions, too. The knife was thrusting methodically under the bed, when you knocked. I heard the window open just before you burst in. The intruder has undoubtedly scrambled down our giant oak tree on this side of the house."

Pointing to the dotted fabric square in Martha's lap, Celeste said, "Is that something you grabbed from the intruder?"

Belle thought, *I was right to be careful of this one. She is observant.*

"I don't remember grabbing anything. It must have been wound around the neck or perhaps over the face as a mask," Martha said.

"Good, then we can identify your early-morning visitor by finding out who owns this," Belle said, grasping at the only bright spot in the ghastly past few hours.

"Well done," Jane said. And Celeste gave a short, quick, celebratory clap of her hands.

Martha shook her head. "If only it were that easy. One of my jobs, as mistress here, is to provide clothing. I bought several bolts of this fabric and, with help from some of the women, sewed clothes for all of our families – negro and white - out of it. Everyone on this plantation owns clothing made of this," Martha said.

They all groaned and for the second time tonight Belle said, "O folly, fudge, and flummediddle." After a pause, she said, "You did the right thing, Martha, and it probably saved your life. Did you get any sense of your attacker? Tall? Short? Fair skin or dark? Did he speak?"

"No, but whoever it was, they moved very fast and smelled of cinnamon. That's all. It was pitch black."

"Was your door locked? And your window?" asked Celeste.

"Yes, they were. However, I know from Sadie...uh... my experience in Enterprise, that these locks can be opened by a wide variety of keys."

Mary said, "We need to get some better ones. In the meantime, each of us can prop a desk chair against the bedroom door at night."

Martha said, "And I'll bring each of you a couple of those agate marbles that I keep to entertain children. Balance them along your windowsill. Anyone coming in your window in the dark would knock them to the floor, making a noise and also creating a tripping hazard for the intruder."

Mary said, " Oh, and I can bring you some sharp tacks to scatter below the window, too. I read that sailors used to scatter them on deck when they were worried about being boarded at night by hostile natives."

Martha said, "Oh, Mary. You've been reading too many books. Do you really think an attacker, climbing our oak tree and into a window, would be barefooted? Besides, my attacker came in by the door."

"First, there's no such thing as too many books. Second, he might come back by the window. Put them on the windowsill. Getting stuck with sharp tacks in his hands would startle an intruder enough that he would lose his hold on the tree and fall. It would serve him right, creeping in through the window with black intentions."

"I don't like the idea of being vulnerable," Celeste said.

"Nor do I," said Martha. "Belle, didn't you and Jane and that Pinkerton lady share techniques for warding off an attack? We have a killer in our midst. You really must teach us."

"All right. Meet me tomorrow, I guess I should say 'today,' after dinner in the back parlor and I will show you ways to defend yourselves," said Belle.

"Better make it before dinner, because we're all going to the dance after dinner," said Mary.

Belle said, "You are going on with the dance?"

"We need it now more than ever," Mary said.

"Then our lesson will be before dinner," Belle said.

Jane yawned.

Martha turned to leave, saying, "I'll be right back with some of those things for you. Will you accompany me, Sister?"

Belle said, with more confidence than she felt, "Let's all go to bed now and get some rest. I'll talk with each of you tomorrow."

And what are the chances that one of you is our killer?

CHAPTER NINE

June 2, Morning After Séance at Cypress Pointe Plantation, Eau Gallie, Florida

Belle rose early and, while she dressed, she thought about Martha's attack. *It must be connected to Philippe's murder. Could the killer be one of the little group gathered in Martha's room or do I rule them out because they showed up so quickly?*

Jane has no motive, as she just arrived with me. I can't see Mary wanting to harm her sister, though I suppose that's possible. The thought of that little lady with wispy white hair climbing up and down trees... no.

What motive could Celeste have to hurt Martha? None, that I can see, but she is agile. Martha's attacker would have to be fit, to get down the rain-slick tree from a second-story window. And if it's Celeste, she'd have to be fast, to get back to her room in time to come out and act innocent -- and dry.

She opened her window a couple of inches to fresh air and an overture sung by a mockingbird. As she sat down to read the statements from the night before, weak light filtered onto her desk and a cool jasmine-scented breeze ruffled her hair.

Quite a variety, she thought. *Most of Martha's guests have excellent grammar and handwriting. John's is very stilted, while the statements of Albert, Tom, and Old Nanny are incomplete and so creative they're hard to understand.*

She sat thinking, then stood and made her way to Jane's room, where, after a soft knock, she found her friend ready for the day. Belle said, "Good morning. I just remembered some details of evidence on Philippe's body. Can we go over this together?"

Jane said, "Yes. Just a minute" She retrieved her gray sweater from an ornate mahogany bedpost and shrugged into it.

In Belle's room they pulled out their "Evidence' and 'Questions' pages. Belle said, "When the footmen moved Philippe's body, I saw cobwebs on his clothes. I haven't seen so much as a fleck of dust around here. Where did he get cobwebs? In the old barn or sheds?"

Jane said, "Those are the obvious possibilities."

"And that's not all," said Belle. "His boot soles were covered in dried black muck. Isn't the soil here sand or clay?"

"Yes. Muck would suggest that he was in the Ever Glades."

"What was he doing down there? Was he there to discuss sugarcane agriculture?"

"Martha would know. Maybe he delivered Cypress Pointe Plantation rum."

"Did the sisters say anything to you about him selling in the Ever Glades?

"No. I got the impression that most of it went north, to the railroad spur in Baldwin. Maybe he was going into business for himself?"

"Hmm. Theft. That would explain a few things."

"From the Glades, rum could easily be sold to a sailboat captain who would resell it outside the country."

"After breakfast, I'll ask Martha if he was authorized to travel for them or to negotiate sales for Cypress Pointe Plantation."

"Speaking of breakfast, I'm ready to go down now."

In the cheerful chintz morning room, chafing dishes were waiting for them on the sideboard and Belle smelled coffee. Mary sat alone on a sturdy white wicker chair positioned in a weak pool of sunshine. She looked up when they entered. "Good morning. May I have a word?"

"Yes. Let us get some bacon and eggs and we'll be right there." Belle and Jane filled their plates and carried them to Mary's table. After the usual pleasantries, Mary said, "Celeste sometimes irritates people. It's her investigative nature, which makes her a good journalist. In case you were wondering about her, she held my hand firmly, to reassure me, every minute during the séance."

Belle said, "Ahh. Good to know. Thank you."

The older woman said, "And I need to tell you something else. This may be nothing. It just seemed like an embarrassing family matter at the time. A while back, I was taking an early morning walk and overheard Philippe threatening his son."

"What happened?" said Belle.

"It was a beautiful warm clear day and finches filled the air with song. I had stopped to sit and think in the shade of some gardenia bushes. My chair was hidden and I was enjoying the sweet fragrance, when I heard Philippe's loud bass voice. He said to Albert accusingly, 'Did you tell her?'

"Young Albert said, 'No. Not yet. I will.'

"Philippe said, 'You tell her today... or tomorrow I will.'

"Then Albert said, 'I hate you. I should have stayed in France.'"

Belle said, "What were they talking about?"

"I can only guess that Albert was going to get in trouble if he told something he had done."

"That being?"

"He was always poking around where he didn't belong -- the old barn, the boats at the dock, the molasses shed. Maybe he broke something?"

"Thanks. I'll ask him about it," Belle said. "And where would I find Nanny this morning? I want to ask her view of the séance. She didn't write much of a statement."

"No, she wouldn't. But she has a well-developed sense of right and wrong and has been part of the family since my father was a boy in South Carolina. No one knows how old she is. You'll probably find her in the kitchen out back."

"Thank you, Mary. We need to go over your statement, too. When is a good time?"

"I'll be in my room writing letters later this morning. Until the workers clear away the fallen trees and debris, and repair the damages from the storm, I think we will all be compelled to stay inside. Please come anytime it suits."

Belle and Jane opened the door to the kitchen and were inundated with the smells of frying bacon and sausage. House staff members looked up curiously from the long table where they were eating their breakfast.

Old Nanny said, "Miss Belle, I need to talk to yer." She moved to the end of the table and indicated two empty chairs.

The ladies sat and Nanny said, "Now then. Philippe was quite the ladies man -- had 'em flockin' roun' 'im. That Miss Terra, wot's stayin' wit 'er sister over at the Crews' place, *The Landin'*, was sweet on 'im fer a while, then it went sour. I wasn't no eavesdropper, nor nothin', but I hear-ed Terra tellin' Mr. Philippe to drop dead. Jest like that, she said it. They was outside in the hallway afore the séance. An' I seen Miss Phoebe cozying up to Philippe, while her husband done been taken prisoner by the North." She stopped for a breath, then continued full tilt.

"Don' rightly know how Mr. Ben takin' that, see'n as how he's home now. Mebbe he's too weak to fight it much, but he must kin 'is wife's actin' the coquette wif Philippe an' thuh hurt's boun' to be there. Now Tom's been a grumpy goose ever since 'is wife run off with thet salesman, some 15 years back. But I seen fer meself that Crozbi was makin' eyes at Philippe, too. Then he was sent off to school." The tiny woman stopped to shovel in some scrambled eggs.

"Crozbi?"

"Tom's wife, don'cha know."

Belle gulped. "My goodness."

Before Belle had an opportunity to say more, Nanny was off on the subject of John Crews' business dealings. She explained that his plantation *The Landing* was a refuge and staging area for blockade runners during the war.

"They took goods from the Indian River to the St. John's River an' t'other way roun'. Nowadays, the family's taken Northerners huntin' and fishin', fer a price, o' course. And they's those rich'ns, wot likes the nature -- Mr. Crews guides 'em aroun', like. An' he was trying to get Philippe to help him." She finally ran down and started on her breakfast again.

"Nanny, did you blow out the candle at the séance?"

"Laws a mercy. Now why would I do a fool thing like that?"

"Thank you for your information. I will take all this into consideration. And now a question for all of you." Belle looked around at the other faces at the table. "Who would want to kill Philippe and why?"

"Gotta go. Yes, indeedie." And Nanny was gone.

"Whew," Jane said.

Everyone else looked down at their plates.

"All right. Thank you, folks. If you think of anything let me know. We'll be going, too."

As they headed back to the house, they heard raised voices. Phoebe said, "I don't know why they didn't fit you with one at the hospital."

"I told you, they don't have such a thing."

Phoebe's voice rose in anger. "Oh, they most certainly do. I read all about artificial limbs, 'prosthetics' they are called. You just strap one on and you are as good as new." Now, practically yelling, she said, "You must get one. Do you want everybody's pity? You'll be shunned."

Belle peered over the hedge at the couple.

Phoebe flung her final barb, saying, "Half a man is never tolerated under the chandeliers."

Belle saw Ben flinch under the assault. He closed his eyes momentarily, then said, "So, now I am half a man? Trust me. There are prosthetic legs, yes. But no arms -- just hooks. Do you really want to be married to someone with a hook?"

"No, but ..." her voice trailed off as the couple walked farther away.

Belle said, "She's right, you know, about the general attitudes of our society. Perhaps with so many loved ones suffering amputations and worse, we will become more patient with those who have suffered disabilities."

Jane said, "At least it removes jealousy."

"I disagree. The disabled person can still have attributes -- creative talent, good looks, money, property -- that might cause jealousy in others."

"I see plenty of jealousy around here. And it's a good motive for murder," said Jane.

Belle said, "True." She stood thinking. "Jealous sisters might play bad tricks on each other, like putting pepper instead of poppyseeds all over a plate of pudding, but stabbing? They do have the strength for it, but I doubt they have the heart."

"You think it's more likely to be a man? Men do tend toward physical extremes, stabbing or shooting each other, when they're jealous," Jane said.

"Yes. Though we don't even know that Nanny's story about Philippe and Tom is true. And it all took place a long time ago. Let's focus on 'now.' Her point about Ben being jealous of Philippe sounds likely. Also, we need to ask Martha or Mary about the relationship between Albert and Philippe."

"Terra can tell us if that child was holding his hands on the table the whole time."

Belle said, "Yes, but I wonder if he would be capable of stabbing his own father?"

CHAPTER TEN

June 2, Assassin at Cypress Pointe Plantation

The assassin was restless. *Now I have another to eliminate — and soon. I must finish this.*

Belle and Jane made their way to Martha's room. Jane said, "I've been thinking about Miz Phoebe's birthday. In view of the rather basic fare we've been served here, I am guessing their cook doesn't have much experience with pastries and cakes. Would I be out of order to offer to bake something special for us to celebrate with her?"

Belle said, "I think that's a splendid idea. Let's ask Martha." She knocked on Martha's door.

Both Martha and Mary welcomed them in and invited them to sit. "Thank you. We have a couple of questions for you. Jane, who as you know is an accomplished baker, would like to make Phoebe happy by baking a special confection to celebrate her birthday. Would that be appropriate?"

Both sisters exclaimed, "Oh, yes." Martha said, "That's a kind and generous offer, Jane. I'm sure our young cook would love to learn some of your secrets.

Mary said, "I'll take her down to the kitchen right now and introduce them."

When the two were gone, Belle said, "Martha, where would Philippe get cobwebs on his clothes?"

"Probably in the old barn, but I don't know why he would've been in there. We haven't used it for years."

"Hmm. And his boots have a layer of muck, which would indicate he's been in the Ever Glades. Did he have plantation business there? Perhaps he was there delivering your rum?"

"Good heavens, no."

"I see. And why do you think there were puddles of water on the floor below the locked window last night after the séance?"

"Well, Tom was dripping wet when he came in from the storm. And he stood beside Philippe there by the window."

"Yes. You haven't had any difficulty with that window leaking in the past?"

"As far as I know it's watertight."

"Did you plan to have someone blow out our lone candle?"

"I did not. I don't know who blew it out, but that certainly contributed to the chaos. It seems like something Albert would do for fun."

"Yes. Tell me about the relationship between Philippe and Albert."

"Philippe bullied him and Albert often yelled that he hated his father. I think some stern guidance would have gotten better results."

"Who do you think killed Philippe?"

"I don't know. I still can't believe it happened. Sadie...er, Belle, please say you will stay here and help us. You found Luther's killer at Enterprise. I know you can find out the truth."

You have much more faith in me than I have in myself. "I think you must continue to think of me as 'Belle.' I can only promise to do my best. Where will I find Albert?"

"Go down this hall. It's the second room on the right."

Belle did as instructed and knocked on the door, but got no response.

"Albert? It's Belle. I'd like to talk with you. Will you open the door, please?"

Knock, knock.

"Albert?" She tried the door knob. It turned. She pushed the door open in time to see Albert's foot disappearing over the windowsill. "Oh folly, fudge, and flummediddle."

Now what? Do I climb down the giant oak after him? In this long skirt?

Next time I won't give him a chance to run away.

Instead, she went to find Mary, who was just leaving the kitchen.

"Mary. How are the two cooks getting along?"

"Polly seems to be a bit in awe of Miss Jane and her capabilities. And Jane is stifling laughter at some of Polly's superstitions. But other than that, they are getting on fine."

Belle said, "Would you like to take a short walk? Maybe you can help me find Albert. He ran away from me just now."

"All right. It's a nice day for a walk. Tom said we lost the roof off one of the sheds. But aside from that and all the downed trees and litter everywhere, you'd never know we had a terrible storm yesterday."

"Yes. Everything is washed fresh and clean."

Mary said, "I'm sorry he ran away. That boy can be skittish as a colt sometimes. He frequents the old barn and the molasses shed. Let's see if the way is clear of obstructions and rubble from last night."

As the two left the house, Mary said, "Did you want him for anything in particular? Is he in trouble?"

"No. I just want to ask him about his written statement -- it's hard to read. And I want to see what he says about his father."

They made their way around fallen trees. The sweet burbling songs of finches proclaimed a new morning.

Mary said, "Oh, good. They have cleared the area for our dance tonight." The men were cutting up logs and placing them around as benches for temporary seating.

Belle said, "Mary, I found puddles of water on the floor below the locked window at the séance. It was under the curtains, way past where Tom stood in his wet galoshes and a wide segment of the curtains was really wet. Is there an easy explanation for that?"

"I've read that ghosts sometimes leave plasma trails."

"Ahh. Hmm. And there's the candle...I think a real person blew out the candle. Who do you think did that?"

"Somebody at the other end of the table by the window, probably."

"Philippe was at the window. I suppose he could have done it. Nanny and Jane had their hands next to his. I'm sure Jane didn't do it. Ben, next to her might have, but he and Nanny both look frail. I don't think they would have the energy to blow that hard. Do you have any ideas about who killed Philippe?"

Mary said, "In the short time that he'd been back, he had gotten entangled with a great many ladies. It must have something to do with that. Oh, look." She pointed toward Albert, who at that moment disappeared behind the old barn.

"Excuse me," Belle said. She picked up her skirts and ran through the weeds to the barn.

A minute later, she came back holding the boy by the collar. "Ouch. I haven't seen sand spurs anywhere on this plantation except here. Let's get these stickers off of you," she said and began carefully pulling burrs from the boy's pants legs. "Why did you run?"

Albert thrust out his lower lip and said, "You're that séance lady. I don't want to talk to you."

"Why not?" The three of them started back to the plantation house, with Albert firmly guided between the two women.

"Because I do not want to become a cooper and make barrels my whole life, like my father wanted. If he had gotten medicine for my mother when she was sick, I'd still be there with her."

Mary said, "Was your mother Crozbi? She was crazy about Philippe before she ran away."

"What? No. Maman was Marie Claire, the most beautiful of French ladies. She was good to me. And I should still be with her in France."

"I think your father wanted you to tell me something. He threatened to tell me himself. What is it you need to say?"

"Um... I took out one of the cat boats and Papa saw me turn over out on the water. He paddled out and saved me. He said I have sorry skin. But now the boat is lost. It's on the bottom of the river. I'm sorry."

"Oh, Albert. Don't you know that the boys can bring it back up, if you tell them where it is? And if you want to learn to sail, all you have to do is ask."

His thin shoulders hunched up to his ears and tears trickled down dirt-smudged cheeks. Then the floodgates opened and he sobbed.

Mary comforted her nephew with a tight embrace.

Belle thought, *He seemed the most likely suspect. Hate of his father is a powerful motive, but this poor mixed up child couldn't be a killer -- could he?*

CHAPTER ELEVEN

June 2, Accident at Cypress Pointe Plantation

Belle left Mary and Albert and went in search of Celeste. She approached the parlor and heard Phoebe say, "Ha. I threw a six and all the shells are up. We are going to beat you, Terra. Your turn, Sister. Throw the cowrie shells."

She entered the room and found Celeste partnered with Phoebe against Terra and Virginia in a spirited game of Pachisi.

"I'm glad to find you together. I have a couple of questions. "Terra, Phoebe, did either of you blow out the candle at the séance?"

"No," said the two sisters in unison.

"Terra, did Albert's hand touch yours on the table the whole time during the séance?"

"No. Not after the candle went out and it went all black in there. He jumped up."

"What do you think he was doing?"

Terra said, "I couldn't see well, but he was just larking about."

"Did you see what he was doing, Phoebe?"

"I couldn't see a thing. But I think Albert killed Philippe. That nasty child yelled all the time at his father."

Belle nodded, then turned to Virginia. "What did you see from your vantage point?"

"Nothing that would identify the killer, and apart from the few moments John checked around his seat for wires, he and Nanny kept their hands on the table continually."

"Did you or John blow out the candle at the séance?"

"Absolutely not. Do you think I'm a ninny? I don't like sitting in the dark. And why would John blow it out? The answer is no."

"No, of course not. Virginia, who do you think killed Philippe?"

"That young man was making quite a name for himself -- running after anyone in a skirt. Maybe a protective brother or jealous husband did it. How they managed it with all of us in the room is another question."

"Where are your husband and son this morning?"

"I think they went out to help the workers clear the storm debris."

"Ah. Good of them to pitch in. Terra, how well did you know Phili..."

Ben barged in. "Belle! Mary says, come quick. In the molasses shed, an accident. Come," said Ben, clearly out of breath.

They all jumped up and trooped out of the plantation house. Belle entered the yeast-and-alcohol scented molasses shed in time to see John and Tom pulling the dripping, unmoving form of Albert out of a large vat of brown sticky goo. The two brawny men stopped momentarily with their burden on the platform above the pool.

John said, "Here. Dangle him head down and I'll give him a good shake." They shook the poor young boy like a rag doll, while dark, oily, viscous material trickled from his lips.

Then they carried him down the access steps and laid his limp body on the ground. His head lolled to one side and John leaned his forearm on the boy's chest, bringing more liquid from his mouth.

Dear God. I just talked to him, thought Belle.

The child turned his head and coughed.

"Hooray," "Yay," and "Bravo," came cheers from everyone.

Mary said, "Celeste, will you please go into the shed next door and fetch a board to carry him?"

"Right away, Aunt Mary," she said, and she hurried out the door.

Mary said, "Albert, you poor boy. However did you end up in the molasses?"

Belle said, "Who found him?"

Tom said, "I did. He was poking around the distillery again. It hadn't been 10 minutes since I said, 'Albert, if you aren't going to make yourself useful, then clear off and as of now, this area is off-limits.'"

"What happened?" said Belle.

"I came to check the progress of our molasses fermentation. It takes 12 days to two weeks, before distilling can begin and I have to keep a close watch. I found him floating face down. The fermenting barrel full of molasses and yeast is covered with a large special-made cloth."

"I don't see any cover," Belle said.

"No. I guess he took it off to look inside. He must've fainted from the fumes. Looks like he fell in and got tangled in the cloth."

Martha said, "Albert was curious about the rum. Oh dear. That boy always seems to be in a place where he shouldn't be."

"I told him to stay out, but he kept showing up. You've heard the proverb, 'Curiosity killed the cat?'" said Tom.

Belle noticed more sand spurs on the boys sodden gluey pants legs. *We got all those off of him not an hour ago. He must have gone back to the old barn.*

She bent over and examined the boy. "He has a large bump on the back of his head. I see nothing that would have caused that during his fall."

Amid a loud babbling of voices, she climbed up the stairs to the platform and picked up a loose brick lying there. She motioned and mouthed to Martha, "Come up here a minute."

Belle showed the bloodied brick to the plantation owner. In a soft voice she said, "Look at this hair stuck to the brick. It's the same color as Albert's. This sticky stuff looks like partially dried blood. I think someone hit him with this brick before he toppled in. Somebody tried to murder him."

"But why? He's a mere boy. What could he have done that would cause someone to kill him?"

"I don't know, but he had more burrs on him after we just pulled them all off, so it must have something to do with your old barn. It's time we get a good look at that place." Using her stage voice, loud enough for everyone to hear, she said, "As soon as we move him to the plantation house and clean off all the molasses, I want everyone to join me for a tour of the old barn."

Suddenly it was quiet. A horsefly could be heard buzzing up high against one of the cheese-cloth-covered windows in the mostly open shed.

Tom frowned and said, "It's off limits because it is unsafe. The roof could fall down around us at any moment. And the ghost..."

Belle said, "You all heard Charles Merritt say the feared spirit is now happy. And I've seen you go in there, Tom. I want to know what drew Albert there."

Martha said, "I do, too."

Celeste appeared with a wide pine board and they transferred the boy onto it.

"Everyone is welcome to join me at the barn as soon as we make Albert comfortable," Martha said. "We'll see what's so interesting in there. You two, bring him and follow me. Careful, now." She turned and marched back toward the plantation house, with the others parading behind her.

CHAPTER TWELVE

June 2, Kitchen at Cypress Pointe Plantation

In the kitchen, Jane, usually shy, was in her element. Cypress Pointe Plantation cook Polly Butters was a tall, gangling girl of 18, with reddish brown pigtails escaping in wisps from under her gathered white cap. Big ears stuck out from under the hat and big hands made her a little clumsy. But her contagious wide smile and sparkly blue eyes endeared her to everyone.

Jane, pointing to the baskets of fresh carrots and okra from the garden, said, "Those look good. I was wondering ... do you have anything special in mind for Miss Phoebe's birthday today? I'd be glad to help."

"Oh, I didn't know." The girl looked worried. "I didn't... I don't... I don't suppose the regular puddin' would do?"

"Yes, or I could help you make a buttermilk chocolate cake."

Polly brightened. "Oh, that would be wonderful. I never made anything so fancy before."

"What else did you have in mind for the menu for this evening?"

"The fellers brought in some deer an' I was gonna stew it with them carrots and okra."

"Would you like to try something different? In Cuba I learned a recipe for venison steaks with beef gravy and bacon. And I used to make zippy carrots for Mrs. Bird, the lady I worked for in Enterprise. She couldn't get enough of them."

Polly whooped. "Glorious day. I'm just frabjous with the thought of learning how to make all of that." She twirled around the kitchen, then stopped her impromptu dance long enough to look out the window.

"Laws a' mercy. Look at everybody following along behind Miz Martha. They are all coming up here to the house," said Polly. "I 'spect they'll call for a jug of lemonade pretty soon." The girl resumed her lively dance.

"You sound happy, Polly. Let's get started on that cake. We need two eggs, a medium bowl, and a big birch rod."

"We don't use no birch rod no more. We have a whisk." From a drawer, she proudly produced a wire whisk."

"Great. You get busy beating the eggs and I'll put the butter, cocoa, and water on the stove." Jane removed what she needed from the shelves, then glanced up at Polly. "You must have a melody in your head," said Jane, with a laugh. The girl beat the eggs for the cake, while dancing a fast jig around the kitchen.

"Yes, I was thinking of the last time I attended a dance. I hope our fiddler has some good tunes tonight," said Polly, her yellow dress flapping as she whirled.

"Oh, my goodness. Belle would love your colorful socks," Jane said. Yellow, green, blue, lavender, black, red, and orange striped socks peeked out, as the girl's dress and apron rode up.

"Thanks. I made them myself, using the last bits of yarn from projects of everybody else on the plantation. Miz Mary taught five or six of us to knit. She and Miz Martha, they sew and knit for the plantation. These eggs are frothy. What next?"

Jane continued stirring the butter, cocoa and water on the stove. "Measure a spoonful of baking soda into it. And put in one and a half teaspoons of vanilla and half a coffee-cup of buttermilk. Then beat it all together," she said.

Jane watched in amazement as Polly measured the baking soda into the bowl, then took another spoonful and threw it over her left shoulder. She reached into the pepper jar and pitched a generous spoonful of pepper over her shoulder, while executing a joyous pirouette. She still whisked the ingredients.

Jane removed the saucepan from the stove and set it to the side to cool. "I think you've beaten that enough. Take down another bowl and a fork for the flour, sugar, and salt."

Polly stopped dancing. "A fork?"

"Yes, we are going to fluff those dry ingredients and add as much air as we can to this cake."

"Oh. I see." She set down her buttermilk bowl and brought a clean one. Then waiting for instructions, she stood on one foot with the other foot tucked up under her skirt and hopped up and down.

Tell her fast before you laugh and hurt her feelings. Jane said, "Put in 1/4 of a teaspoon of salt, two teacups full of flour and two of sugar."

She watched as the girl measured her salt, then cast another pinch of salt over her left shoulder. The flour and sugar had the same fate -- some in the bowl, some over her shoulder. *That is just plain wasteful, and messy, too,* thought Jane. *I have to say something.*

"Why are you throwing ingredients on the floor, Polly?"

"I'm throwin' it in the devil's eyes, don'cha know." She vehemently tossed another pinch of salt over her shoulder. "He sits up there on my left shoulder trying to make me do things wrong."

"Isn't that wasteful?"

"My friend said that a long time ago in Bible times, salt was precious --that means expensive. Spilling it was almost sack-ree, sack-ree..."

"Sacrilegious?"

"Yes, but now it isn't expensive. And it's good to throw some because the devil doesn't like it. I fling salt in his eyes and he goes away. I figured he wouldn't like flour, sugar, or baking soda in his eyes either. Maybe I should throw a pot. That'd knock him out all right and he'd stay away for longer. Knock on wood," Polly said, and she rapped on the table.

Short, rotund Jane tried to match Polly's sincerity as she looked up at the towering girl. She was Buddha peering up at Lincoln. She said gently, "That is superstition."

"What do you mean? Super-sti-tion?"

"I mean a lot of people believe in magic like that, but it isn't true. A better way to avoid mistakes is to think about what you're doing. No need to throw things."

"Oh, good. It does seem awfully wasteful. But I can still knock on wood, right? Trees have good spirits, ya know. Jesus's cross was made of wood. It was good luck for all of us. And that's why I cross my fingers when I wish for something good. It's a cross I can make myself."

"Polly, that's good to know." She rapped her knuckles on the wooden table. "From now on, I'll do it, too. Knock on wood and cross your fingers, to your heart's content."

Polly resumed her dance, but stopped again in front of the window. "Where are they going now?" she said, as she stared at the procession, now going the opposite direction.

"Belle mentioned something about seeing what's in the old barn. Have you ever been there?"

"Heavens to Betsy. No and I never will. They's ghosts a-haunting that place."

"Albert didn't seem to mind the ghosts and everybody's wondering why he was drawn to that barn. He was metal filings pulled to a magnet."

"He is a nosy fellow, to be sure," said the young cook.

Jane said, "Mmhmm. Now, about this cake..."

After they put the cake in the oven, Jane said, "Wash and scrape those luscious fresh carrots, and slice them into half-inch rounds. Meanwhile, I'll cut this venison into steaks and then butterflies."

"Butterflies?"

"Yes. Give me a minute and I'll show you." Jane pulled the whetstone pendant from its peg on the wall, wet it, laid it on the worktable, and used both hands to glide her knife over the stone. After several passes, she said, "All right. This knife is sharp enough."

She cut off the fat and gristle. "Now I'll cut steaks the width of my thumb." She sliced the piece of meat.

"Then we butterfly each of them, slicing them even thinner, like this. I start from the small edge and carefully cut towards the bigger side, leaving enough to connect the 'wings.' And we will have to hammer them some, to get them tender."

"They look pretty."

"They'll taste good, too, when dredged in egg and milk, then seasoned flour, and then breadcrumbs. About half an hour before serving time, we'll fry them in bacon drippings and smother them with gravy. When you're finished with the carrots you can leave them in the large crock. Next, wash the okra and slice it into thick rounds. We'll fry it right before we do the steaks."

A few minutes later they removed the cake from the oven and let it cool. "Let's get the skillet ready to sauté the carrots. We need to melt some butter, add brown sugar and mustard with a pinch of salt. Then just heat and stir until they are glazed."

Polly followed Jane's instructions, then removed the carrots to the serving bowl. A quick taste and she said, "I can see why Mrs. Bird loved these. I could eat the whole bowlful." She wiped her sticky hands on a towel. "How long are you staying for?"

CHAPTER THIRTEEN

June 2, Barn at Cypress Pointe Plantation

"He's clean and comfortable and Belle gave him some medicine. I think we've done all we can for now. The poor boy seems to be asleep," said Martha quietly to her small crowd of helpers in Albert's bedroom. "Let's go see what's been drawing Albert to the barn."

Belle said, "Lead the way."

John Crews III said, "I'm with you Martha, but I doubt there's anything in that old barn, except for cobwebs, mice, and a snake or two."

Snake? Aaa, thought Belle. Stop that. I have to get over my fear of snakes. Being in that pit with rattlers should have cured me. She shuddered. "Coming, Martha."

As they all traipsed down the track, avoiding or climbing over fallen trees, Belle said, "Terra, how did you meet Phillippe?"

"It was at a song and dance party three months ago, about halfway through my visit with Phoebe. I played violin to accompany my sister's singing. He was so charming and paid me a lot of attention, saying he expected to be master of Cypress Point soon."

"Did you fall for his charms? Were you in love with him?"

"I suppose I was, a little, at first. But he soon started paying more attention to my sister."

The pretty petite blonde pursed her lips. "The flirt. She grabbed him away from me. I heard her tell him that she was terribly lonely since her husband was away in a Union jail -- Ben was captured running the blockade."

"Was there any rivalry or jealousy between you and your sister?"

Terra paled. "Er, why no. Of course not."

Hmm. "Who do you think killed him?"

"Well, it wasn't me, if that's what you're thinking. Have you asked Ben that question? There must be a string of jealous husbands from here to France." She strode away from Belle.

At the barn Tom opened the rickety doors as wide as they would go. Fredrika trotted out in a stately manner -- with a mouse dangling from her jaws.

"Eww. Don't put that dirty mouse in your mouth, Fredrika," said Phoebe.

Terra said, "That's her job. Don't fuss at her, Sister."

"Whew. This is worse than I remember," Martha said. "It's dark and smells of rats." From the interior, a crow took wing and flapped out over their heads. "Tom, please go first and hold the lantern high."

"Yes, ma'am. But I don't see nothing in this old barn except old barn." His hand, held aloft with the lantern, became tangled in a swath of cobwebs. "Blast it all."

"Martha, look at this," Belle said, as she pointed at the floor. "Someone has been in here recently, moving something heavy in this corner. See the scrapes on the floor. Tom, will you please shine the light over here. Ahh. More of those 'Black Ball Rum' labels. And aren't those your barrels?"

"What in the world are they doing out here? They look new, too." Martha said.

Belle pushed at one of the barrels and found that it was heavy and it sloshed, obviously filled.

"I'd say someone is stealing your rum and storing it here temporarily, until they can haul it away. They must be making plans to sell it under their own label."

"I can't believe anyone would do that. And who could get away with it?" Martha said.

Mary said, "Maybe our new 'manager' went into business for himself, when we left for vacation."

"He wouldn't dare," said Martha.

"Well, somebody did, because there it is," Celeste said.

"Tom, what do you know about this?" said Martha.

"Nothing at all, Ma'am. We don't store any barrels in here for fear of the roof caving in. But we make a great many of them barrels in the run of the year. I can see how a few wouldn't be missed. I'll ask our coopers if they made any extras.

"You do that," said Martha.

Mary said, "This would explain why some of the workers saw dark shadowy figures around here at night."

Tom said, "No, Ma'am. The workers have been afraid of this place for years. They wouldn't be caught dead in here, let alone moving barrels in. But Philippe wasn't aware of the ghost stories. He could have put some barrels of rum in here. Maybe he liked the idea of having his own private stash. I think the spirits killed him for being disrespectful."

John Crews III said, "Don't be daft, man. It wasn't a spirit that stabbed Philippe."

"That's right, Father," said Ben.

With some heat, Tom said, "Oh, really? Then how do you account for the fact that the man was killed in a closed room, while everyone's hands were on a table? You were in the middle of a séance calling up the spirits of the dead!"

"Well, I, I..." John spluttered.

Martha, ever the unruffled hostess, said, "Gentlemen, thank you for your thoughts. I think we are finished here. Belle has kindly offered to allay some of our fears concerning our safety. Will you gentlemen resume your important efforts in clearing the river and roads, please? Ladies, we have business in the parlor."

CHAPTER FOURTEEN

June 2, Parlor Lessons at Cypress Pointe Plantation

"Martha, didn't you say that Virginia is coming?" Belle said.

"Yes. She was going to encourage Terra and Phoebe to come, too. Oh, there they are now."

Belle smiled at the latecomers. She said, "Scared? I think we all are. Did you know you can control your fear by controlling your breath?"

"Breath?" said Mary.

"Try it. Everybody breathe in for four counts through your nose, hold it for four counts, breathe out slowly through your lips four counts, and hold for four more counts before you repeat. Let's do it together. In, two, three, four. Hold, two, three, four. Out through the lips, two, three, four. Hold, two, three, four.

After they repeated it four times, Celeste said, "I do feel calmer. Where did you learn that?"

"I have worked in big cities and I had a teacher who taught ways for a small person to resist a larger attacker. Controlling your fear is the first step. You can calm yourself that way, then focus on action, instead of being paralyzed by fear."

"Martha could have done that breathing to be more calm when she was attacked last night?"

"Yes. Always focus your mind on what you must do. And she did the right thing. Always, always your best defense is to run away or hide. If that isn't possible then you must stand and fight back as fiercely as you can."

Phoebe said, "Oh, I thought you were going to give us some way to avoid all that, all that ...violence. An incantation to bring someone from the spirit world or a charm to protect us."

"No, I don't have anything like that. I <u>can</u> help you learn how to resist an attack. You must practice and be prepared."

Mary said, "What do we have to do?"

Belle said, "Let's start with stepping."

"Stepping?" they chorused, as they passed dubious looks between themselves.

"It's a matter of balance, because it's really important that you don't fall. First, never cross your feet."

"Hmph. I do that all the time. It looks dainty," said Virginia.

"I know we've been taught that it's ladylike, but it puts you at a disadvantage -- if someone attacks you," Belle said. "Next, no matter which direction you're going, move the closest leg first. It's faster and leaves you balanced. And take small to medium steps, like normal. If you will all spread out in a semi circle facing me, I'll show you what I mean."

"I don't like all this talk about limbs," said Phoebe, with a pout.

Terra said to her sister, "Quit fussing, Phoebe. You are always against anything new."

They all moved to face Belle. "Good. Now put your hands on your shoulders and notice how wide they are. That's how wide your feet should be apart. Imagine your feet are hands on a clock. Point your right foot at 12 o'clock towards me and put your left foot back a little, pointing at 10 o'clock. This turns your shoulders, so that you're a smaller target. Take a small step back with the left foot. Now try that with your left foot in front, your back foot aiming at 2 o'clock. "

"It feels quite comfortable," said Celeste.

"Now I'm going to step back away from you and I want you to step forward toward me. Remember to use your front foot going forward and follow with your back foot, so you are in 'Clock' position. Good. Everybody looks balanced. Now I move toward you and you step back a medium step, back foot first. Good. And if I move this way, you do too, using the closest foot first." Belle looked into their eyes and watched them concentrate, while they moved around the room in this fashion.

"Next, think about defense. Any nearby object can be a weapon. Look around this room now and see how many things you might use as a weapon. Look in your pockets, too... or your hair. Name them."

"The pen on the desk could be a poking weapon," said Celeste. "As could the pin in my hair."

"Knitting needles," said Mary.

Martha said, "The bronze figurine on the mantel would be nice and heavy for hitting someone."

"I'd just pick up that lamp and whack the attacker with it," said Phoebe, getting into the spirit.

"What about that heavy mug. That would do a lot of harm if I thumped somebody with it," Terra said.

"The flower arrangement has a heavy brass vase that would crack bones," said shy Jane.

"And I had a spoon that found its way into my pocket after giving medicine to Albert. If I turn it around, it can be a weapon, too." Belle clapped her hands in glee. "Yay. I want you to practice in the next few days looking around you and finding possible weapons."

"But what if we don't have time to reach for a weapon?" said Martha.

"If none are handy, use what God gave you," said Belle. "Some ladies file their fingernails to points, rather than round or oval. They are, in essence, claws. You could do that -- I have a file.

"When you scratch, fold your thumb into the palm of your hand and make your four fingers stiff and hard, like claws." She demonstrated.

"Eww. That's ugly. A proper lady would never do that," said Phoebe, with a shake of her head.

"A lady would, if she wanted to avoid being hurt or possibly killed by an attacker. Now you try it. Scratch the underside of this leather saddle, Phoebe." Belle picked up and held a small saddle at chin level.

"Oh, Belle. I can't do that," Phoebe said.

"Sure you can. Imagine I just tried to choke you and the saddle is my face."

"Oh, all right." She reached over and gave a half-hearted scrape.

"That's a good start. Remember to step forward with your forward foot. Now Celeste. Let's see you fold in that thumb and claw this bad man. "

"I will, Belle. I'll just imagine it was that last idiot who tried to grab me in New York." She swiped hard right, left, right, left at the saddle.

"Great. Who's next? Can anybody scratch harder than that?"

They all took turns and, as inhibitions lifted they tried to outdo each other. Friendly competition kicked in. By the end of the third round they were fierce -- more like wild, angry cats than soft, sweet Southern belles.

"That was good. Next we are going to hit imaginary things. Let's step outside the French doors and do this on the lawn. Spread out and give yourselves room to swing your arms. Keep your arms in, close to your sides, until you're ready to hit. Stand balanced in 'Clock' position and make your rear hand into a fist like a hammer."

"A hammer? Good Lord," said Virginia.

"Yes. With our fist hammer, we can hit four ways: down, across diagonally, sideways, and upward. First we'll practice 'down.' Bring that fist up from the back, around up high and hit down from 12 o'clock to 6 o'clock, stopping about chest height -- you are hitting at your attacker's collar. Twist your body and put everything you have into that blow. Bring your fist down and repeat that 10 times."

"Oh, my Great Aunt Nelly! People will think I'm a feminist. If anybody sees me doing this, I'll just die," said Phoebe.

"Hush," Terra said. "You could die if you can't do this."

"Now put your other foot forward. Yes, I know it's harder, but we must train both sides. Do 10 strikes and put your whole body into it. See if you can hit with more force each time. Can you SCREAM as you hit?"

The screams were hesitant at first, but got louder with practice. Belle warned away well-meaning people who came to investigate. "We are all fine. We are playing a game," she said to them.

"Good. Change feet again and for this round make diagonal strikes across your imaginary attacker."

"10 times?" said Celeste.

"Yes. And then put your other foot forward and do 10 more." After that they practiced hitting sideways and upward.

I think my delicate ladies are getting tired, thought Belle. "Let's go back in and everybody have a seat."

"Thank goodness," said Martha.

"While you take a short break, I want to show you something else. Elbows are sharp. Your elbow makes a good weapon if you strike with your full body weight behind it. You can spike an elbow up with the lead or rear arm. The lead elbow is quicker, because it's closer to the target. But it lacks the power of the rear elbow, that uses more body rotation like winding up to throw a ball."

"I'm good at ball throwing," Phoebe said.

"Great. Use that skill, Phoebe," Belle said. "We'll play a game -- the scoundrel versus the lady. Right foot forward, everybody. You are going to 'throw' your left elbow, now in back, into the scoundrel's stomach. In a minute you will get a partner and grab one of those big upholstered pillows. We will take turns being the scoundrel, who holds the pillow in front and threatens, like this." She held a pillow and made a frightening face, while advancing on Martha.

Belle said, "When you are 'The Lady,' wind up by twisting back, like you are going to throw a ball. Then spring forward and jab your back elbow into the pillow as hard as possible. Don't just poke your elbow into the pillow. Put all of your body weight behind your blow. Try that, Martha."

Belle's hostess hauled off and elbowed the pillow hard enough that Belle lost her balance and fell on the couch. "Hooray," Belle said, with a laugh.

"Now everybody pair up and choose your roles. And add a scratch. Think 'left elbow, left scratch. After 10 of those, put your other foot forward and do 10 more. Then switch roles. Scoundrels, stand with your backs to the couch or an upholstered chair so you have something soft to fall on when the ladies really ram you." They all laughed.

Martha said, "And, so the upholstery doesn't suffer too much from the scratching, find the part of the pillow that doesn't see the light of day and hold that part toward the fierce lady, please." More laughs went around the room.

Belle said, "Hold pillows firmly at the top at eye level. Ladies, don't hold back. Ready? Go."

Everyone had a chance to practice elbowing, scratching, and hammer fist pounding. Looking somewhat disarrayed, they finally sat. "Another useful and easy technique is to clap your hand on your attacker's ear. That will make his ear ring and give you a chance to run away. You can pop him hard on both ears, if you can get to them. Now turn to a neighbor, cup your hands a little, reach out, and gently clap your hands over their ears. Imagine you're doing it much harder to an assailant. As you go in to dinner, imagine different positions in which you could clap someone's ears. They are bending over to pick up some thing. You imagine clapping them on the ears. You are walking behind them and imagine reaching up and clapping them on the ears."

The ladies practiced, then talked excitedly about their experience. "Would you like to do this again?" Belle said. "I have more I could share with you."

Flora the parlor maid knocked, stepped into the room, and with her big brown eyes open wide in surprise, announced, "Dinner will be in 30 minutes, Ma'am."

"Thank you. That's all we need right now, Flora," said Martha. And to the other ladies present, she said, "Oh, my goodness. I must look a fright, but I've had a really good time. And I feel much calmer. I think the physical movement has done me good. Thank you, Belle."

Terra said, "Yes, and the knowledge that I'm not at the mercy of an attacker does me good. Thank you, Belle."

"Now, I really must get ready for dinner," Martha said.

"I'll go look in on Albert," said Belle.

Belle turned the door knob and opened Albert's door quietly. She thought, *Poor boy. Who hit you and pushed you into that vat? Have you wronged someone in the short time you've been here? You have carried years of resentment toward your father for his failure to understand and care about you. But he's gone. This attack on you can't be the result of viciousness between father and son. Who did it, then?*

The boy's very dark skin contrasted with the bleached linens. He stirred but didn't open his eyes. Tall and slender for his age, he was in many ways the opposite of the Merritts. Tight curls of brown hair were cropped close to his skull. With a long narrow face, aristocratic nose, and sensuous, moody mouth, his was the face of a dreamer.

"Sleep well, Albert. We are all anxious to hear what you know of your attacker," Belle said very softly. She turned and hurried off to get ready for dinner.

CHAPTER FIFTEEN

June 2, Dinner at Cypress Pointe Plantation

T he séance group had ten for dinner. Missing were only Philippe, for obvious reasons, Albert, who was still recovering from his swim in the molasses, and their revered old Nanny, really a denizen of the servants' hall. She had used her position and age to finagle a seat at the intriguing séance table.

In the dining room, the chandelier's many candles glowed yellow bright above ladies' shiny pastel silk dresses and gentlemens' charcoal or navy woolen suits. Martha and Mary, seated at either end of the highly polished mahogany table, surveyed their guests along the place settings of crisp embroidered linen napkins, shining crystal goblets, silver flatware, and their best china. Fresh flowers, artfully arranged in two low vases down the center of the table, perfumed the air. Light glinted from the silver coffee service on the buffet and they were all reminded by these social cues that politeness was expected of everyone.

"We have a very special meal tonight, to celebrate Phoebe's birthday," said Martha. "Let's raise our glasses in a toast to Phoebe. Happy birthday neighbor, and we wish you many happy returns." They all toasted as the footmen served the chicken noodle soup.

"How is Albert?" said Virginia.

Belle said, "He was still asleep when I looked in on him. I hope it does him some good. He suffered quite a shock."

"Do we know how he came to fall in?"

"Tom thinks he was overcome by the fumes," said Mary.

Martha changed the subject. "I was glad to see that they have cleared an area in front of the servants' quarters for the dance tonight. The roads and the river are still blocked with trees and debris. You all may be stuck here, but at least we'll get to eat well and hear that light-hearted fiddle music tonight. We all need that."

Ben said, "I heard that fellow playing his fiddle while your workers were chopping logs and clearing out the brush today. That was some mighty good fiddling."

Flora, Paul, and Zack served the venison with bacon and gravy along with glazed carrots and fried okra. "Oh, that looks delicious," said Mary. Murmurs of approval came from all around the table.

"Mmm, it is delicious," Terra said.

"This is the best venison I've ever had," said John Crews III. "And I've eaten a lot of venison in my time," he said with a hearty laugh.

Celeste said, "I like this better than stew, Auntie. Did Polly make it? I didn't think she knew how."

"She does now," said Mary, with a laugh.

"I heard that fiddler, too. But I also heard ladies screeching and screaming. It sounded like murder was happening out on the lawn," said John. "The lads and I stopped what we were doing and hurried to save you, but you all refused to be rescued. I never heard such laughing."

"Oh, we were just playing a game," said Belle quickly.

"That was some violent noisy game," he said.

Terra said, with a slight wink to Celeste at her side, "Yes, we were laughing and having so much fun, that we forgot to be demure ladies. And we are going to do it again soon."

"Well, tell us beforehand, so we will know not to come running," said Ben.

Martha, steering the conversation gently, said, "Happy Dan is an exceptional musician. I'm looking forward to the dance tonight. Is everyone planning to go? I think moving to his fun music will do us all good."

Celeste said, "Yes, I'm going. But what do we wear to an outdoors dance?"

"Let's all agree to wear something simple and comfortable. Our workers will be there and they won't have fancy clothes," said Martha.

Phoebe said, "I don't have anything suitable to wear, then."

"I have just the thing, Sister," said Terra, giving her sister's hand a little squeeze. "You must go. It's your birthday."

At that moment, Flora entered with the festive birthday cake, aglow with candles.

"Happy birthday, Phoebe," said Martha. They all joined in congratulating Phoebe and toasting to her good health. She clapped her hands in delight.

"Oh, this really is the best birthday ever," she said.

As everyone swooned over the taste of the luscious cake, Martha asked Flora to go get Polly from the kitchen. When the young cook appeared, Martha said, "Jane will you please stand. Let's show our appreciation to Polly and Jane for an exceptionally delicious meal," and she started the applause. Then everyone wished Phoebe many happy returns of her birthday.

Mary stood and approached Polly. She said in a soft voice, "Dinner was divine. As we all know, no young lady should go to a dance without the protection of a married lady or an elderly gentleman. After I have finished dressing, I'll come and help you get ready and be your chaperone for the dance. We'll do something pretty with your pigtails - a curly coiffure, perhaps."

Polly said, "Oh, thank you, Miss Mary. I'm ever so grateful. But whatever can you do with this vexatious hair?"

CHAPTER SIXTEEN

June 2, Dance Evening at Cypress Pointe Plantation

The moon shone bright silver over the front of the servants' quarters. The comfortable structure was built on stilts for airiness and to accommodate the occasional flooding of the river. Polly came down the front steps with Mary. "Oh, my. So many stars. I could never count them all," Polly said, marveling at the thousands of pinpricks of silver in the dark velvet sky overhead. "I don't go out at night. I'm afraid of the dark."

Some distance away, posts had been erected around a flat gathering area. Lanterns, swinging from the posts, swayed back-and-forth in the breeze and illuminated the small 'dance floor.' Mary and Polly were drawn like moths to the cozy glow.

"Hello Belle, Martha. It does look pretty," Mary said.

Martha said, "I like that we have a variety of social classes -- plantation owners and guests, servants, cane workers, tenants, and a close neighbor or two."

"They must be hardy souls. It would require hacking their way through the storm debris to get to Cypress Pointe Plantation," Belle said.

People milled around in anticipation.

Celeste had dance-calling experience and volunteered her service as dance leader. She walked under a lamp and said, "Welcome, everyone. Take a partner for the first dance, please. Stand beside your partner, gents on the left, ladies on the right. Take two hands with that partner and all couples form a big circle.

Short, wiry, dark Happy Dan began a lilting melody. He looked dapper in his top hat and he jauntily propped one foot up on a log, where his shiny black shoes gleamed in the moonlight. The air held the piney smell of fresh chopped wood. A whippoorwill announced continuous blessings over the proceedings... or, more likely, called to his shy lady love. Above the music, Celeste called out, "Promenade around the circle anti-clockwise until the music stops."

When Dan stopped playing, Celeste said, "Gentlemen, bid farewell to this partner, walk past one lady and promenade with the next." Dan played 16 bars more of his jaunty music, while dancers promenaded, laughed, and flirted. The music stopped again. "Tell her 'goodbye,' pass one, and promenade with the next." They continued this way around the circle and then Celeste said, "Say 'adios' and turn the next in an allemande right for eight counts before you promenade."

Ladies fanned and flirted. Gentlemen smiled, bowed, and chatted. At the end of the mixer, Belle was partners with Tom. She said, "Oh, folly, fudge, and flummediddle. We're going to have to rescue the fiddler from Fredrika. Look at that cheeky gray cat. She's draped around Happy Dan's shoulders and is batting at his shiny red suspenders. How can he fiddle like that?"

With a noticeable lack of concern, Tom said, "It doesn't seem to be slowing him down much. And I think I hear Fredrika purring. I didn't take her for a music lover."

"That is a front row seat. She could conduct the whole shebang from up there," said Belle, with a laugh. "And now that the music has stopped, I can hear her loud rumbling. That cat must enjoy the music as much as we do," Belle said, showering the neighboring dancers with her musical laugh.

Celeste announced, "Choose partners for the Virginia Reel. We need all the gents on one side in a line and all the ladies on the opposite side facing your partners."

Tom bowed and said, "May I have the honor of the next dance?"

Belle gave a little curtsy and said, "Yes, thank you."

Tom led her to the ladies' line, then took his place with the men.

"Our head couple at the top is here, nearest the fiddler. Raise your hands, head couple." She pointed to Martha and John Crews III, who waved cheerfully. "We will walk it once. We're going to start with a forward and bow, then back into your place. So let's try that. Forward, two, three, and bow. Back, two, three, and stop. Right elbows now for eight counts and then left elbows. Ready? Go around, two, three, four, five, six, seven, eight. And left, two, three, four, five, six, seven, and eight. Stop right there."

"Who is that handsome fellow with Polly?" Belle said in a soft voice. *He seems infatuated with our young cook.*

Tom said, "That's Abe Miller. He just bought a small plot from John Crews close to the Cypress Pointe property line. He's growing produce for markets up north."

"That girl is positively glowing tonight. I almost didn't recognize her without the pigtails," said Belle. *She curled her pretty red-brown hair and left some ringlets around her face.*

"Now two hands and we go clockwise. Ready? Two, hands and, circle, four, five and, six and, seven and, eight. Then comes our do-si-do. Back to back with her, around the right shoulder. Right, shoulders, three, four and, five, six, seven and, eight. Then seesaw with the left shoulders... Now head couple take two hands and, while everyone claps, skip or slide between those two lines, all the way to the end of the set for eight counts, then back again for eight."

Belle noticed Winston, the tall, lanky, and very dignified butler, by himself in the shadows at the end of the set, buck dancing! *Has he been sampling the rum?* Except for the occasional "whippoorwi-i-i-ill," the evening was quiet as everyone paid courteous attention during the walk-through. But the rhythmic thump and scuff of dance steps pitter-pattered like a well played drum, as Winston hopped and clogged to a tune of his own. Dancers in the line nearby quietly cheered him on.

At the end of the walk-through, Dan played lead-in music on his fiddle and the dancers were off, bowing and twirling.

When the head couple slid to the end of the set, they grinned at Winston and danced around the vigorous buck dancer. Everyone clapped and encouraged him with a chant, "Yay, Winston. Kick those, heels." The thunderous sound of all those clapping hands and shouts encouraged the energetic skipping couple and emboldened the syncopated steps of the butler.

"Whew," said John Crews III as he escorted Martha from the "floor" at the end of the dance. "Let's find you a seat on a smooth log and I'll get us some lemonade."

Later in the evening, Belle spied her shy Cuban friend Jane partnered with Winston. *Oh, good. They seem to be having fun.*

"Now, gents. Look around and find a lady who hasn't danced with you and invite her to honor you as your partner in the graceful Lancers Quadrille. Four couples form a compact square. We need another couple over here, please. Thank you. This is a proper dance, couples side-by-side with gents on the left. We will walk through it once. All four couples take two hands with your partner and promenade anticlockwise with 16 slide or gallop steps around your square, and back to your own place. Gents three chassez steps to the right. Ladies three chassez to the left, with gents passing behind the ladies."

The evening was enjoyed by everyone -- young and old, rich and not-so-rich. Virginia Crews was seen doing a lively polka with a cane worker, a grinning boy, who looked to be about eight years old and was an excellent dancer. Flora the parlor maid danced a spirited gallopaede with Ben Crews. And Terra danced a hornpipe with Zack. It was one way to forget, at least for an evening, the hardships of the fiery trial that was the Civil War.

Happy Dan ended the festivities with a waltz, considered by some to be inappropriate, because of the close position of the dancers. For this beautiful, lilting, but scandalous waltz, most gentlemen chose 'that-special-someone' as a partner. Some ladies let it be known through their friends that they would like to dance with a certain gentleman.

As she watched people swirl, dip, and glide, Belle thought, *I wish Noah could be here. Folly, fudge, and flummediddle. We seem to be traveling in different orbits. I suppose I did leave him and come here. I'll just help Martha find this murderer and then I can go back to Enterprise. What will it be like if I accept a job as a Pinkerton agent? Will I ever get to see him?*

The dance ended with everyone tired and happy. Dancers were relaxed. As Mary escorted Polly back to her quarters, an owl hooted. "Who hoo hu hooo." And the smell of honeysuckle was strong in the air. She noticed a sniffle coming from the girl. "What's wrong, Polly?"

"A-Abe," said Polly, mumbling.

Mary wasn't sure she had heard correctly. "Did you say Abe? Abe Miller?" Mary said.

In the silver moonlight, Mary watched Polly nod, clasp her hands under her chin and moan, like the end of the world was coming. She then burst into tears. "Y-yes."

Mary stopped abruptly. In the moonlight she held the young girl gently by the arms and stared into her face. "Did he do something inappropriate? What did he do?"

Through great heaving sobs, Polly said, "He, he..."

"What did he do, Polly?"

She bawled even harder. "He asked me..."

"Yes? Go on. He asked you what?"

She took a big breath and then blurted "He asked me... to marry him."

"To marry you? For heaven sake. Have you known him long?"

"Yes, Ma'am. About a year. He comes over sometimes to bring his fresh vegetables and I give him a bite from the kitchen. We talk."

"There's nothing wrong with that. He seems a nice fellow. Don't you like him?"

"Oh, yes Ma'am. I do."

"Then why in the world are you crying?" Mary offered her handkerchief. "Here. Wipe your face."

"'Cause if we marry, he'll get to know everything about me," she said.

"Yes. That usually happens. But surely, that's a good thing."

Her anguished sobs began again in earnest. Through an abundance of tears and snot, Polly said, "But then, he, he won't like me."

"My dear, that's nonsense. Dry those tears. Come. It's been a long day." Mary pulled her along, anxious to finish their short walk. "I'll visit you tomorrow in the kitchen and we'll sort this when you're rested. Here we are." Polly walked slowly up the steps of the servants' quarters.

"G' night," the girl said in a desultory manner.

"Good night."

Mary continued to the plantation house and breathed in deeply, as she listened to the sounds of cheers and laughter floating on the evening air. She stepped down the hall to Albert's room and opened the door quietly. Fredrika was curled atop the lump of covers that was Albert. *Still asleep. I wonder if you will ever be right again, young Albert? Won't you awake and tell us about your attacker?*

CHAPTER SEVENTEEN

June 3, Early Morning in a Pigeon Loft at Cypress Pointe Plantation

Little Jaz, a boy in brown-and-white polka dotted bib overalls, ran around the small pigeon loft enclosure waving his arms. "C'mon down, you," he said, following the erratic flight path of a newly arrived pigeon. "Come down here where I can see ya. Come and get this here cracked corn." He pointed to where he had sprinkled grain on the floor. The bird flew. The boy chased.

Finally, he stood out of breath, with his hands on his knees. The bird lit on the handle of his rake, where he had leaned it in the corner. Jaz pounced. "I knew you wanted to come to me."

Cypress Pointe Plantation's pigeon master Pablo, a short dark fellow, who wore a luxuriant long, droopy, black mustache, unlatched the loft door and slipped in. "Good morning, Jaz boy. You're about your chores early this morning."

At the sight of the excited boy holding a gray messenger pigeon out in front of him, Pablo said, "Oh, ho. What are you doing with that pigeon? You're just supposed to rake and put corn in the trays."

"She come in jest now, whilst I was raking the sand on the floor, sir," said Jaz. "Don't they know the war is over?"

"They're probably just checking to see what damage the storm did here. That bird is named 'Dawn.' I took her to Caleb in Jacksonville the last time I went. Don't hold her so tight, Son. She might…"

A blast of slimy yellow-white bird poo dribbled down the little boy's fingers, covered the front of his shirt, and dripped on his feet.

The shocked boy burst into tears, but maintained his hold on Dawn, out in front of him. "I jest wanted to pet her."

Pablo said, "Easy, Jaz. Hold her easy. Seeing as how you got her in hand, so to speak, and saved me the trouble of getting her from her box, please hold her still so's I can get the goose quill out from under her longest tail feather. Cradle her in your arms."

"Eww. Up next to me?"

"Yes, but not too tight."

Jaz took a deep breath, squeezed his eyes closed tight, looked away, and rested the bird next to his messy shirt.

Pablo's mustache almost brushed his chest as he leaned over the bird. He untied strong sewing thread from the slight notches in the hollow goose quill and removed it from the bird. "You can put her down now, Jaz. You best get yourself to the pump and rinse that stuff off. Then take this to Miz Martha right away. Be careful with it and do not tarry."

In her bedroom, Martha found her tweezers by the early morning light and carefully extracted a tight roll of microfilm from the quill. Fredrika wound around her ankles as she separated a microphotograph and placed the delicate one-and-a-half-inch-wide collodion film between two thin flat glass plates. That glass sandwich she inserted into the Magic lantern and projected the image on the bedroom wall. "It's for Sadie, asking if she's all right, Fredrika," said Martha. "Be patient, my affectionate companion. You can sit in my lap as I transcribe."

Belle awoke that morning and opened her window. She heard birds murmuring in the tree outside and paused to appreciate swaths of purple and pink painted across the morning sky. Gardenias in a border below perfumed the air. A soft knock sounded at her door.

"Belle. I thought I heard you stirring. Are you awake?" came Martha's voice, almost a whisper.

"Good morning, Martha. I'll get my robe and be right there," Belle said. A moment later she opened the door to her friend, who handed her a folded sheet of paper. Fredrika zipped in past her and disappeared under the bed.

"This letter came for you," Martha said.

"Came? From where? And how? The roads and river are closed."

"Ummm. We have other means of communication."

Really? Belle's brown eyebrows flew up and she stared questioningly at her friend.

"Oh. I knew I was going to have to tell you. We belong to a sort of secret club of people who keep homing pigeons. Some Cypress Pointe birds have been caged and transported to members in various towns around the state and the country. When they are released, they unerringly fly home to us -- with messages attached."

Belle blinked. "Are you telling me that this letter came here by pigeon mail?" said Belle.

"Yes. This message came from our member in Jacksonville."

"On a pigeon?"

"Don't sound so surprised. It's a great collaboration between man and animal. After someone writes a message, a photograph is taken on microfilm. That reduces the size of the message by five times or up to as much as 40 times, depending on the equipment used. The film is very carefully rolled into a tight bundle and put inside a waterproof goose quill, which is then tied to the longest tail feather of the bird. The tail feathers remain stationary while a bird flies. The bird is then freed to fly home with the messages."

"Martha, I've heard of microfilm, but I have never seen it. How in the world did you ever find out about such a thing, let alone learn how to use it?"

"In 1851 Mary and I attended the Great Exhibition of the Works of Industry of all Nations in the Crystal Palace in London's Hyde Park. The photography exhibit display, in my opinion, showcased the most remarkable discovery of modern times. We were fascinated and talked with photographer/astronomers, James Glaisher and John Herschel in depth about their work. We purchased chemicals and apparatus there and had them sent home."

And my aunt was probably in the thick of it. This explains, Aunt Cora, why the top of our boat house at Snow Bird Cottage has a pigeon loft. "You, my friend, are full of surprises," Belle said. "Will you show me your camera?"

"Of course, my dear. I'll be glad to."

"And you must show me how to use it." Belle became thoughtful. "Who sent a letter to me, using such valuable resources?"

"Don't worry. It was a last-minute addition to a dispatch of other information that was ready to be sent. And it's from Noah, of course. He is worried about you."

"Noah?! You read it?"

"Yes. Think of it as a telegram. Our pigeon master brought it to me and I transcribed it for you. I'm amazed that Noah found our agent. That took a lot of doing. You can send a message in return, if you wish. Get it to me by the end of the day and I will photograph it and send it on."

"Thank you, Martha."

"You are quite welcome. I'll leave you to read it," Martha said.

The door closed, and Belle sat at the small desk. Fredrika sauntered out with a streeeeetch and yawn. "You heard all that, did you?" The feline hesitated momentarily, before pouncing to Belle's lap. She stomped around with slow, jab-like pokes, as if wearing miniature hobnail boots on her dainty feet. Belle stroked her and she settled. Belle said, "Kate Warne told me that I needed a photographer. If I play my cards right, I'm going to become one, Fredrika, my heavy-footed friend."

Belle opened her amazing missive.

To Sadie Snow c/o Martha Merritt

From Noah Asbell

June 2, 1865

Dear Sadie, HOW ARE YOU? I confess that I've worried about you since the storm. Not knowing if you are alive and well, I've had to make myself stop making up stories and accept 'not knowing.' When I realized that I could get a message to you and possibly get a letter in return, I was relieved and happy.

To my knowledge all our friends and neighbors are coping well with the destruction from the storm. It left a great amount of damage on the St. John's River. I'm concerned most about the several people who are missing.

I've known about Caleb's pigeon post for quite a while. When I saw the devastation in Palatka, I immediately thought of your safety and realized that Caleb's hobby could be very useful. The "Darlington" has also docked in Palatka for the night and is heading for Jacksonville in the morning. I will hand this letter to Jacob Brock with instructions to give it to Caleb when he gets to Jacksonville.

You'll be happy to know that, with help from some of my crew, I put in your new Yale locks at Snow Bird Cottage. That was the evening after our wonderful dance in Palatka. I have folded my memories from that magical night into a sparkling packet and put them on the table in the entryway of my heart, where I can take them out and examine them often.

More good news from your cottage -- Percy has been diligent in feeding your chickens, and they are looking plump. My plans for building your henhouse have been put on hold, due to this storm. I may be able to start it when I dock in Enterprise on the sixth or the tenth. Don't worry. I'll find the time. Meanwhile, they are safe in the boat house.

During the storm the *Katie Asbell* was traveling from Jacksonville to Palatka, and as the river is much wider there, we ran into very little debris. But we sharpened our axes that night in anticipation of the need to chop away downed trees on our journey back up the narrows to Enterprise. The crew and I spent many hours clearing, to make our way through. We sang some of the music from the dance to keep ourselves going, and that kept the work from being too onerous. The happy tunes running through my head bring back all my feelings from that night. I'm looking forward to seeing you soon.

Is your work at Cypress Pointe nearing completion? I hope that, as soon as the waterways can be cleared, you will return to Enterprise. I have a surprise for you, which will prove helpful and, I think, please you, dear sweet and so very capable lady. Anxiously awaiting news from you and Cypress Pointe Plantation, I remain

Your friend,

Noah Asbell

Belle's heart beat faster. *Who knew he could be so poetic? And he called me sweet. How did he find Martha's contact in Jacksonville? He is resourceful and smart, as well as very handsome. And what kind of surprise could he possibly have for me?*

CHAPTER EIGHTEEN

June 3, Attack at Cypress Pointe Plantation

At breakfast Belle focused her attention. *Let's find this killer.* She said to Celeste, "Did Philippe tend to gamble or owe money to anyone?"

Fredrika, who had trotted along behind Belle to the morning room, hesitated momentarily, wobbling from side to side, and then launched herself into Celeste's lap. "Traitor," Belle said to the cat.

With raspy, pink, sandpaper tongue, Fredrika licked the young journalist's hand. "Never mind. She is lapping at the last of my bacon sandwich. Er, did Philippe gamble? Not that I ever saw. Sorry. That's not much help."

"Did you happen to blow out the candle at the séance?"

"No. I was too far away."

"Who do you think killed him, Celeste?"

"I've been thinking about that. How did any of us do it, with all of our hands touching on the tabletop most of the time and the room closed?"

"I can't answer that yet."

"Then, answer me this. You are presenting yourself as a medium, but Aunt Mary said you're a Pinkerton agent. The two -- medium, immersed in a world of spirits and ghosts versus Pinkerton agent, who deals with harsh realities, is masculine, calculating, and tough -- are complete opposites. You are not either one of those, are you?"

Belle was suddenly a wild horse, eyeing and shying away from a noose thrown above her head. *I knew this woman would be trouble. I can't afford to have my former life as an actress on stage at Ford's Theatre publicized. I did nothing wrong. I'm NOT going back to Washington under police guard.* "What do you think?" said Belle.

"I think my aunts trust you, whoever you are. And we are all stuck here. Even though you don't look anything like a normal Pinkerton agent -- I mean, you aren't a burly man with a cigar -- you are making a good show of investigating."

Ooo, that's way too close for comfort... except I AM investigating. "Well, let's get on with the show, shall we? Did Philippe spend a great deal of time alone, such that no one knew where he was?"

"All right. I'll play your game for now, but I <u>will</u> find out. Mmm, now that you mention it, he did disappear sometimes. He was secretive and often didn't turn up for meals."

"Did he ever explain his absence?"

Phoebe, in high spirits and a very strong cloud of floral perfume, burst into the room ahead of Ben, interrupting the conversation. "... and the cake was so luscious. Imagine. They did all that for me."

"Good morning, you two. Come sit with us," Belle said.

"Belle. I want my jacket back," Ben said.

"Yes, of course. It's over there, on the side table," the sleuth said, pointing to a pile of jackets. As soon as he was out of earshot, she said, "Phoebe, how long was Ben jailed in the north?"

"I was all by myself over a year. I was so lonely."

"I can imagine. What was your relationship with Philippe?"

"With Philippe?" the woman said, in a voice that sounded like a squeak. She flushed a pretty shade of red. "We were just friends."

Ben appeared with two plates loaded with ham, eggs, biscuits, and gravy. He placed one on the table in front of his wife and one at his place, then took his seat.

"Oh, Ben. You know I can't eat that much of this rich food," Phoebe said. She opened her mouth to continue her protest.

Oh folly, fudge, and flummediddle, thought Belle. *What's wrong with, 'Thank you, thoughtful husband?'* "Ben, did you write letters to your family while you were in jail in the north?" Belle said.

"No. I got one letter the whole time," Phoebe said.

Belle rolled her eyes. Phoebe didn't notice.

"I told you before, my dear. I wrote every week. They must have gotten lost," said Ben quietly.

Phoebe sprang up and put her fists on her hips. She stamped her foot. "Benjamin. One letter in the whole year? That's no kind of writing at all."

Belle jumped in, saying, "Ben, did you blow out the candle at the séance?"

"No. I've had enough of darkness in my life."

"Ben, who do you think killed Philippe?"

"I don't rightly know. But I learned one thing in the war. Stab wounds are caused by knives wielded by real people. I don't know how, but I can guess the why. I've been told that he was getting too familiar with a good many ladies. He was probably stabbed by a jealous husband, who was spying on us from a closet." He looked at his wife. "Or, a lady he no longer favored popped out of a hidden compartment and attacked him in a jealous rage."

"I checked the room before and after the séance, Ben, and there are no closets. But I will look for hidden compartments. Thank you for the suggestion." She looked up. "Here come your parents. Good morning Virginia, John."

Virginia said, "Belle, you must give us some more lessons, this very day, immediately after breakfast... if you will, I mean. Did you hear? Terra was talking with your upstairs maid Lucky last night after the dance, when a man grabbed Lucky and tore at her bodice. Terra clapped his ears and used her fist-hammer, like you taught us. She pounded and scratched the man, until he ran away. Now several of the maids are asking for lessons."

John Crews III said, "Terra? That little thing? The one with the mop of blonde curls piled on top of her head? That wisp of a girl couldn't scare a rabbit."

"Well, evidently she did. Belle taught us how. Brutes of the world, watch out," said his wife.

"Are the ladies all right?" said Belle anxiously.

"I think so. I just overheard Lucky telling the housekeeper Bertha about it this morning."

Belle stood and said, "Excuse me please. Ladies, will you pass the word that we will have lessons in half an hour in the back parlor and ask Petunia to bring an old bed sheet. I need to do a quick check on Albert and Terra before we start."

Belle muttered to herself, "Philippe, Martha, Albert, and now Lucky. The ladies are right to ask for defense lessons."

Is that boy awake? Can he remember how he got into the molasses? My intuition and that bloody brick are telling me that someone hit him and pushed him in.

Lucky's attack sounds different. Was it the same person who killed Philippe and went after Martha... and Albert? How are any of those linked?

After breakfast Belle met with Jane in Albert's room.

"Good morning, Jane. How is our patient this morning?"

"He's awake, but he doesn't remember anything about the attack. He says he wants me to stay here and hold his hand. I guess I can do that, but he's hungry. Could you go get us some breakfast?"

"Of course. I'll be right back." She opened the door and stepped into the hall, where she met Mary. "Good morning. Off to the morning room?" said Belle.

"Not yet. I need to go to the kitchen first and have a word with Polly."

"I'm headed there myself. Let's walk together." They moved toward the outside door. "Is Polly planning some more fancy food? She and Jane really outdid themselves last night."

"I'm not going to plan meals. She has some fool notion that I need to discuss with her."

As they walked, Belle said, "Are you aware that Lucky was attacked last night on her way back from the dance?"

"Oh, no. What happened?"

"I think Terra scared off the man by clapping his ears and using what we talked about before dinner last night. As a result, your guests, plus some of your employees are requesting defense lessons. Those little ladies do need to learn that they don't have to give in. Perhaps your workers might be excused from their jobs for an hour to join us this morning? Ah. Here we are. Mmm, I smell apples with cinnamon, one of my favorites. May I please have a taste of that, Polly? I actually came to get plates of food for Albert and Jane." said Belle.

Mary said, "Yes, I think more defense lessons is a practical way to adjust to our predicament. We are all frightened of being stuck here with an evil person among us. Tell everyone that the staff may join us. They can catch up on their work later. That goes for you too, Polly. Belle is teaching us how to fend off attackers."

"We will start in about half an hour in the back parlor," Belle said.

"You can find a stopping point in your meal preparations, then leave your work and join us," said Mary.

To the astonishment of both women, Polly burst into tears.

Belle said, "Whatever is the matter, Polly?"

"You're both so kind," said the young woman.

"Does this have anything to do with what you told me after the dance?" said Mary.

Polly nodded. "Yes."

Mary said, "Please tell us what's worrying you."

Polly shook her head and wiped her eyes. "Sorry, I am being silly. Let me get those plates of food for Albert and Jane. I guess that boy's waiting on you and he is not a graceful wait-er," she said, as she scurried around the kitchen readying the plates. Soon she handed Belle a covered tray with a sprig of Queen Anne's lace from the vase on the counter. "I put you some apples on there."

"Thank you. That's pretty and the food smells divine, Polly. I'll see both of you in the back parlor for our lessons. 'Bye." She shot an encouraging look at Mary as she left the kitchen.

Belle hurried on her way back to Albert's room. She could imagine the intense hunger pangs that sometimes drive a teenage boy. She knocked gently and opened the door.

"Finally. I'm starving," Albert said. He released Jane's hand. Belle removed Jane's plate and her own apples to the small table and then handed over the tray with a heaping plate to the boy. He immediately tucked in, with a zeal that proclaimed him to be a growing boy. Jane and Belle sat at the little game table.

Between mouthfuls Belle said, "Jane, are you about ready for some self-defense lessons? The ladies and some of the staff are clamoring for more. It will only take us a little while, Albert."

"Mmm. This is delicious. Yes, I'm ready for a break. Do you need anything else before we leave, Albert?" Jane said,

Albert shook his head to express a negative answer and with a mouth full of food, said, "Mfpak ptoo."

"You are welcome."

The ladies cleaned their plates, stacked them, and pushed away from the table. "We'll be back. Meanwhile, please rest," Jane said.

After they exited the room, Belle said, "We need to stop off and have a word with Terra. That spunky little botanist used my fist-hammer and scratching techniques to chase off a man who attacked Lucky last night."

"Oh, my."

They walked a few steps down the hallway to Terra's door and knocked. "Who is it?" said a quiet voice from inside.

Belle said, "Belle and Jane. May we come in a moment?"

The petite botanist opened the door and ushered them in. Belle said, "I understand you did some extra practice on our ladies' lesson last night. What do you remember of the attacker?"

"Lucky and I were strolling along talking and he appeared out of nowhere and started grabbing at her. His back was to me, so I jumped up and clapped his ears hard, like you said. He just stood there, so I hammered upward on his ear with my fist and clawed his neck. He finally turned and ran."

"He was taller than you?"

"Everybody is taller than me," Terra said.

Belle laughed. "Good that you stayed calm and used what we talked about. Was he fat or skinny? Long hair or short?"

"On the hefty side, very muscular. Short hair."

"Do you remember anything he said, or the smell of cologne he wore?"

"Oh, yes. He smelled very strongly of rum and he grunted like a bear."

"Can you remember anything else about him?"

"No. That's all."

"Are you ready for lesson number two? We are going to the parlor now to practice and add something new."

"Absolutely. Let's go."

CHAPTER NINETEEN

June 3, Lawsuit at Cypress Pointe Plantation

Belle, Jane, and Terra headed down the hall towards the parlor. As they passed the Crews' room, they heard angry raised voices. Virginia said, "Well, it doesn't matter now, does it? He's dead."

The three ladies slowed their pace.

John said, in a bellow, "Yes, it does. It's still blocked. We can't get anything bigger than a canoe through there. I want it unblocked."

"Why don't you just talk to Martha about it? You don't need a lawsuit."

Outside the door, six eyes opened wide. The ladies lingered.

"Because I want a strong bargaining position. And the lawsuit against Cypress Pointe Plantation is already in place."

The mouths of three ladies dropped open and eyebrows flew up in surprise.

"John, you say I know nothing about business. But I do know that it's never a good policy to bring a lawsuit against a neighbor, instead of sitting down and having a reasonable conversation. You were going to tell them about it when?"

"I guess when the law clerk can get through to serve the papers."

"You are really going through with it? You're going to sue your good neighbors Martha and Mary?"

Belle thought, *This gives John a motive for murder. He says not but, with Philippe out of the way, he can make peace with Martha and save money on lawyers' fees. Only old Nanny and Virginia were between him and Philippe at the séance.* She reached up and knocked on the door. This was greeted with dead silence. "Virginia? Virginia, are you ready to go? We are headed for the parlor."

Virginia opened the door a crack. "Did you hear?" she said in a quieter voice.

"Yes. Why don't you tell us about it on the way to the parlor," Belle said, calmly. "Are you ready?"

"Let me get my big pillow. I'm coming."

As Virginia joined them, she said, "This was none of my doing. John got in a tussle with Philippe, who said our large tourist boats are noisy and are scaring away the deer and trout."

"Bah. Tell 'em all of it. Everyone will know soon enough," John said in a more civilized tone from behind the closing door.

"John said he sees plenty of deer and trout every day -- enough for everyone. But up river from your docks, Philippe had Cypress Pointe cane workers put boulders in the river to block river traffic."

"That was pretty high handed," Jane said.

"It isn't completely blocked, but we can't use our tour boats. John said the man wouldn't listen to reason. Tourism and nature guiding are our livelihood. We have to be able to take wealthy northern sportsmen and naturalists hunting and fishing. So, John went to our lawyer and brought suit against Philippe, Mary, and Martha."

That gives John a reason for wanting Philippe out of the way.

CHAPTER TWENTY

June 3, Late Morning Lesson Cypress Pointe Plantation

As the ladies entered the parlor, the gray tabby cat Fredrika ran to the sleuth and wound around her feet. Belle stooped and picked up the friendly animal. "Thank you, Martha and Mary, for giving your staff ladies a break from their duties to learn this. Petunia, did you bring a sheet?"

"Yes, Ma'am. It's on the table." She pointed to a mahogany pie crust table.

"Thanks. Let's start with our calming breath. Breathe in for four counts through your nose, hold it for four counts, breathe out slowly through your lips four counts, and hold for four, before you repeat. We'll do four rounds of that."

"Are we going to blow them attackers away with our breath? We probably need some onions and garlic for that," Lucky said. The ladies erupted in laughter. Fredrika twisted and fled from Belle's arms.

"No. We are going to banish the fear and focus on actions to defeat the attacker." She reviewed how to stay balanced, to choose handy objects as weapons, to fold thumbs in and make hard claws, to strike with a closed fist like a hammer, to twist and poke pointy elbows with bodyweight behind them, to clap ears of an attacker, and to scream as they hit.

"Now, put a hand out in front of you and press your thumb next to your hand. Always keep your thumb in. Bend your hand back as far as it will go. If this were a foot, it would be the heel. We'll strike with this heel-of-your-hand on an attacker's chest or upward on his jaw, while we shout. And, while I admire the creativity in some of the shouts I heard yesterday, let's be more clear than 'Just try it, you rapscallion,' and 'Not today, geezer. Go suck an egg.'"

"Try for something short like, 'NO' or 'GO AWAY' or 'LEAVE ME ALONE.' If he keeps coming you can strike him in the throat, nose, eye, or ear. Driving the heel of your hand, with force, into someone's nose can stop, injure, or even kill him."

"Wait. Wait. I couldn't kill nobody, Miss Belle," said Flora.

Martha said, "My attacker intended to *kill me.* Lying under that bed, I was petrified. His knife kept slashing back and forth. I would have fought tooth and claw to stay alive, but I didn't think of something as simple as looking for a weapon under there. If that happened today, I would grab my slipper and knock that knife right out of his hand. He'd have a hard time finding it in the dark. I want to learn more effective ways to stop an attack, and if striking him on the nose does the trick, then I'm all for it."

"You must assume your attacker has evil intentions," Belle said. "Decide now if you're willing to do everything you can to stop him. Your mental response will dictate your actions, and it's best to figure that out ahead of time."

Lucky said, "I was petrified, too."

"The special breathing is to help get rid of that, Lucky, and let you think what to do. Now get a pillow and a partner. Out we go to the lawn. We are playing 'Lady versus Scoundrel' again. The scoundrel holds both pillows in front of chest and face. Ladies twist back, then lunge forward for that heel-of-hand strike. Scream 'NO' or 'LEAVE ME ALONE' and drive your palm into his chest. Practice striking six different places. Think Chest. Chin. Throat. Nose. Eye. Ear. Change hands and repeat it. Then reverse roles. Remember to keep your thumbs in."

The yard looked and sounded like a deadly pillow fight was underway. The screams got really terrifying.

While they practiced, Belle slipped back inside and brought out the sheet and several long couch cushions. She spread the sheet on the patio and placed cushions end to end on top. She sat on them, then stretched out fully. Some questioned her with curious looks, but no one said a word.

From her prone position, she said, "Now let's see you jab those hard, pointy elbows into soft parts of your attacker. If a scoundrel is facing you, twist to your right, then pound him in the stomach with your left elbow, with all your body weight behind it. Or twist back, then fire your elbow up and hit an imaginary target in front of you. Good. Try it again and this time draw your arm across your upper body and drive your elbow to the side. Your elbow should travel close to your body."

Phoebe said, "That's a more girly way to fend off an attack."

Impatient, Terra said, "Oh, yes. As if we are really worrying about being feminine here, Phoebe."

"Well, I prefer being feminine over that terribly unladylike behavior," said Phoebe, pointing at Belle.

Belle chuckled and said, "I understand what you mean, Phoebe, but consider Martha's attack, which landed her on the floor. We need to practice all the things that you've just learned from different positions -- sitting and lying down. The spider lilies smell wonderful from down here, and I detect a hint of lavender from the sheet. Who's first to practice elbow jabs from down here? "

"You must be joking. I'm not doing that out here in the open, where everybody can see me," said Virginia.

Martha said, "Well, I will. Scoot over, Belle."

Belle jumped up and Martha lowered herself carefully onto the cushions. She jabbed and hammered and shouted. Soon she was joined by Celeste. Most of the ladies eventually took a turn and tried this very undignified practice.

Terra was still lying comfortably on the cushions, when Phoebe, the hold out, plopped down beside her. "See? I can do it, too," and she thrust her elbow forward. "This reminds me of when we were little. Remember your nickname?"

"Don't you dare," Terra said, and she playfully poked her sister sideways in the ribs. "No nicknames, Sister."

Phoebe wiggled her fingers in front of Terra's face.

"No, Phoebe. You wouldn't," Terra said.

Phoebe reached over and began to tickle her sister.

"Hee, hee, hee, ha. Oh. Stop. Hee, hee, hee."

"What are you going to do about it, Gertrude Giggle Guts?"

Terra shrieked in laughter. "Stop tickling. It's not 'ladylike,' she gasped, as she tried to roll out of reach. "I'm warning you. I'll tickle back."

Everybody chuckled with them as the two dissolved in fits of giggles, rolled on the grass, and tickled each other, as only sisters can. They ended in a heap, with their arms around each other, embracing in a big hug. "I love you, sister. I want you to be safe... and happy," Terra said in a whisper.

"And I want that for you, too, silly girl. I'm glad our ever-so-proper mother can't see us now," Phoebe said.

The onlookers clapped, and Belle said with a soft chortle, "If you ladies are finished entertaining us, I have one last thing for today. You all know how to stomp your foot down hard when you're standing on the grass. Try it. Everybody stomp. Drop all your weight onto that heel."

Phoebe stood and gave a demonstration.

"Phoebe is really champion at that," Terra said. "Because she has had so much practice."

"Never mind your sister, Phoebe. Keep stomping. Now imagine doing this from sitting, or on your hands and knees, or even from lying down, which is a very vulnerable position."

Terra quickly sat up.

"Terra, you have just pushed up to sitting. Now keep pushing yourself up, lifting your hip up until you can get your knee up and stomp down on an imaginary target's fingers or knee cap. You are trying to get up and he's trying to grab you or your skirts. Now get up on your hands and knees, pull up your knee and slam your foot down on that scoundrel's face."

"Stomp somebody's face? I couldn't," said Virginia.

"If he's trying to hurt me, he must expect me to resist and even to hurt him," Terra said.

"Whomp." Terra flattened the cushion.

"Yay. Even if you don't want to do this here with people watching, find time to do it in private. Kick and stomp like a donkey."

When they had practiced everything, they reconvened in the parlor, dresses crushed and hairpins dangling. Belle said, "Remember that running away or hiding is always best. But if that doesn't work, be calm and strike fast. Practice on your own." She thought, *They're flushed and disarrayed but they appear to be happy and relaxed.*

As she exited the room, Celeste said in a soft voice, "Today you sound much more like a Pinkerton agent than a medium." She pursed her lips, mimed pulling a fat cigar from her mouth, and laughed, her mouth a perfect 'O.'

As they left the room, Martha said, "Thank you for teaching these things that everyone considers unmentionable. You said you learned all this in New York. Do many New York ladies know these techniques?"

"No. Not many, because it's considered unladylike. I was taught by a friend from the orient who worried about my safety in that big city."

Virginia said, "Did you ever have to use it?"

"No. Most scoundrels are lazy, and I think they recognize that, with me, they will have a tough fight on their hands. I guess it's the alert and determined look in my eyes. It's easier for them to choose someone who will give in right away. Virginia, I've been wondering what it's like to own a big plantation. What's your main job at *The Landing*?"

"It's kind of like being mother to 200 people, isn't it, Martha?"

Martha said, "Yes. I have many hands to help, but I make clothes for all the workers, their families, and for us, too. I see that everyone has what they need. And I oversee the running of the plantation - planting, harvesting, and processing of sugar, molasses, and rum. We have our overseers. And Virginia has her men folk to help with that last part."

"Yes, thank goodness. The plantation is like a self-sufficient city. My day-to-day activities include gardening, dairy activities, salting pork, preserving fruits and vegetables, mixing medicines, the making of candles, soap, rugs, pillows, linen, and bedding. There's never a dull moment. We make everything- almost everything - that we use, and our workers are talented in that way."

"Ours are multi-talented, too. We've been paying our workers since we took over three years ago. They could go somewhere else, and some of them have, but most have stayed here. I like to think it's because they're treated fairly. Oh, there's John."

"Good morning, ladies. Have you finished scaring the birds?" he said, in a loud boisterous voice.

Belle said with good humor, "Yes, Mr. Crews, we are finished for today, and I know you are glad to have your good lady wife and daughter-in-law safer from scoundrels. But be careful sneaking up behind them."

"Yes, well... I came to get a drink and some biscuits for the workers. The river is partially cleared, but it will be another day or two before we can get through. Some massive old oaks came down across the river in several places."

"John, I'll walk to the kitchen with you and help you carry it," Belle said.

"I don't want to put you to any trouble, Miss Belle," John said, eyeing her.

"No trouble at all. I'm happy to do it," Belle said, ignoring the topic they both avoided.

"Well, that's mighty kind of you, Miss Belle."

As they walked, Belle said, "I understand your plantation *The Landing* was a refuge and staging area for blockade runners during the war. That must have been dangerous work."

"Yes. We did our best to keep people here stocked with necessities."

"Mmm. And the Confederate troops, too. Martha says you have a thriving guide business now. Do you ever take anyone to South Florida? To Key West?"

"No, we are mostly local. People want to go birding, fishing, and hunting."

Polly provided them with a large bucket of lemonade and a bag of lemon cookies. "This orter keep them fellers going for a while longer."

"Thank you, Miss Polly." John slung the sack over his shoulder and carried the large heavy bucket with bails. Belle balanced two stacks of cups on their way to the dock. "Careful now. The ground is uneven here," Mr. Crews said.

"Virginia explained about the lawsuit. What were your business dealings with Philippe?"

"When he first arrived, I tried to hire him to help in guiding visitors, but he wasn't interested."

"Were you angry with him for being overly familiar with your daughter-in-law?"

"I think that marked him as a man of no integrity, and I was displeased. But I didn't kill him, if that's what you're getting at."

"Did you blow out the candle at the séance?"

"Oh, of course not. Why would I do such a plum fool thing as that?"

Belle thought, *Were the two of you transporting stolen rum to the Ever Glades?* Instead, as they neared the dock, she asked him, "Who do you think killed Philippe?"

"No doubt about it. He was killed by an irate husband. I don't know how, since we were all holding our hands on that table."

"I'm beginning to have a theory about that," Belle said.

"Are you sharing?"

"Not yet."

CHAPTER TWENTY-ONE

June 3, After Lunch Cypress Pointe Plantation

Belle made her way back to the plantation house. *I have to solve this murder soon. If I don't, we could have another murder on our hands. And Celeste. I need to steer clear of that smart girl. I can't let her find out I was Evangeline Bright, actress extraordinaire in Washington at the scene of Lincoln's assassination.*

That would mean, besides the obvious trip to Washington in leg irons, all my possible suspects will lose respect for my detective work. And I will lose the ability to steer this investigation toward the truth.

She knocked on Albert's door. *Hurry up and figure it out -- all of it.*

"Come in," Albert said.

"I'm glad to see you awake. Have you thought any more about how you ended up in the molasses?"

"I did remember something, Miss Belle. I was standing on the platform, staring down at all that sticky stuff. The cover was off. Two days ago it just looked like a vat of molasses. This time it was moving around, like it was alive. Anyway, I heard a noise behind me and started to turn around. Then my head hurt and everything turned black."

Ah-ha. Just as I thought. "Who was behind you?"

"I don't know. That's all I remember. Maybe I'll remember more later," said the boy.

"Did you blow out the candle at the séance?"

"I don't think so. If I did, I don't remember it."

"You said you spent time at the boat docks. Did you see anything unusual there?"

"Only that biggest cat boat was in-and-out and in-and-out."

"What do you mean?"

"Late at night it would be gone. But in the morning, it would be back."

Another ah-ha. "Who did you see when you were out late at night?"

"Well, my father and Tom. They were always busy at something."

"Wouldn't that be normal? They were both managing the plantation."

"I guess. I'm just telling you they were in the old barn and around the boats late at night. Mr. John and Mr. Ben have done some late-night prowling, too. Oh, my head hurts something fierce. Do you have any medicine?"

"Yes, of course. I'll be right back." As she went to fetch her bag of medicines, she thought, *If our killer learns that Albert is remembering, that boy could be in real danger. Who can I get to stay with him?*

She returned with willow tincture, her faithful and fearless friend Jane, her friend and hostess Mary, and a cricket bat.

Now a letter for Noah. Back in her room, she penned this:

June 3, 1865

To Noah Asbell

From Belle

Dear Noah,

I was thinking of your safety, too… and that of the *Katie Asbell* during the recent storm. Imagine my amazement and relief when I got your unique letter saying you are all right.

You called me "sweet," but I don't think many here would agree with you. Some might consider me "hard."

The work here has turned out more involved than I anticipated. The Merritt sisters' half brother Philippe was killed during our séance, and, until a law officer can get through to us, I'm investigating the murder.

Philippe's 14-year-old son Albert, Martha, and an upstairs maid Flora have since been attacked. I'm frantic to find the culprit, or culprits. The women here are very nervous. I'm helping them by giving lessons on methods to protect themselves.

And I am to receive lessons, it seems, in this marvelous subject of photography. Martha has been doing microphotography and will instruct me.

When I think about you and our Palatka dance under the stars, I sigh. Oh, what I wouldn't give to be carefree and moving with you to that happy melodious music right now. Happy Dan played for a dance here. He has been stuck with the rest of us at Cypress Pointe Plantation since the storm. I hear him playing sometimes and think of you.

So much has happened since then. I started out being a séance medium. That's a role I'm still playing. Now that I am being an investigator, too, some have questioned that duality. I'll be glad to finish and come home.

Thank you for putting in my Yale locks. You and your crew members are very thoughtful. I'll think of a way to repay you when I get home.

Everyone loves a surprise, and I am curious about yours. What can it possibly be? I remain

Your friend,

Sadie

CHAPTER TWENTY-TWO

June 3, Kitchen at Cypress Pointe Plantation

B elle folded the letter and headed to find Martha. Down the hall she knocked on Albert's door. "Mary?"

When Mary came to the door, Belle said, "Where might I find Martha?" Belle lowered her voice. "She's going to show me how to take a microphotograph."

"Then you're going to need her bedroom next to yours. That's where the camera and dark room are."

"Miz Mary. Come quick. I went to the scullery to get a mop, and I saw that vegetable feller hurry out of the kitchen. Now Polly's all in a fit of tears," Flora said.

"Thanks for telling us, Flora," Mary said. "We'll take care of it. You can go back to work." She lowered her voice. "Belle, I'd feel a lot better about this if you'd come with me."

"Certainly. What can be the matter?"

In the kitchen Mary said, "Polly, what happened? Why are you crying?"

"I can't talk about it," the girl said, between sobs.

"You must talk about it. Did someone upset you?"

"I promised I wouldn't tell nobody."

"You can't go on like this. Please tell us what happened."

Polly hiccuped, covered her face with her hands, then said, in a weak voice, "You're just like him. I can't tell him either. He would get the wrong idea. I like him so much, but if I tell him my secret, he won't come to see me anymore."

Mary started to speak, but Belle put her finger to her lips to signal silence.

As if a dam had broken inside her, Polly said, "I can't tell you. I could tell you, but then you'd think I'm a loose woman. Martha said it was all right. But she might forget she said that an' I could lose my job. Then what would Maggie and I do?"

Mary said, "For heaven's sake, girl. Tell us what secret you're talking about. We'll decide for ourselves. And who is Maggie?"

The girl looked down at the floor in front of her, and her shoulders sagged. "Maggie is my secret. Her real name is Magnolia, and she's my baby. She's a year old now." Polly looked up, and the sparkle was back in her eyes. "She has curly blonde hair and blue eyes, and she's the bright light in my world."

Mary said, "Are you telling us that you have a daughter named Magnolia?"

Polly nodded.

"Where is she, Polly?" said Belle softly.

"Nanny takes care of her in Lulu's house, and I go down there every day."

Mary said, "Our cane worker Lulu?"

Polly nodded again.

"How did I not know this?" said Mary.

"Miss Martha said that salesman took advantage of me. We was dancing, and the next thing we was in the hay with his hands on me. Magnolia grew inside me, but nobody took much notice, 'cause my clothes didn't ever really fit. She got big and was kicking me something fierce. I was at Lulu's, and I hurt real bad. Lulu said Magnolia was comin', and she got Nanny and Miss Martha. That's why they're the only ones who know. And it's a secret, so people won't say bad things about Magnolia and me."

"Polly, may I give you a hug?" said Belle.

"Oh, please do," the girl said, sucking in a big shaky breath and blowing it out in a whoosh. "Now you see why I can't tell Abe Miller."

Belle released the girl from the hug and said, "What does this have to do with Abe Miller?"

"I really like him, and after the dance he asked me to marry him. But he doesn't know about Maggie. I could never ever leave her here. As long as I have breath and she needs a mother, we will stay together. We would be a package. And what man would want to raise someone else's child? No one."

"Great folly, fudge, and flummediddle," said Belle. "If he loves you, he won't care. He might even be overjoyed at the thought of having a lovely daughter. The only way you'll know is to tell him."

The tears started to flow again. "But I don't want to lose him as a f, fr...friend."

Mary said, "If he takes against you because of Maggie, then you don't want his friendship anyway. Tell him."

"Miss Mary, I just can't."

Belle said, "Polly, what will you say when he asks you for your answer?"

"He done asked me today. I told him I don't know. I need time to think about it."

Belle said, "You can either say 'no' without an explanation, which is going to stomp all over his hopes and dreams of having a life with a charming, fun-loving, hard-working, fine woman -- you. And it will make him feel like there's something wrong with him, that makes you reject him. That will be a real hurt to someone that you care about. Or you can say 'yes' and tell him about sweet Magnolia."

"Oh, I'm so confused. I don't want to hurt him. And I don't want to lose him as a friend."

"It sounds like you think you'll be rejected by Abe. You don't know that he'll feel that way. You're just guessing at his feelings. I want you to tell your story to Mary, and when you finish, say 'Nothing is wrong.' And then tell it all over again. And then tell it again, and again, until it loses its power to make you feel inferior."

Belle said to Mary, "Please just listen to her. Don't agree or disagree. Don't judge or suggest what to do. Only listen."

"All right," Mary said.

Polly covered her face with her hands and said, "Can't you just tell me what to do?"

"No. No one can. Only you know your heart. But telling your story, until it loses its power over you, will free you."

Belle left them, sitting side-by-side, with Polly chattering and Mary listening. As she made her way back to the bedroom wing of the house, she thought, *I must get this letter to Martha. And it's about time I search Philippe's room.*

CHAPTER TWENTY-THREE

June 3, Dark Room at Cypress Pointe Plantation

At Belle's knock, Martha opened her door. "Belle. Come in. I've been expecting you."

On her desk by the window was a pretty argand lamp, and next to it stood a magic lantern. Fredrika lay curled in a furry gray ball between the two, and she flicked an ear, then opened one green eye to see who interrupted her nap.

Martha said, "Did you bring your reply to Noah's letter?"

"Yes, and I'm very curious about your micro photography."

"It's rather involved and will take a while for you to learn. You don't have to make the film, Belle. If you prefer, I'll do it for you and save you the bother. I am accustomed to it."

"Oh, please Martha. I want to learn."

"Very well, if you're sure. Put your letter on the table and come next door. I'll show you how to prepare a wet plate." She walked over and opened a closet door, behind which a heavy curtain hung. Fredrika silently inched from her perch. She licked one forepaw and then the other.

"How long will it take?"

"We use Frederick Scott Archer's collodion method, which he published in "The Chemist" in March 1851." At the sound of the name Frederick, very like her own, Fredrika stretched languidly and jumped to the floor.

"It requires the photographic material, in this case a glass plate, to be coated, sensitized, exposed, and developed within the span of about fifteen minutes. So, we work quickly, and the room must be dark."

She parted the curtains to reveal a table with a small polished mahogany box camera, and a wall full of shelves with rows of bottles. The stealthy feline streaked in ahead of them. "No, Fredrika. You know you're not allowed in here. Come down from there. You get your claws out of my curtain." She reached up, carefully extricated the cat, and placed her back in the bedroom.

They went inside and closed the door and curtains behind them.

"Whew. I might be in a hospital," said Belle. A pungent smell of chemicals engulfed them. After her eyes adjusted to the dark, Belle noticed more equipment on the table behind the camera.

"Yes, you might. You're smelling a trace of my solvents -- ether and alcohol. Collodion is a flammable syrupy solution of nitrocellulose in ether and alcohol. The flexible type of collodion is often used in hospitals as a surgical dressing or to hold dressings in place."

Ah, yes. I've seen my friend, Doctor Mary Walker, use this in the hospital in Washington.

"Meow," the cat said, from outside the door.

Martha said, "Yes. I know you like to be in the middle of everything, kitty. But not now.

"Where was I? Oh, yes. Nitrocellulose, also known as guncotton, acts as a binder and carrier for photosensitive salts of silver, while making wet collodion images." She picked up a glass beaker full of cottony, fluffy stuff and held it out toward Belle. "Hold this nitrocellulose, while I unstopper my mixed solvents."

"I thought gun cotton was a replacement for gun powder," Belle said, as she received the container.

"It is. Miners use it as a low-power explosive."

"Folly, fudge, and flummediddle," Belle said, in alarm.

"Don't worry. It's also used as a lacquer finish on furniture and musical instruments."

"Aren't you afraid it will explode?"

"No. Watch it dissolve." She poured in the premixed solvents. "Now stir that. I'm going to add in the potassium iodide and then we have to coat this glass plate very quickly. Once the solvents evaporate, we are left with a colorless, transparent, flexible film."

"That's what the birds carry with the messages?"

"Meow, meow."

"It is. I roughened the edges of this glass plate with emery paper to help the collodion adhere. I will hold it by the corner while you slowly pour the iodized collodion near the middle. Careful. Now I tilt the plate to each corner to make the puddle flow around and cover the plate. That looks perfect. Now I'll lay it level on this table and let it set for a short time."

"You said it's very flammable. Aren't you worried about it catching on fire?"

"I don't do this next to a fireplace, if that's what you mean," said Martha, with a chuckle. "It's set. Now we place it on that ribbed glass dipper, bent on one end to hold the plate. You try. Just like that. And lower it into the silver nitrate bath, this tall skinny tub, in one continuous movement. The silver nitrate combines with the potassium iodide in the collodion to produce silver iodide."

"Which is light sensitive?"

"MEOWRR."

"Yes. Now, turn that two-minute egg timer over, and then we get to dance or do whatever we want for two minutes," Martha said, humming an Austrian zweifacher dance tune. "Let's go twirl with Fredrika." She danced out the door and scooped up the poor unsuspecting feline.

"That reminds me of Palatka and my dance with Noah," Belle said, sighing wistfully.

"You really like him, don't you?"

"Yes, I'm afraid I do."

"I've seen how he looks at you. There is no doubt he's sweet on you," Martha said, joining hands with Belle, and holding Fredrika between them. "One and, two and, three and, one, two, one, two. Whee. A triple swirl."

"For all the good that does us. He's destined to captain his boat on the river, and I will always be somewhere else. We're headed in different directions and want different things out of life, I think."

"Are you sure about that?"

"I..."

"Oop. Our two minutes are up. Down you go, kitty cat." Fredrika dug in death blade claws, twisted out of their arms, and leapt gracefully to the floor."

"Ouch," said the two simultaneously.

Rubbing sore arms, Martha said, "Now back to our plate."

They were careful to close the door behind them. "Take it out, put it on that rack to drain a little, and then we are ready to expose it. That should do. Put it in the camera here.

Good. Now we take the camera outside to the window." She carried it to her desk in the bedroom.

"Is this bright sunshine what we want?"

"Yes. Put your letter here. Now we focus here. Have a look. That appears sharp. We open this to expose it a few seconds --three will be enough."

"That's all it takes? I thought it would be much longer."

"That's one of the beauties of collodion. Now we go back to the closet. Close the door and the black-out curtain tightly behind you. Your turn to hold the slide. Take it out of the camera and hold it the same way I did when we coated it with collodion. I'm going to flow this developer onto the plate. Keep it in motion by blowing on it or tilting the plate." Martha poured and then picked up a piece of white paper from the table. She held it beneath the plate, while Belle blew.

"Why the white paper?"

"That's so we can see when it's properly developed. That looks good. Now we wash it with water in this tub. Dip and swirl. Then dip it in that tray over there -- it has sodium hyposulfite solution. Swirl it and then we give the plate a thorough wash in this tub of fresh water."

"I'm not sure I can remember all that."

"I'll write down the chemical names for you and the order. The last bit of magic is gutta percha in benzole. Hold the plate while I pour it over the image. Tilt it to cover evenly. Now we leave it to dry. Later, when we immerse that plate in water, the collodion will separate from the glass plate."

"That's brilliant. I wondered about that from the first moment you told me that pigeons were carrying photographs. All the photographs I've ever seen were on metal or glass plates --not really suitable for loading onto a pigeon."

"We could print these on albumen paper, but the words would be tiny and you would need an expensive microscope to read them. This way all you need is a simple magic lantern."

"This is clever. May we examine Philippe's room while we wait for the plate to dry?"

"Yes. I'll get the key. But what can you hope to find in there?"

CHAPTER TWENTY-FOUR

June 3, Aboard the Katie Asbell

"Where is that stench coming from?" said Joe, a fit, smart deckhand in blue denim overalls. He wore his shoulder-length brown hair pulled back with a leather tie. Working with him on the freight deck of the *Katie Asbell,* his shipmate Pete said, "It's upwind of us. Maybe a little critter died under some of those crates we took on. Ugg." He turned his head full of black curls downwind, held his blue flannel sleeve over his nose and mouth, and held his breath.

"It'd have to be a big critter to smell this bad," said Joe, pinching his nose. The two walked upwind and rounded a corner. The stink hit them full on.

Noah stood unrolling seven-foot-long strips of rawhide on the deck. "Hi, fellows. Will you help me lay these out and tie them to the railing? I need to soften them."

"Uh, Boss. All right, but these really reek. What is this?" said Pete.

"They're from that black bear Curly trapped. He skinned the hide and tanned it. Something he put on it stripped all the hair off. So, he just cut it into thin strips for making whips."

"Whew. They smell gamey." They unrolled and laid out a long thin strip.

Pete said, "Thunderation. These things are making my eyes water. You can't carry a whip that smells like that. Hold on a minute. Leave those other strips rolled. I'll be right back."

He returned moments later with a bottle, a bucket, and a bar of oil soap. He lowered the bucket over the side and brought up a small amount of tea-colored water. Into this he poured liquid from the bottle. "Here. Dip them in this vinegar water then rub them one by one over the soap." He pulled a small brush from his pocket. "I will hold my breath and rub it in using this. When we finish with all of 'em, we can blast them with the fire hose."

They followed Pete's directions, and when they finished, Noah said "They're a little vinegary, but they definitely smell better."

"Agreed," Pete said. "Now, we loosely coil these fresh-as-a-daisy bear hide strips and put them in the shade to dry,"

"Thanks, Pete, Joe. I have work to do, now. I'll be back later to do the braiding."

"I will help. I've never seen anybody braid bear hide before," Joe said.

"You're on," Noah said, heading for the companionway.

He climbed up the ladder. His next errand took him to visit swarthy, former circus performer, John, 'Cookie,' Lane. "Hi, Cookie. I'd like you to make me some special biscuits."

"Sure, Noah. What kind? Chocolate? Ginger snaps? Lemon drops?"

"No. I want savory cookies made with liver and they need to be small, the size of a big Aggie marble."

"Don't have many calls for liver cookies. When do you want 'em?"

"I need them by Jacksonville."

"You got it. Are you going to trap some critter with these?"

"I'll tell you later," he said, with a smile, and he headed up to the wheel house.

A stiff breeze ruffled his brown curly hair as he reached the highest deck. "How's it going, Shorty?"

"All is well, Noah," said the first mate.

"Good, because we need to run a "man overboard" emergency drill. I am going below and remind everyone what to do. When I ring the bell, I want you to circle the *Katie Asbell* back and cut the engine. I'll have all hands practice retrieving items from the water with the boat hooks. I'll ring the bell again to signal that we're finished. Questions?"

"No, sir, but we just did one, and the crew did right well at retrieving Luther Grimes' body from the river. I don't think the deckhands have forgotten how to do that. Are you expecting any guests in particular to go overboard in these gator-infested waters?"

"I'll tell you about it tomorrow, Shorty." He grinned conspiratorially and headed down to begin the drill.

When they docked at Green Cove Springs, a flock, called an earful, of extremely social Cedar waxwings twittered in a mulberry tree by the dock. As the deckhands began to load freight, Noah strode down the gangplank and visited the lean-to of potter Patty White. The building was nearly obscured by a profusion of fragrant gardenias interspersed with red and yellow ruffled hibiscus. The tall brunette, wearing a white duster covered in smudges of various colors, answered his knock at her door.

"Do you have any unbreakable bowls?" Noah said.

"I sold Jacob Brock several heavy little ones for service on his steamer. They aren't exactly unbreakable, but they will stay on the table of a steamer without much sliding around. Come in and look around," Patty said. They went into her work room.

He pointed out some bowls on a shelf. "I need a couple like that, only bigger," Noah said. "They need to hold about a quart apiece."

"What about these?" She went through a curtain and returned with a beautiful blue-glazed bowl in each hand. "Jeb carved some pine blocks to fit this size. That makes 'em take up more space on the table, but they don't slide none. They are real good for serving vegetables."

"I'm not sure I know what you mean."

"Let me show you." She went into her store room again and came back bearing two squat pine pyramids with cut-outs for bowls. She set them on her table and nestled the bowls down into the holes.

"Perfect. I'll take them."

She stacked one on top of the other and offered them to him. "That'll be a dollar. I can make you a whole set by the time you get back. And I'm experimenting with glazes. I can give you other colors, too."

"Thank you, but this is all I need for now." He paid her and came away carrying two heavy, quart-sized, blue-glazed bowls that fit into stabilizing pyramids of pine.

When he walked up the gangplank balancing the two pyramids, Adam said, "Hi, Noah. Need me to take those to 'Cookie' for you?"

"No, thanks. I'm going to stow them forward, under a small net I put there. See that they don't disappear, would you?"

"Yes, sir," he said. And after Noah had gone, he said to Abel, "I wonder what in the world those are for?"

CHAPTER TWENTY-FIVE

June 3, Gun at Cypress Pointe Plantation

In Philippe's room Belle moved to the window and pulled it open. "Whew. This place smells stale." She ran her finger over the surface of the dresser. "And it's dusty."

Martha said, "That's to be expected. It's been closed. What exactly are we looking for?"

"Anything that would tell us where he got all that silver. Signs of a smuggling operation, perhaps," said Belle.

"I'd like to know where he has been for the last 15 years and what he's been up to."

They searched cupboards and clothes drawers. "He has many fine pocket handkerchiefs and linen shirts, but common socks. I'd say he spent on things to impress others. He was thrifty on things that didn't show."

Looking in his dresser, Belle said, "This top drawer has only clean underwear. I was hoping for private letters - ones too personal to mix with bills and casual correspondence in the desk. But -- there's nothing."

Martha said, "All I've found is a pig skin toilet kit and a set of silver-backed brushes."

They had been looking for 10 minutes when Belle said, "Look at this old letter from 'Lycée Pape Clément' with an address in France. It's directed to Charles Merritt, stating that the school expelled Philippe for theft. Did your father ever mention getting an expulsion letter?"

"No. He was proud that Philippe was being educated in Europe. I know he kept sending him money."

"How would Philippe get the letter, and why would he keep it?"

"He must've stolen the official notification, so Daddy would never see it. Perhaps he was proud that he tricked us and the school?"

"These clothes look more appropriate for a sailor than for a plantation manager," Belle said, fingering the items in the highboy. "Although, this one suit of fine cut and quality shows that he was possessed of good taste. Perhaps he didn't have the purse to indulge it to the fullest."

From far down in the yard came the shouts of men engaged in loading fallen tree trunks onto a cart.

Martha said, "By Jove. I don't believe it. In this bottom drawer… a bullet mold and a gun." She picked up the weapon and a folded document. "And look at this. Papers for a slave named Marie Claire. Albert called his mother Marie Claire."

She put her face in her hands, then rubbed her temples. "Oh, Philippe. Did you buy a slave and then bed her, when you were supposed to be studying in France?"

"We can ask Albert."

"Belle, I don't know how much more of this I can take." She looked up. "I need to get away for a little while. I'm going to take a cat boat out for a quick sail. It won't be possible to sail very far downstream before I run into sweaty men with axes clearing fallen trees, but it will be a break. Would you like to come?"

"Thank you. I'll go with you as far as the dock for the fresh air and to stretch my legs. Then, I have something else to do."

Fredrika, tail standing straight up, trotted along behind them as if to say, "Don't do anything fun without me." Cardinals called to each other in the trees above as they strolled to the boat dock. "Do you really think you can find this killer?" Martha said.

"Yes. I've been developing a theory."

Tom approached them. "You ladies are not planning a sail, are you?"

Martha said, "Yes. I'm aware of the debris. I'll be careful."

"Yes, ma'am. See as how you do."

Belle thought, *That man is impertinent.*

Fredrika pondered, stalked Martha's feet, then pounced.

"Come on, you scamp." Martha scooped her up and stepped into the boat. She cast off, and as soon as she was out of hearing range, Tom said, "Miss Belle. I've been meaning to tell you about Ben."

"Oh?"

"Before the war he drank somethin' fierce and gambled on anything. It's only gotten worse since he returned from that Yankee prison. I reckon he had a real good reason to take against Philippe, what with Miss Phoebe castin' her eyes that direction."

"I see. Thank you for telling me."

"I just thought you ought to know."

"Tom, during the séance how did you manage to come along to the dining room and hear the shouts over the noise of the storm?"

"I was just doing my normal night rounds, making sure everything was secure."

"In that horrible storm?"

"Why, yes ma'am. You never know what kind of trouble a storm might bring -- fire, flood, ripped off roof, animals in a panic."

"Did you find any animals in a panic that night?"

"No, ma'am."

"I see. Thank you, Tom."

Belle headed for the plantation house and Jane's room. *I wonder how much of that is true?*

When Jane opened her door, Belle said, "May we talk? I want to go home. And before we can do that, we must figure out the truth in this case."

"This urgency wouldn't have anything to do with a certain handsome boat captain, would it?"

"Well, maybe a little. I got a letter from him, and he said that he put in our Yale locks. And he has a surprise for me."

"A letter? They finally cleared the river and the wagon paths?"

"No, they haven't. That's the extraordinary thing." Belle told her friend about microfilm and the pigeon post. "Do you know if Aunt Cora used carrier pigeons?"

"She did keep pigeons as a hobby. They lived above the boat house, but I never helped her with them. That would explain the occasional bad smells from the little room in back of the boat house, though. I was curious, but I didn't pry. It doesn't surprise me. She was an extraordinary woman."

"I am finding that out, more and more. Let's look at what we know about this case."

Jane went to the small mahogany desk in her room and brought out their lists made the evening of the séance. "It all started with Philippe's death. With the door closed and the window locked, it had to be somebody in that room."

"Agreed."

Jane said, "Some of this evidence can be explained quite easily. For instance, one would expect puddles of water next to Philippe's chair, because Tom was soaking wet when he came in and he stood behind Philippe. He even dripped on me."

"Yes, and that might explain why the curtains by the window were damp. Perhaps Tom brushed against them. But does that explain the big water puddle by the window the other side of his chair? That was a great deal of water to drip off of one oilskin," Belle said.

"So that's an unexplained item," Jane said. "And something else is troubling me. We had water on the floor at the doorway leading around BOTH sides of the room to Philippe's chair. One was from Tom's entry, but the other is a mystery."

"Yes. Note that. And we haven't been able to explain the path of blood drops on the west side of the room from the window to the door. Philippe did not move. How could there be a blood path?"

Jane said. "I can imagine that some of Tom's clothing absorbed blood from the puddle on the table, where Philippe's head rested, or on the floor beneath him. It might have made a path as he left."

"But he didn't leave right then. I requested that he remove his wet oil skin and write his account of the affair. He put the raincoat on the hook behind your chair. You didn't report a wet spot or blood there. He must have shed most of his water behind Philippe's chair, and he didn't transfer any blood," said Belle.

Jane said, "Still, we have an unexplained blood path from door to window."

Belle said, "It could have been the other way around -- window to door. Or, maybe the blood path could be explained if Tom had a wound that was dripping blood as he came in? But he didn't say anything about being hurt or act injured."

"I'd have noticed. Aside from being wet, he looked perfectly normal," Jane said.

"We know that window was locked. I checked it before and after the séance. What if someone unlocked it and locked it back in the dark. What if somebody came in that window, leaving a puddle and letting in rain, which wet the curtains. Did they kill Philippe, and then ...what? Climb back out? If so, who relocked the window? They would need an accomplice," Belle said.

"Or they carried the dripping knife ... where? To some hiding place that we haven't found?"

"Maybe. We need to search that room again."

"Out the door?"

"Impossible. I checked everybody before they left. And if someone other than invited guests was there, where did that 'somebody' go? Into thin air?" Belle said.

"I don't believe in ghosts, but this looks very ghostly."

"My intuition is saying that someone else was in that room with us."

"Well, I can't, for the life of me, see how or who," Jane said.

Sigh. Belle said, "So why is there a blood trail? What are we missing? We haven't found the murder weapon, which must have had Philippe's blood on it. Folly, fudge, and flummediddle. I looked for a knife before everybody left the room. I don't think it was hidden on anyone's person. And we have searched that room. Where did the knife go?"

Jane looked at her sideways. "Did it go into thin air in the hand of the unexplained 'somebody?'"

CHAPTER TWENTY-SIX

June 3, Braiding Aboard the Katie Asbell

"What are you going to transport in all those orange crates you bought from Curly at the general store?" Adam said.

"I'm going to take them apart and use the wood. I need to make a box," said Noah, examining for flaws several slatted wooden orange boxes he had temporarily stored on the main deck. Intended to transport heavy loads of citrus fruits, the crates were very sturdy.

"Excuse us, please," said a gentleman vacationer in a boater hat. Following him, a lady, who shepherded three young children, said, "Sorry to be in your way."

"No, the fault is entirely mine. Let me move these things out of your path," Noah said.

He moved four boxes aside, making a path, and nodded to the gentleman and lady, who were paying guests. After they passed, he thought, *The rule is one hand on the ladder at all times. That leaves one hand free to hold a crate. I don't want to make eight trips.* "Will you please help me move these boxes down to the freight deck, Adam?"

"Yes, sir."

Noah grabbed an orange crate and mounted the ladder at the companionway. He looked down the rungs, where Adam stood below him on the cargo deck. With a whistle to warn him of incoming, the captain tossed the orange crate to his deckhand, who handily caught it and set it aside. One by one they moved the crates down to the lower deck. "Thanks, Adam. You saved me seven trips up and down that ladder."

"Glad to help. Need anything else?"

"No, thanks," Noah said, as he cleared a working space on the after deck. Then he headed for the companionway once again.

Up in his cabin he hurriedly rummaged in his utility locker until he found a hammer, nails, handsaw, measuring tape, a brass buckle, small shackles, D-ring, and a sailor's fid. Everything went into pockets or hanging from his belt.

Then he headed back down to the freight deck, where Adam had stacked his orange crates. Finally, he removed tools and supplies from his belt and pockets.

Noah worked quickly and skillfully, measuring twice before cutting. The hammering and banging were hardly noticeable over the sound of the engine and the threshing of the water wheel.

Soon he had made a box, slatted on the bottom and three sides. The fourth side had a door with a sturdy latch. The top was solid.

"Did he say why he's making boxes?" Abel asked his brother.

"Nope. But that one looks like a trap to me. Maybe he's planning to trap rabbits, or chickens, or something."

The second project was one inch deep. A shallow slat-bottomed box, two feet by two feet, took shape quickly under Noah's hands.

When he finished, he placed the larger box forward under the net in the shade of the freight deck. "Hey, Joe," Noah said. "Do you still want to braid?"

"Yes, sir."

"All right. I am all set to do that. I just need to stow my shallow box back there, near the fire hose." From under his net he removed coils of rawhide, a bucket for water, and a tin of salve.

He said to his deckhand, "This bear hide is really stiff. I need to rub some of this beeswax and fat preparation into all of these straps to soften them some."

They proceeded aft where he dipped the bucket overboard and brought up some water. From his pocket Noah produced two squares of sheepskin and tossed one to Joe.

"I use this to put the wax on." He dipped his square into the water, then into the salve. He pulled a strip through the loaded applicator, then pulled it through the other direction. "While you soften that one, I'll get the buckle."

Joe said, "These smell much better."

"Yes, and the beeswax will help, too. Find the middle of that leather strip. Then fold it there."

Noah held the buckle in his left hand and threaded the middle of his strip through it. "Now I loop it around the buckle and pull the ends of the strip to attach it. Now, your turn. Push the fold of yours through the buckle and secure it."

While Joe fastened his, Noah took out his hammer and a two-inch-long nail. "Bang. Bang. Bang." He hammered the nail into the boat's railing. "All right. Drop the prong part of the brass buckle onto it, and we will weave these eight tails."

They began with five strips on the left and three strips on the right. "The pattern is four steps, though the first two are almost the same, as are the last two. Starting on the top left, I take the strand under one, over two, and under one. Then on the top right, you take the strand under one and over two. Step three, again on the top left, I take the outside strand <u>over</u> one, under two, and over one. Step four on the top right, you go <u>over</u> one under two. And that's it."

After two passes they had a huge tangle below their braid on the deck.

Joe said, "Stop. Let's straighten out this mess of loose strands. How did Curly ever get such long strips from a bear, anyway?"

"I watched him mount a very sharp knife next to a guide. Then he started right in the middle of the big hide and cut thin strips around and around."

"Well, these blasted ends are all snarled up together. After we separate them, we can tie each tail into a loose loop, and save ourselves a lot of time."

"Good idea."

They untangled the strips and resumed braiding.

"We are almost finished with this part. We have to stop and taper the ends."

Using Noah's sharp knife, they trimmed the remainder of the weaving strips to 12 inches and sliced the tips into long vees. They finished their braid and tucked the tails back into the braid.

"Now we attach two more strips." They each waxed another piece of rawhide. Noah buckled the braid into a circle. With the buckle on top at what, on a clock, would be 12 o'clock, he attached the folded rawhide strips at nine o'clock, then again at three o'clock, measuring and adjusting the length between. "Now we weave back, except we have to stop midway and attach the D-ring."

They finished the project quickly. "You're really good at this, Joe. Your tension is perfect, and you are fast. Do you want to learn to weave a round braid?"

"Yes, sir."

"Wax two extremely long coils of wider rawhide and find the middles, while I find that shackle I bought." He rummaged in his pockets and produced the small brass fitting, useful for connecting ship rigging. "Slip your folds through this, attach them, and put the brass down on the nail to hold it secure. Begin by spreading out the strands -- 12 o'clock, 3 o'clock, 6 o'clock, and 9 o'clock. Swap the top and bottom strands. Then swap the left and right strands. That's it. Just repeat the same process."

Noah watched his deckhand deftly manipulate the strands. "When you have about 30 inches of tail left, you can start a flat braid. Take the top left over one and under one. The top right goes under one. Repeat those two steps until the tails are only six inches long. Taper them. Fold up the flat braid back on itself to create a handle and secure it by weaving your tails into the braid. Questions?"

"Nope," the clever deckhand grinned from ear to ear. "Can I have the extra short pieces we cut off earlier?"

"Sure. I have to go up to the wheelhouse for a few minutes, but I'll be back."

When Noah returned Joe had produced a long round braid like a whip, with a shackle on one end and a handle on the other. And he was wearing a shiny shell amulet on a braided necklace, secured by a wire hook and loop.

"Very nice, Joe," Noah said. "You are a creative one."

"Yes, sir. I've been lookin' for a way to make some of my treasures, shells and animal teeth that I found, into jewelry. Those end pieces worked fine."

"Thanks for your help. Take the rest of those coils. I bought extra because I didn't know how much I would need. And I'll leave the nail there for your future projects. But find something to put over the top, please, so no one gets scratched on it." He neatened his work area, then picked up his tools and leather projects. As he strode forward and added the rawhide to his collection under the net, Adam said, "What in the Sam Hill is he going to catch with all that?"

CHAPTER TWENTY-SEVEN

June 3, Cypress Pointe Plantation Afternoon

Belle said, "And then we have the candle. Mary and Martha didn't blow it out. They were sitting by me. I asked everyone else -- Nanny, Virginia and John, Ben and Phoebe, Terra, Celeste, and Albert. They all said they didn't."

"Maybe Albert jumped up and blew it out and then forgot ...or lied about it."

"I really think we have to rule him out because the dried wax droplets look like it was blown from the window-end of the table. The boy was sitting at the opposite end of the table up near Martha and me. Unless Philippe blew it out himself, I guess we are left with a ghost."

"You know that's impossible," Jane said.

"Yes, I do. And yet it was blown out. I suppose Philippe could have blown it out. But why?"

"That's another unknown. And our biggest mystery is where is the knife?"

"We may never find it, but let's look for hiding places in the dining room today. We'll summon all our ingenuity and imagine ourselves looking for a hidey-hole during the sporadic on-and-off lightning of the storm. Meanwhile, we can list people who could have done it. Nanny was sitting next to Philippe. And she was fussing at him. But why would she kill him, and further still, is she strong enough?"

"I am listing Nanny, but I don't think she did it. Virginia could have leaned over Nanny. Perhaps she developed a hate of the man because he was compromising her daughter-in-law. That sort of thing reflects on the whole family."

Belle said, "Yes. Good. Number two -- Virginia. Next to her was John. He dropped hands and was ostensibly checking for hidden wires. I suppose that would have given him an opportunity to leave his chair and kill the man who was threatening his livelihood by closing off the river."

"And he's certainly strong enough to do it. Number 3 - John. Next to him was Terra. Nanny said Terra told Philippe to 'drop dead.' Was she angry enough to plot his murder? She could have stabbed him, while John was checking for wires. Albert was on the other side of her, and he was creating a disturbance. With all the other distractions in the form of storm noise and screaming, she could've gotten away with it. Number four -- Terra."

"We know that Albert, sitting next to Terra, had serious issues with his father. He has to be number five. But if he did it, we must ask, 'Why did someone push him into the molasses?' He says Philippe, Tom, John and Ben all have been skulking around the old barn and the dock late at night. I suspect it has to do with theft, and I aim to find out."

"All right. What about Martha and Mary? Philippe was obstructing their plans to modernize."

"Yes, but they were sitting on either side of me, and I'd swear that they didn't get up. If they planned to kill him, why bother to bring us here and stage a séance? And who threatened Martha that night under the bed with a knife? No, Jane. I think we can rule them out. Who else? Celeste. Mary swears that her niece was actually holding her hand the whole time. I think that lets Celeste out, too, unless they were both part of a grand scheme to rid the plantation of Philippe."

"Hmmm."

"That brings us to Phoebe and Ben. I think either of them could have killed him, given their motives and all the interruptions of the evening."

"Ben was jealous of Philippe. I have seen jealousy make people do crazy things. Phoebe was jealous of Philippe's attention to her sister and began to throw herself at the man, making it clear that she was available in Ben's absence. So, both of them go on our suspect list."

"Do you think the attacks on Martha and the others are linked to Philippe?"

"Yes, they must be. But I can't think about that right now. Let's go to the dining room and look for that knife."

Jane carried a step ladder, a feather duster, dust bin, and cleaning rags borrowed from the kitchen scullery. She followed her friend into the dining room. Belle said, "What I really want is to find a distinctive knife that clearly belongs to a certain owner. One with initials in the handle would be ideal."

Jane lifted an eyebrow.

"But that is just so much wishful thinking. Besides, if it was hidden in here, the culprit probably moved it by now," said the faux séance medium.

"We need a friendly ghost to show us the hiding place," Jane said, setting down the ladder. "If Charles is a ghost, he's probably furious over all of this business."

"Be serious. Where would we hide something if we didn't have much light? Turn over that extra chair that was next to Philippe," Belle said.

"Nothing under here," Jane said, examining the chair's structure. "But these chairs have wheels. They could have been mixed around to accommodate cleaning. We better check the rest."

One by one they examined chairs and eliminated them. "I don't know how to check for secret rooms, like priest holes, but I suppose we knock on the walls and moldings. You start on that side, and I'll start over here. We'll take turns and compare the tones."

They rapped and tapped their way around the dining room. "If there's a secret hidey hole in here, I can't find it," said Belle.

"No. It all sounds like 'wall.'" Jane said.

"I did a cursory look in this buffet after the séance, but it was suggested that some furniture might have hidden compartments. Let's start by pulling out the drawers."

"All right. This cutlery is for dining, with rounded knives. Those wouldn't be any good for stabbing. Here's a great big carving set. Too big?"

"Yes. The knife that killed Philippe has a thin pointed blade. Did you know that King Louis XIV banned the use of sharp pointed knives at the dinner table? That's why we have rounded ones. Since people couldn't skewer food with the rounded knife, the fork with four prongs was created."

"Interesting. Hmm. Nothing underneath or in the back of this drawer." They pulled out the middle drawer. "No knife, but look here, stuck fast to the bottom of the drawer. An envelope." They looked at each other. "Should we open it?"

"Yes. This is a murder inquiry." Belle carefully removed the envelope and took it to the bright sunlight streaming in the window. Inside she found two sheets of crumbling, yellowed parchment paper. It read, "...do certify that on this day ... with such proof, I am of opinion and do adjudge that the aforementioned Deleila is free according to the laws of this State of..."

"Charles freed her. Why in the world didn't he give her these papers?" Jane said.

"Folly, fudge, and flummediddle. Another secret."

"He probably had second thoughts and was afraid she would leave him."

"I don't think so. My guess is that he meant to free her and she died before he could do it. Then he was sorrowful and couldn't bring himself to destroy the papers. He left them in this secret place, where he could read them when he wanted to remember. This tells something of his character. It doesn't matter now. I'll put them back. Is there anything behind this other drawer?" She pulled it out and held it up.

"No. Just a bit of cobweb. Here let me get my arm in there and knock on the back of the cabinet. Oh. My arm is too short. You try."

Knock. Knock. Knock.

"This sounds solid to me. I think one would really have to know his way around this room to be able to pull out a drawer and deposit something in a hidden compartment behind it in the near dark."

"True, but we are checking all possibilities." The sun went behind a cloud, making the room a bit darker.

"I don't remember these used pencils being on the counter. I saw some in one of the drawers." She pulled out a drawer. "Ah. Here." Belle put them away with others in the drawer. "On to the cabinets below."

They opened the left door and removed the contents. "No knife."

Jane began emptying the right cabinet. "Hello, Fredrika. Come to help?" The friendly feline examined the items spread on the floor, but found nothing of interest. She then, with fur standing on end, prowled the dark space inside the cabinet. "What's wrong, kitty?"

"Martha must be back from her boat ride. Ignore that cat's 'ax-murder-er-over-your-right-shoulder look.' Tabbies have a tendency to do that. I don't think they mean to scare you." The sun came from behind its cloud and suddenly shown blindingly bright on the large white porcelain serving dishes displayed in the hutch atop the cabinet. "Shoo, Fredrika. We have work to do." The cat backed further into the cabinet. "All right, then. <u>You</u> tap on the back of the cabinet and let us know what you find."

"Meowrr."

Belle reached in, removed the cat, then examined the cabinet thoroughly. "I can't find anything even vaguely suspicious. Let's put these things back."

They clambered around, retrieving and rearranging folded linens and odd shaped dishes intended for serving all manner of foods. Jane stood and pointed at the countertop. "How did those get there?"

"What are you talking about?"

"Didn't you replace those pencils in the drawer?"

"Yes I did. Why?"

"These three pencils on the counter are forming an arrow pointing at the middle of the hutch. If I didn't put them there and you didn't put them there, how did they get there?"

"Are you joking?" Belle said, as she stood. Then she grimaced at the sight of the pencils.

"We must really have a friendly ghost. Many people in Cuba believe in such things. It's telling us to look up here in this hutch. Quick, let's take down these big serving dishes."

They removed terrines and lovely big white platters. The ladies did not find the knife they sought. They did find some big black beetles lying on their backs. "What did we do with those cleaning cloths?"

They had just finished straightening the hutch, when the sun again shone on the hutch in the top of the cabinet, flooding the plate rack with light. "My goodness. The sun is making the edges of those plates glow. I like that rack. It's a good design for showcasing those pretty plates, while keeping them safe," Jane said.

The rack was attached to the underside of the top cabinet and to the wall for additional strength. Fancy silver-rimmed plates were resting in slots that accepted only a single plate per space and no cabinet door covered the rack.

Fredrika leaped to the countertop, stretched up to her full length, and began to scratch at the slots.

Scritch. Scratch. Scratch. Scratch.

Belle watched the cat a moment, then said, "What in the world?"

"She must have detected something that we've missed. We need a piece of wire to check those slots. I'll go find some."

"Great. I'll take the plates out and stack them." While she was engaged in this, Belle noticed several slots were already empty. After she finished, she picked up Fredrika and stroked her soft gray fur. "Are you trying to tell us something?"

Jane returned and they fashioned a hook that could reach to the back of each slot.

The no-nonsense Cuban lady scraped her hook across the insides of the first empty slot. Nothing. She repeated the process. Again, nothing. The next time her wire caught on something and she struggled to pull it out. After some manipulation and to the astonishment of both young women, an eight-inch long, razor sharp, pointed knife blade with a polished and monogrammed silver handle clattered to the countertop. Dark brown stains covered part of the monogram.

"We need to preserve this knife just like it is. Stay here. I'll be right back with Martha and Mary," Belle said. Fredrika streeeeetched and yawned. The sleuth swept up and hugged the furry kitty.

"I'm not sure, but I think you showed us the location of our murder weapon. You must have keener senses than I do. If I hadn't seen it, I wouldn't believe it."

As if to say, "My work is done here. No accolades necessary," Fredrika squirmed in her arms, jumped lightly to the floor, and sauntered away.

Belle turned to go fetch the plantation owners. *This knife has a unique monogram. It looks like PC. Who, besides Philippe Cooper, has those initials? Phoebe Crews? Surely not. Petunia? Paul? Polly?"*

Chapter Twenty-Eight

June 3, Pedigree of a Knife Cypress Pointe Plantation

Belle rushed out of the dining room and hurried down the hall. Mary came out of the library, and the two nearly collided. "Mary, I need your presence in the dining room, please. And have you seen your sister?"

"Yes. She just came in. I think she said she took out one of the boats and needed a wash. I would check her room. What's wrong?"

"Nothing's wrong. Maybe something is finally right. I hope it's the evidence we need to identify our killer. I'll meet you in the dining room as soon as I find your sister." Belle dashed off before she could hear any reply.

She charged up the stairs and to Martha's door.

"Knock, knock."

"Martha, are you there? Martha. It's urgent."

The door swung open, and the odor of lavender greeted Belle. Her hostess stood there with a towel. "What is it? What's happened now?"

Belle lowered her voice. "Jane and I have been searching the dining room. I think we've found the murder weapon. Hurry and dry your hands. You must come. I am hoping you can tell us who owns it."

"Good gracious. Give me a minute, and I'll be right with you."

They stopped en route at a linen cupboard, and Belle pulled out a small pillow case. *Mmm. Lavender again. Maybe it will calm our nerves. I mean, 'my nerves.'*

"Slow down, Belle. I doubt it's going anywhere before we can get there. What does it look like? Does it have a maker's mark?"

"It looks very sharp and expensive. I noticed a lovely tree shape stamped at the base of the blade. That should tell us where it was made."

"That sounds like the kitchen knives that Mary and I saw in shops all over Europe. I'm not good at that sort of thing, but I'll bet she will know where it was made."

At the dining room Belle said, "If you've no objections, I'm going to lock the door to avoid interruptions."

"Fine. Now tell us how you found the knife."

Jane and Mary stood looking at the knife where it lay on the buffet counter. "It was lodged in one of the slots in the plate rack and fell out when Jane scraped her makeshift tool across the bottom of the slot."

"Well, I never would have found it. We hardly ever use those Spode plates," Mary said.

Martha said, "Isn't that the same pretty knife hallmark that we've seen in shops in Europe, Mary?"

"Oh, yes. That's one of those expensive Böker chef knives. Those are made in Germany, but I read an article recently about that company. It has split, with a branch of the family immigrating to North America and setting up plants in Canada, Mexico, and the United States. All the German and North American factories produce similar beautiful knives and use the "tree brand" trademark."

Jane said, "Can you tell if this one was made in Germany or here?"

"No. They all look the same. But the ones we saw never had initials."

"Who here, besides Philippe, has the initials PC?"

Mary said, "Petunia, my maid, is the daughter of Chombo, so she is Tom's half sister. Chombo was a Cooper. She is Petunia Cooper, PC. Where would she get such an expensive knife?"

"A lucky find or possibly theft from a plantation guest or from someone during your travels -- I'm not accusing. I'm just listing possibilities," Belle said.

"It sounds like you are suggesting she stole it and killed Philippe. Number one, what are the chances of finding a knife with your own initials on it? Number two, why would she want to kill him? Number three, how? She wasn't at the séance, and you said yourself there are no hiding places," Martha said.

"Mmm. All good additions to our list of unanswered questions. Who else has the initials PC? Polly?"

Mary said, "I can't imagine our Polly as a killer, no matter what the circumstantial evidence."

Martha said, "She's Polly Butters, so there's no need to defend her. But our footman Paul Carter certainly has the strength and cunning to do it. He, too, could have found the knife in the street, won it in a game of chance, or lifted it from a guest, but the likelihood that it would have the initials PC are very remote. Purchased with savings? He could have had it monogrammed later. Not impossible."

"How did any of them get a Böker knife with their initials on it? The monogram looks very professional. Could a jeweler do that well? If so, at what cost? And have we found a motive for any of your staff to do away with Philippe?" said Belle.

Mary said, "Not yet. I'll think about it. Up to this point, I've not even considered the staff as suspects. You were wondering about the initials. Böker isn't known for making one-of-a-kind special orders for individuals. It is not cost effective. The German company sometimes makes small runs of specialized knives, for a school or the household of a rich nobleman."

Martha said, "We need to consider the possibility that the knife was Philippe's, and that brings up the questions we have hesitated to ask. What was he doing during the 15 years that he was gone from here? What were his finances? Was he wealthy? Or lucky in cards? Or a thief?"

Mary said, "That's an expensive knife. It says sterling on the blade. Maybe he worked for a rich nobleman."

"Given what we've seen of him, I would think it more likely that he won it playing cards," Martha said.

"Or stole it from a rich cathedral or a nobleman?" Belle said. "What was the name of that school he attended?"

"Lycée Pape Clément. It's in wine country. The vineyards, lands, and all the barrels of wine are owned by a very rich cleric. He supports the school. Daddy used to say Clément was one step away from God."

Jane said, "Pape Clément. PC. He would be rich enough to have sterling knives with his initials on them. I should think Böker would be happy to make a short run of specialized knives for him."

Belle said, "Are you thinking what I'm thinking?"

"That Philippe stole this knife from his school," Jane said. "How does that knowledge help us, though? He didn't stab himself."

Belle said, "I think the question is, who had the opportunity to steal this knife away from Philippe?"

Martha said, "The staff would have ample opportunity to steal it out of his room. But others could have taken it. If caught, a guest could just claim they were mistaken about the room. A better question is, why kill him? And better yet, how did anyone do it? Even us. If the window was locked, the door closed, and everyone's hands were touching on the top of the table, even if the knife was Philippe's, how did it end up in his back?"

CHAPTER TWENTY-NINE

June 4, Zippy Surprise on the Katie Asbell to Jacksonville

Early in the afternoon Noah turned to his first mate in the wheelhouse and said, "Shorty, we need to have another emergency drill. No guests have fallen overboard recently, but we're about to have one that might. I'm going below and spread the word. When you hear, 'Man Overboard,' please circle back and cut the engines. I'll have the boys practice retrieving things with the boat hooks again."

"All right. You're the boss," he said skeptically as Noah went down to announce the drill.

The *Katie Asbell* made good time that day and steamed up to the Jacksonville dock by early afternoon. Noah left the sternwheeler in Shorty's capable hands and hurried down the gangplank.

"He sure has been secretive the last couple of days," said Adam.

"He's lovesick, if you ask me," said Abel. "I'll bet he has a new girlfriend in Jacksonville."

"Ya think? I thought he was pretty set on that redheaded Sadie."

"Yeah, but she's gone isn't she?"

While the gossip and conjectures continued behind him, Noah headed for the Jacksonville Mercantile. Warm wind swirled strands of his hair forward, and his pants legs flapped in the breeze. He nodded at several strangers, including ladies in fashionable bonnets and balloon skirts and a gentleman in a top hat. He continued past shops in the early stages of renovation.

A bell on the door jangled smartly when he entered the store. He was greeted by owner Billy Bob McPherson, a tall lanky ginger fellow with a scar through his eyebrow. "A good day to you, Noah. How do ye find yoursel' today?"

"As well as can be expected. And yourself?"

"Fair to middlin'. I got that big package of cork for you. And a letter came for you. I put it on top of your package. Here it is, right at the back of this shelf."

He pulled out a big croker sack, closed with twine. "Says it'll float 25 pounds. What are you planning to float?"

"Well, eventually eighty to a hundred pounds. But this is a start." He put the letter in his pocket and paid for his package. "Is your cousin in the back? He promised my special order would be ready today."

"Aye. Go through."

Noah carried his package to the back of the shop and knocked on the door. It was opened by a giant of a man, clean shaven and with mid-length gray hair. He wore a formerly white work apron, stained with random globs of red, yellow, blue, and green paint. "Good day to ye, Noah. Come in."

"Hello, Angus. How are you? Have you been doing much sail making?"

"I am good, thank you. Business is picking up. I got a new order just today. And I just painted a colorful family crest on the center of a spinnaker. Your little jacket is finished." He produced an odd red canvas jacket with sturdy buckles and a flat handle stitched into the back. A small reinforced loop also stood out on the back. The entire outside surface was covered with big, long, deep pockets, closed with button flaps.

"It looks a little bit big, but that will allow room for growth. Your workmanship is impeccable, Angus. It's very pretty, and it looks rugged. Thanks."

"It was my pleasure, Noah. If I can't be a'makin' sails, I'm happy to be makin' safety clothes for the wee seafarin' doggy."

Noah gave him a bank note. "Please keep the change. I may need alterations later," he said, with a chuckle.

"I thank ye for your custom. Haste ye back."

The boat captain hurried out, waving at Billy Bob on the way. Jingling the door's bell again, he carried his unusual purchases to his favorite Jacksonville café, Cantique.

When café owner Gabriella Pharay saw Noah, she said joyously, "Oh, I'm glad to see you. She has grown so much since you were here last."

He laid the red jacket and his big sack of cork on a nearby table. "Good. Good. I can't wait to see her. I sure hope she likes her new temporary home with me."

Gabriella darted through a door to the back of her café and up a short flight of stairs to her rooms. She came down laughing and cradling a fuzzy red bundle, who was licking her chin and trying to give her great slobbery kisses. "Her brothers and sisters are already gone to their new owners. So, I've had this heap of energetic joy all to myself." She placed the baby bloodhound on the floor, and the uncertain boat captain surveyed the bouncing pup.

"Let's see how her new red canvas coat fits," he said, holding up the garment. He unbuckled it and held it out to Pepper, who sniffed once and took off racing around the café.

A café customer came in, and Pepper made a beeline for him. The big blond fellow, who wore a red plaid shirt, said, "Oh, ho! Hello, Pepper." He, too, was treated to big wet kisses. "I'll have the usual, Gabriella." He held the pup out at arm's length and ruffled her fur, scratching her behind the ears.

"Coming right up, Lars." Turning for the kitchen, she said back over her shoulder, "Do you want something to eat, Noah?"

"Not until I get this pup settled, thanks," he said.

"Hi, Lars. I'm Noah, Pepper's new owner. Could you hold her still a few minutes, while I put this jacket on her and fit cork into the pockets of her new flotation vest?"

"Sure. So that's what that is. I was curious. With the long pockets all around it, it could be a fishing vest -- a very small fishing vest."

Noah managed to buckle the jacket onto Pepper. "That's good. It doesn't restrict her movement." The pup wiggled happily.

"Nope. I'd say she's not restricted at all. But you better hurry with that cork. Here. Come back here wiggle worm." Pepper twisted out of his gentle grasp and charged around the room between the chair legs and through the door to the kitchen. "Whoo. You're going to have your hands full with this one. Why the vest?"

"I'm the captain of the sternwheeler *Katie Asbell*. Pepper is a gift for a friend, but she's going to live aboard for a while until my friend can take her. The vest is just a precaution."

"Good luck with that. Let's round her up." He headed for the kitchen, but Pepper streaked from the kitchen out into the café and started doing laps.

"Whew. Energetic, isn't she?" Noah said, with a big laugh. "You block off the kitchen route so Gabby can cook, and I'll chase her. She's bound to run down soon." Ten minutes later she was still evading him as she raced under tables and chairs around the big café.

When a new customer opened the door, Pepper bolted out onto the dusty city streets of Jacksonville with Noah right behind her. "Whoa! Whoah," he shouted at horse and carriage traffic.

The pup dashed across the street, barely escaping the hooves of horses and fast-moving carriage wheels. A family with a young boy emerged from a shop. "Grab that pup," Noah said, and the youngster, whose thatch of blonde hair was easy to spot on the street, took up the chase. Down in front of the shops they raced.

Now, other onlookers joined the rush to save the baby bloodhound from the dangers of the street. A shop door opened in front of Pepper, and in she bolted.

"Eek." Screams from the shopkeeper and the shoppers arose in her wake. The dusty dog was making her way around bolts and bolts of pristine silks and linens. The door was still ajar, and she dashed out again, straight into the arms of the young lad. "Gotcha," he said gleefully.

Pepper wiggled, but the boy held tight. Noah, panting, approached. "Thank you for saving this little firecracker."

"She streaks like a shooting star," Lars said, coming up alongside Noah.

Noah said, "Gabriella told me that all her pups tended to need two hours a day of jogging or running. I was skeptical, but Pepper has made me a believer. We are going to be wearing out the decks of the *Katie Asbell*."

Lars gasped in, then gave a huge belly laugh. "I believe that. Well, now that she's safe I'm going back to my meal."

"Right. I'll be with you in a moment." Noah turned to the youngster and pressed on him several coins. "Thank you. Buy yourself something special." Pepper's tongue lolled out, and she reached up to coat the child's face with a thin, protective layer of puppy spit. He giggled and reluctantly turned Pepper over to Noah.

The boat captain reached into a pocket and pulled out the braided rawhide leash, which he attached to the loop on Pepper's jacket. "No, you can't eat that." He gently put his hand over Pepper's muzzle. Cradling the happy wiggly puppy, he walked back to Cantique.

Lars and Gabriella stood watching him as he entered. "I'm really going to need your help to get this cork into those pockets."

"Let me have her," said Gabriella. She said to the pup, "Have you been leading the big tough men on a merry chase, my little Pepper?"

"Let's do it," Lars said. Noah hurriedly unwrapped the great packet of flotation material. He and Lars fit together circular strips of cork. Pepper lay perfectly still in Gabriella's arms.

When all the cork was in the pockets around Pepper's jacket, except for the small bit she ate, Noah said, "Thanks you two for all your help. Gabriella, has anyone introduced her to the river?"

"No. She doesn't particularly like splashing in her bath, though."

"Good luck, mate," said Lars.

Noah shook the man's hand, and Gabriella passed over to Noah the puppy, who immediately began to wiggle. "We are going for a swim. 'Bye."

Noah carried Pepper to the river's edge and set her on the ground. "Here. Try one of these." He offered her a liver treat, which she gobbled.

Roo. Roo. Aroo.

"Oh. You like those, eh?"

He took off his shoes and socks, rolled up his trousers legs, and stepped into the shallow water. "Come on in, Pepper," he said, giving an encouraging nudge with the leash. She didn't move a muscle.

"No? Come on. You'll like it." He bent forward and swirled the water in front of him.

"All right. Will you come in for one of these?" He pulled from his pocket another liver treat and held it out.

Kersplash. Splish. Splat. She happily rushed in for the cookie, wiggling and paddling joyously.

"Oh, ho. So, you can be bribed," he said, and laughed. They played in the water. She paddled enthusiastically, and he fed her more treats.

The little roly-poly in the red vest attracted the attention of several passersby, who coaxed her out of the water, only to be showered as she shook the water from her coat. She dashed happily to the end of the leash, then rushed back into the water and paddled to his arms. *She isn't afraid. And she's's going to be a good swimmer,* thought Noah.

While the puppy played, he opened his letter. *From Sadie. She is all right. Thank God.* He read and daydreamed about what might be.

Pepper splashed up to him and shook vigorously. "Aww. I guess I do need a shower," he said, with a laugh. He pocketed the special letter. *For later.*

"So far, so good, Pepper. Now to introduce you to the crew and your new home."

June 3, Ben's Trouble at Cypress Pointe Plantation

Fredrika wasn't allowed in the dining room at dinner time, but when Flora, carrying a fully loaded tray, opened the door, the sneaky cat whizzed past the maid's feet and hid under the table. Belle was mulling over recent discoveries and failed to notice the feline. Though the chandelier glittered and the crystal and china gleamed as before, several guests were subdued in thought, and one of them was downright sullen. Dinner was a quiet affair.

Ben finally said, "What's wrong with everybody tonight? Come on. Let's drink to good friends." He raised his wine glass and drained it. "Hey, Paul. How about more wine over here?"

"Not that my father is acting like much of a friend at the moment," he said. "Good friends don't sue each other. I'm surprised Martha hasn't thrown him out by now."

Martha and Mary looked thunderstruck at this very improper outburst, but remained quiet, as did the rest of the company.

Into the embarrassed silence Phoebe said, "How wonderful the lilies smell tonight. What kind are those in the table bouquet, Martha?"

Ben raised his empty glass and his voice. "What does one have to do to get a refill around here?"

"Ben, hush. You're embarrassing us," Phoebe said.

"I am just telling the truth about dear old Dad," said the inebriated Ben. "But I need more vino."

Terra said, "I think we've all had enough wine right now, Ben. I'm looking forward to the fish course."

"Who asked you, anyway? Can I get some wine over here?" he said in a louder voice.

Under the table, Fredrika patted Terra's foot, testing boundaries. "Tap, tap, tap." The imp hesitated momentarily. Then she pounced stealthily onto the available lap, stomping around in circles on heavy feet until she was finally satisfied. She found the perfect position and settled, emitting a low rumbling purr. Under cover of the tablecloth, the young woman stroked soft, warm kitty fur... and offered an occasional tidbit.

"Oh, I will be so glad to leave all this behind. When can we go home?" Phoebe said.

"You know you have to wait until the big strong men clear the river and the trails, silly girl," Ben said. "... unless you want to take a machete and whack your way through the brush," he said, with a loud belly laugh. "I'd like to see dainty little you do that in your fancy party dress and pumps."

"Oh, Ben," Phoebe said, throwing down her napkin and running from the room in tears.

"Uh, oh. I've done it now," Ben said. "Better go after her. Maybe she'll be sweet and make up," he said.

"Folly, fudge, and flummediddle," said Belle, after he left. "This business is getting everyone down."

Flora and Paul removed the soup dishes and served the salad.

From a distance they all heard Phoebe say, an octave higher than normal, "What are you doing, Ben?" The dinner guests froze in place and listened to the remote conversation in speechless silence.

Ben said, his voice loud and belligerent, "I know they're hiding around here somewhere. Those gall darn Union sidewinders..."

"Put it down, Ben. You're scaring me."

"Look out. It's an ambush. I'll get them, this time. There's one."

Bang!

"That's where they've been hiding. There's another one."

Bang!

"Eeee. Our bed! You shot a hole in our BED. How could you?"

John jumped up. "Oh. Dear God. I thought he was finished with the hallucinations." The man raced out of the room.

"Stop it, Ben. We have to sleep there." Phoebe's shrill voice rent the air.

They heard John say, "Put it down, son."

"No. I can't. I must protect our position. They won't get us this time."

Bang!

In a suspicious voice, Ben said, "Father? Are you joining the enemy?"

Belle sprang to her feet. She ran toward the commotion. Ben's wife stood in the door to their room. Belle said, "Phoebe, go to the dining room. Now. Go to your sister."

The young woman fled past Belle.

Inside the room John wrestled his son. The gun clattered to the floor. Belle swooped in and picked it up.

"It's over. John got the gun away from him, and I gave him something to sleep. I think he was still fighting the war, but he shot holes in your feather mattress, Martha. Fluff is floating everywhere," Belle said. "Let's all finish our dinner and then turn in. This will look different in the morning."

"Oh, really? Do you think any of us will sleep, knowing that the killer is lurking in a room right down the hall?" Celeste said.

"Who says he's the killer? He's just a sad tired boy," said Virginia.

Belle said, "We are not in danger. I took away everything sharp and locked his door from the outside. Put your chair against your door tonight if you are worried." She picked up her fork and stabbed a pole bean.

Martha said, "Flora, please serve the fish now."

After dinner, Jane quietly voiced the concern that had been uppermost in Belle's mind. "Belle, do you think he would have harmed Phoebe?"

"Yes, I think he would. In that state, he could also harm himself. Tom warned me about him."

Jane said, "Maybe he is our killer."

"Maybe."

"I suppose he won't be any more trouble tonight, but I think I still need to follow your plan and sleep in Albert's room."

"Yes. Thank you. It's good of you to offer to do that. Mary had a small bed put in there for you."

"I'm afraid I'm going to regret it. That cot is hard."

Jane snuffed out the candle in Albert's room and lay in the dark listening to the crickets and an owl. Very faint snatches of music filtered in through the window. *Happy Dan must be playing for his own enjoyment. I suppose that's one good thing that came from all of us being stuck here together.* She tried to get comfortable on the cot. She dozed.

The house had been quiet for several hours when she became aware of Albert's mumbling voice. "Hey. What are you doing?"

Jane could see nothing. She heard a scuffle. The boy's voice came again, this time louder. "Get away from me."

Her fingers closed around the hardwood handle of the cricket bat under her pillow. In the pale moonlight she saw a tall figure hunched over Albert's bed. "Stop it," she said, as loudly as she could.

The short rotund woman sprang up. The bat went back over her shoulder, and putting all of her weight behind the blow, she twisted forward and whacked at the tall silhouette.

The figure wobbled and crashed to the floor, taking half the contents of the night table with him. Jane found the candlestick.

Knock. Knock.

Jane recognized Belle's voice and said thankfully, "Come in. The door's not locked."

"Jane? What's happening?" Belle said.

A soft light flared when Jane lit the candle.

CHAPTER THIRTY-ONE

June 4, Pepper Aboard Katie Asbell

Noah shortened the leash in his hand and started up the gangplank extending from the Jacksonville dock to *Katie Asbell's* deck. Pepper followed him until she got to the plank, where she stopped.

"Come on, Pepper. It'll be all right," he said softly to the little dog. The crew began to take notice. Still the pup balked.

"Come on. You can do it." He took a liver treat from his pocket and backed up a few feet.

She followed him onto the gangplank. "Just a little farther. You're almost over." He stepped back onto the steamer's deck, and she slowly followed him. Shorty and all the rest were watching and began to applaud when Pepper stepped onto the deck.

The first mate strode up with eyebrows raised. "Tell me you're not bringing this dog aboard as a passenger. It's just visiting?"

"Well, remember a few weeks back when I mentioned seeing Gabriella's handsome litter of bloodhound pups? I bought one for Sadie, but it was too young to take from its mother. It's old enough now, and I picked it up this afternoon. We will need to keep her for a while, until Sadie gets back."

"For Sadie? KEEP HER FOR A WHILE?" His voice went up an octave.

"Yes. Is there an echo in here?"

"Did you talk to Sadie about this?"

"No. It's a surprise."

"A surprise? Oh, boy. That'll surprise her, all right. Are you sure you know what you're doing? Most fellows get nice jewelry or flowers and candy for their girl. I never heard of anybody getting a pup."

"It'll be great. I always wanted a dog. She'll love this pup. Her name is Pepper, and she's a red bloodhound. Isn't that just perfect?"

Shorty sighed. "So that's what all the 'man overboard' exercises were about. You should have mentioned they were 'pup overboard' exercises."

"I couldn't call them that. No one would take them seriously."

"Do you know how much work it is taking care of a dog? You have to feed and water them at least twice a day. And they have to have somewhere to do their business, or it'll be all over the place. And it takes time to train them. And what about exercise? How do you exercise a pup on a steamboat? Or wash one?" He turned and tightened a slack line.

"I did think of most of that before now, Shorty. I braided a harness with buckles and this leash. I have a washable blanket, two non-slip bowls, and Cookie made her a bag of liver treats."

"Ugg. Where are you going to keep her? You can't just close her in a wardrobe. And they need lots of exercise."

"She'll have her very own place and won't get in the way. I made a box, slatted on the bottom and three sides. The fourth side has a door with a sturdy latch. The top is solid for shade."

"Terrific. You're going to lock her in a box."

"No. I... only at night. And most important, she now has a one-inch-deep shallow slatted box, two feet by two feet, with a thin layer of Spanish moss, our most easily renewable resource. I've seen that stuff absorb more than 10 times its dry weight in water. I gathered a good big pile of it while we were in Palatka. If this doesn't work as a dog toilet, we are in trouble."

"We're already in trouble," he grumbled. Shorty turned and started toward the companionway, shaking his head. "I think you're making a big mistake. Dogs are work. You don't give a girl work."

In the hour before sunset, Noah walked Pepper around every inch of deck space. He stopped to give some directions to Adam. On the passenger deck several strolling guests stopped to pet her. As he carried her down the companionway ladder, he said, "Pepper, you are an absolute people-magnet, aren't you?"

He set her down on the freight deck. "You need to go up and down this ladder yourself, but sundown is not the time to teach you." They resumed their jog. Suddenly she slowed and started circling.

He picked her up and rushed aft. "On the other hand, there's no time like the present to introduce you to your toilet." He deposited her on the piled moss. "Use the moss," he said. She hopped out of the tray and circled. He picked her up and put her back in. "Use the moss," he said again. She squatted, made a puddle, which quickly disappeared, and she stepped out.

"Yay. Success." He praised the little dog and gave her a cookie. "Now, come this way and see what I have for you."

Adam and Joe greeted them on the foredeck. "We thought this would be a good spot for Pepper's box," said Joe. "And I put the blanket inside."

Inside of the spacious box were the two pottery bowls. One held fresh water, and the other was steaming with something savory. Pepper rushed for the bowl, stuck her nose in, and lapped enthusiastically.

"What did Cookie send down here for her? It smells suspiciously like his venison stew with vegetables."

"That's because it *is* his venison stew with vegetables," said Adam with a chuckle.

Joe laughed. "She will be the best fed scent hound in these parts."

Pepper finished her stew, exited the box, and stood with gravy covering all the wrinkles of her face. Her long pink tongue eagerly sought leftovers lodged in the crevices, leaving slobber traces on her satisfied face. "Noah, I can see you're going to have to keep a rag handy to wipe this feisty little pup," Joe said.

He produced a clean work rag, dipped it in her water bowl, and gently cleansed her muzzle. She waggled her head from side to side and slung drool over all three men. "Great Jehoshaphat," said Adam. They laughed and groaned, as they all searched pockets for clean rags, handkerchiefs, bandanas, or even squares of old sheets. Adam took out his own clean handkerchief. "Make that two rags, one for her and one for you.

After they had removed the slobber, Noah said, "All right. Bedtime for you, Miss Pepper." He opened the door to her crate, picked her up, removed her leash, and deposited her inside on her blanket. She snuggled down and looked settled.

"Thanks, fellas," Noah said. "Time to do all those things I put off while I was jogging the decks with her."

"You're welcome. I'll take a turn jogging her around the decks tomorrow. She's fun and a big hit with all the guests," Joe said.

"Thanks."

Noah had just returned to his cabin and his work when he heard - *Roo. Roo. Rooo.*

"What in the Sam Hill?" It dawned on him that he was hearing Pepper. He thought, *She's lonely. I suppose I should bring her up here, at least temporarily.*

When he arrived at the freight deck, she was in full voice.

Aroooo Roor Roooo!

"Aww. Don't like being by yourself, little one? Shhh. Shh. You'll disrupt the whole boat." He removed her from her crate and carried her up to his cabin. He sat on his bed wondering what to do with the cuddly puppy in his arms.

Pepper wiggled from his grasp and snuggled down into his pillow. "Oh, I see. It's not that you don't like your bed. You just like mine better." The little dog, looking so small in her bright red roly-poly flotation vest, closed her eyes and sighed. Noah, with one last comment, went back to his ledgers. "Just don't think this is going to become a habit."

CHAPTER THIRTY-TWO

June 4, Early Morning at Cypress Pointe Plantation

"Is there any doubt that he's our killer?" said Jane. "He was attacking Albert."

"Well, he didn't exactly hurt you, did he, Albert? You said he was bending over you."

Albert, sitting up in his bed with sleep in his eyes and his hair all askew, opened his mouth to reply. The boy never got the chance.

"Ben was attacking him, Sadie. I heard Albert cry out. Why do you insist on defending the man?"

"I am still 'Belle,' please. And I am not defending him. I think he is ill."

"The only reason he is ill is because he has poured himself full of alcohol."

"Alcohol is an escape. Wouldn't you want to escape the memories of being taken away from your family, put in a cold dirty cell, and half starved for a year?"

"There you are. Making excuses for him again. "

"Jane, I think he's that way because our society can't solve its differences without fighting and bloodshed."

"Listen to yourself. Many soldiers return home without scenes and shootings. That man tried once to kill Albert, and he came back to finish the job. End of story. How did he get in here, anyway? You said you locked him in his room."

"I did. When I took him back to his room just now, the door was locked. But when we unlocked the door to put him to bed, the window was wide open. All I can think is that he awoke from the medication I gave him, found his door locked, and climbed out the window," Belle said.

"That big old oak branch does run right in front of these windows. He must've done that. Though, how he scrambled around on it in the dark and in his drunken state, the Lord only knows."

"Having his fill of alcohol probably made it easier. He wasn't aware of the danger."

"What's to keep him from doing it again, Belle?"

"I'm going to deal with that right now. He won't get out that window when I finish with it." She showed Jane a hammer and long nails. "I got these from Tom."

The sleuth bent over and tied her skirts together between her knees. She felt around for the slits in her skirt that gave her access to the tie-on-pockets underneath.

"What are you going to do? You can't go out on that limb. It's slippery with dew."

"I'll be careful. There are plenty of handholds. Just don't let the cat follow me. If there's anything I don't need right now, it's Fredricka underfoot." Belle fitted the heavy hammer head and nails into her pockets, raised the window as far as it would go and, holding onto the window frame, she slung one leg and then the other over the sill.

A few minutes later at breakfast Mary said, "Imagine my surprise when, this morning amidst the early morning bird songs, I heard noises I didn't recognize. I went to the window and saw a barefoot Belle inching her way along the branch outside my window."

"Oh. My goodness. That woman is certainly full of surprises," said Virginia.

Mary shot a glance at Virginia's daughter-in-law with her visiting younger sister, sitting across the table. "And farther out on the lawn were two ladies in their night dresses throwing their elbows and punching up into thin air with high screeching noises." She smiled at the two sisters. "Brava, ladies for your initiative in practicing."

Phoebe stuck her chin in the air and looked at those around the table. "We, er, want to be able to do what Belle showed us."

"Good. I do, too," Mary said. "You've changed from skeptic to a believer in self-defense, Phoebe. But surely now that we know that the killer is Ben, we don't have to practice anymore. I am sorry it was Ben. It would be much easier to think that the killer was some outsider. Thank goodness Belle caught him, and it's all over."

"Not all over, Sister," Martha said. "We are still stuck in this house with a murderer and a dead man."

Virginia said, "No! Our Ben is not the killer. It <u>isn't</u> all over. He may have disliked Philippe, but he would never kill him."

"Dear, you have to admit that he was quite irrational last night. He hasn't been himself, since he returned from that Yankee prison," John said. "And after he made that scene after dinner and shot up the bed, Belle found him in Albert's room leaning over the boy in the middle of the night."

Celeste said, "It was actually Jane who caught him. She knocked him over with a cricket bat, according to Belle."

"But we have only her word for that," Virginia said. "Maybe our boy was just asking Albert a question or offering to get him a drink. Ben would never harm anyone. Jane shouldn't have hit him. She could be brought up on charges."

Her husband said, "Let's not start with the lawyers again. And about this lawsuit -- I'm sure we can figure it out without lawyers. I'm sorry I brought this extra heartache on you, when you have so many other things to deal with."

"Thank you, John. When you've finished clearing the river and the road, get the men to help you remove those boulders from the river. It's not our aim to affect your livelihood that way."

Celeste said, "Hooray. Good sense prevails."

"Here is Belle coming now. Hello. Where's Jane?" said Terra.

Belle said, "She is staying with Albert. He seems fine, but he doesn't want her to leave him, so I will take them some breakfast."

Virginia said, in a quiet intense voice, "No, John. Ben never hurt anybody. He wouldn't. He was always such a sweet boy."

In an attempt to change the subject, John said to the group, "We have almost finished clearing the river and the road. Another day and we should have it open."

Belle thought, *Folly, fudge, and flummediddle. Once transportation is available all my suspects will scatter. A killer -- Ben? -- will go free and possibly harm others. I have to catch the culprit now. Tomorrow may be too late.*

Mary said, "Oh, good. When the law can get through from Saint Augustine to take him away, then it'll be over."

"Take Ben away? To Saint Augustine?" said Phoebe weakly. "What will happen to him?"

"Ben is staying right here until we can take him home," said Virginia. Eyebrows shot up around the table, but not wishing to upset the matron, the assembled guests remained silent.

"What about Philippe?" Celeste said. "I don't think we can wait another day. We are going to have to bury him -- the sooner the better. It would be indecent to leave him to molder in that room."

Martha said, "Under the circumstances, I think it's appropriate to bury him in the family cemetery. He was raised here with this family. Our father was extremely sad when he disappeared."

Mary said, "I agree. Wherever he was and whatever he did during the long years he was gone, he was still our half brother. We can afford him the respect of a dignified burial."

"Show me where you want him buried, and I will get some of the boys to help me dig his grave," said John.

"Thank you," Mary said.

"Oh, I almost forgot," John said. "One of the men from Saint Augustine working from the other end to clear the river chopped his way through most of the remaining debris and wiggled over the rest to see what we need. He says everyone's talking about the trial in Washington. And he handed me this."

John produced a newspaper with a blazing headline -- New Evidence Against Mary Surratt. Will She Hang?

He read aloud, "John Lloyd, who leased her tavern, testified that Mary Surratt hid carbines at the tavern and told him to 'get the shooting irons ready'... Police Continue Search for Missing Actors. If You've Seen Any of These Players, Please Contact Authorities Immediately..."

Folly, fudge, and flummediddle. I never thought I would be upset at seeing my name in the paper. I've got to figure this out and get out of here. Celeste and some of the others are already way too curious about me. Is poor tormented Ben the killer?

How can I make sure? I must do something to make this killer show his hand. But what?

"Martha, may we talk after breakfast? Perhaps you will come to my room as soon as you finish?"

"Yes, of course, but the parlor will be more comfortable."

"I know, but we need privacy."

"All right. But why all the mystery? Is this about your creeping across that branch this morning?"

CHAPTER THIRTY-THREE

June 5, Antics Aboard the Katie Asbell

Adam jogged around the freight deck with Pepper on her leash. *Whew. We've passed that mule three times. Pepper is getting used to him.* The gray mule swished his tail to get rid of a fly.

"Here, Pepper. Come away from that companionway," he said. They looped around the deck again.

On the next pass, Pepper started up the stairs of the companionway. "Tired of this deck, Pepper? You're too little to go up these stairs right now."

The pup struggled up one step and started up the next one, before she stopped, whimpered, and looked back at Adam pitifully. "You just need to grow some, Pepper. It won't be long before you'll be charging up these stairs like a deckhand. Lord help us then. In the meantime, let me help."

Adam bent down, picked up the pup, and was immediately covered with exuberant puppy kisses. "Ha, ha. That tickles." He carried her up to the last two steps and set her down. "Here. Go on up. You can do it."

A small girl with curly brown hair stood smiling and looking on from above. The girl said, "Come on, Pepper. Come up here to me." She went down on her knees and patted her lap for the puppy to join her.

A short scramble later, the little dog jumped into her arms and enthusiastically climbed up to the child's shoulders, where she licked her neck and earlobe. "Why is she wearing this fat red coat?" the girl said to Adam, as he stepped up beside her.

"She's a baby and doesn't know not to jump overboard," Adam said. "This will let her float, until we can get her out of the water, if she falls in accidentally. She needs a lot of exercise. Would you like to walk around the deck with us?"

The child turned to a tall, curly-haired woman who had been watching from a distance. "May I walk with this man and the little dog, Mother?"

"Of course, dear. I'll just join you.

Pepper pulled forward on her leash in her eagerness to explore ahead. Adam followed in her wake, saying over his shoulder, "Oops. Sorry, ma'am. This little dog seems to have only two speeds this morning -- running flat out and stop. I must run with her."

Pepper's short legs churned on until she met a young man throwing a yo-yo. Adam said, "Good morning. You've stopped this pup in her tracks. I think she's never seen a yo-yo."

The clean shaven fellow, in summer tweeds, looked to be in his early 20s. He threw the red wooden toy down and, as it rolled back up, he said, "Really? I'm surprised. Many of my friends have them, and I understand they've been around a long time. In school I saw a picture of something like this toy in Greece from around 400 BC. And I saw a painting of Napoleon throwing a yo-yo before the battle of Waterloo. That was what?... 50 years ago."

Pepper lunged for it, but stopped short at the end of her leash.

"Whoa, there, little chum," Adam said, with a laugh. To the passenger, he said, "Sorry."

A lady in a blue bonnet approached. She said, "Gerald. There you are. Oh, look at this adorable dog." She bent and ruffled the fur behind Pepper's ears. That was all the permission the pup needed to reach up and plant a kiss full on the lady's mouth. She giggled and was rewarded with a plethora of kisses. "Your dog is so friendly," she said.

Adam said, "She isn't mine, ma'am. I'm just exercising her for the captain. And here he comes now."

Noah exited the companionway and strode up to the small group. He nodded and said, "Morning, folks." After pleasantries he turned to his deckhand and said, "Thanks for taking care of Pepper. I expect you're ready for some relief."

"Yes, sir. I'm all tuckered out, but she's still going strong."

The lady said, "I am totally captivated by your lovely little dog, Captain Asbell. She has such a loving nature. I hope you'll let her take the air on this deck often."

"Yes, ma'am. She seems to enjoy greeting my passengers, and she needs at least two hours every day of exercise. So, I expect you'll see one of us leading her on deck frequently. Thank you for your kind words," Noah said.

After Pepper was coaxed away from the lady and gentleman, Noah said, "Adam I'll take over. Able needs some help with the rigging."

"Aye, Captain," the deck hand said, and he headed the opposite direction with a smile on his face.

Noah said, "I'm happy to see that you're charming all the guests, Pepper. I hope Sadie likes you as much as that lady does."

The wind freshened and ruffled fur and pants legs. "After all, what's not to like?" he said, as Pepper got a whiff of a new scent and yanked him forward. She charged ahead, veering over between the rails and into the alligator-infested river.

Kersplash!

CHAPTER THIRTY-FOUR

June 4, After Breakfast at Cypress Pointe Plantation

Belle delivered a breakfast tray to Albert and Jane. *Jane undoubtedly needs a breather and a change of scenery.*

Fredrika was perched on the windowsill eyeing intently a small blue-gray, yellow and white tufted titmouse, who hopped in a ray of sunshine on the branch outside. "Squee-bee-be-be."

Upon seeing her Albert said, "What took you so long? I'm starving."

"Where are your manners, Albert?" said Belle.

"You are always starving," Jane said with a laugh, as the boy began devouring food.

Belle said, "I've brought enough for two people, but I'm sure you can eat it all, Albert."

He nodded and returned his attention to his eggs. Eyeing her friend, she said, "Albert, I'll stay with you while Jane takes a break to have breakfast downstairs with the others." Jane gave her an appreciative smile and gathered her things.

Belle moved to stand beside his bed. "Albert, have you remembered anything more about your fall into the molasses?"

With his mouth full, he said, "I do remember something about a person behind me. It's still just on the edge of my memory, a shirt sleeve, a hand. No. Nothing more, but it's getting clearer."

"Good. Enjoy your breakfast,"

She smiled at Jane and said, "May I talk to you? We can step outside."

"Yes, of course. Albert, we'll be right outside the door. Just sing out if you need anything."

In the empty hallway they conferred using quiet voices. Belle said, "I'm sorry you've been stuck in here so long. Take as long as you want, but I'm worried. If Albert was pushed, then for his safety, we must keep secret the fact that he's remembering what happened to him in the molasses hut."

"Absolutely. But I hear hesitation in your voice. Now that he's getting well, is he again a suspect in Philippe's death?"

"He *was* heard yelling at his father, 'I wish you were dead.' And, to make himself look like a victim, he could have lied about being pushed. Maybe he jumped into the molasses, not realizing that he could be overcome by the fumes. That's the sort of thing a child might do."

"No. I don't think he killed his father. A child might shout in the heat of the moment, but he didn't really mean it. However, he *is* very nosy. Maybe he found out a damaging secret about the killer without even knowing it. I think he's an innocent."

"He's told you more? You're basing that on evidence?"

"No. Call it instinct."

"All right. Then who do you think killed Philippe? I am seeing jealousies, old and new, plus grudges and possibly a need for revenge. Of all our suspects, Martha and Mary are the only ones I can rule out. If they wanted to get rid of their half brother, there are much quieter ways to go about it."

"Agreed."

"I'm going to enlist their help with a plan. We have to make this killer show his or her hand. And it must be now. Once the river and carriage path are open, our suspects will scatter. It has been about that old barn all along. I want to..." She continued in a barely audible whisper.

After Jane left, Belle went back into Albert's room. She sat beside him and said, "Good job. You ate it all. That should bring back your strength."

"I feel stronger already. Nobody ever praised me for eating before."

"You can add it to your list of 'firsts,'" she said with a laugh.

"Miss, I was wondering... about my father. What happens when you die?"

"I don't know."

"Maman took me to a Catholic church sometimes, and I remember what they said. But, what do you think?"

Folly, fudge and flummediddle. I am not equipped for this. "I think you get to keep your real self, but you don't have to worry about your body, or chores, or work anymore. No more cleaning your teeth or washing your clothes. Some people think you get to fly around like a big bird and look down on the rest of us."

"Did it hurt?"

"Yes, I think it did - very much. Albert, why these questions? Did you jump into the molasses on purpose, thinking you'd escape chores and responsibilities?"

He put his fists to his eyes and rubbed them hard. He said, "Oh, no, Miss." He took a deep breath and huffed it out. "I reckon as how I'm in line to be master of this plantation, now that my father is dead."

The room was silent.

Fredrika's tail twitched back-and-forth as she watched her possible prey on the other side of the glass.

Belle stared at the boy. *Why in the world would you think that? Did your father hold that out for you as a possibility? Another motive to kill a father you evidently hated. Did you kill him, Albert? How could you do it from the other end of the table with Martha and Terra holding your hands?*

Jane returned, and Belle went to her room, trying not to think of the danger in what she was proposing. She switched her thoughts to her favorite riverboat captain. *I wonder if Noah got my letter yet. I keep replaying in my mind the feeling of being in his arms at the dance.* She sighed.

There's that warm tingly feeling again, just from thinking about it. I just...feel safe with him. What could his surprise be? A new flowering plant for the garden? Not very romantic. A dress? Too personal. Jewelry?

Knock. Knock.

She was pulled from her reverie and opened the door to her hostess. "Come in, Martha. Please have a seat at my desk." Belle closed the door and perched on the side of her bed.

"Why the secrecy, Belle? Do you know for certain who the killer is?"

"I think I know, but I need your permission to try something," she said.

After a few minutes' conversation, Belle said, "... and will you offer to pay them extra, to add certainty to the plan?"

"Yes, I can do that."

"Then it's agreed you will announce it at teatime?"

"If you think it'll put an end to this business, I'll be happy to."

Polly is popular with the workers at Cypress Pointe Plantation, Belle thought. *It would be prudent to enlist her as an ally.* "Your Polly has her finger on the pulse of the workers. Let's get her thoughts on the matter, and if she thinks they will agree we'll ask her to spread the word."

On their way to the kitchen to see the clumsy cook with the big wide smile and music in her soul, Belle said, "Polly goes every day to spend time with her daughter among the workers. She will know if the séance got rid of their superstitions concerning the old barn."

"Mmm, yes."

In the kitchen they found the quirky girl, dressed in an astonishing purple dress and purple mob cap, with pink and purple striped socks to match. She danced a jig as she stirred a bowl. "Good morning, Mistress Martha, Miss Belle. How do you like my purple dress? I jest dyed it last night." The girl twirled.

"Oh, Polly. Wherever did you get that striking purple? It looks like the new artificial dye called 'mauveine,'" Belle said.

"I think it is, Miss. Remember when that chemist lady visited last year, Miz Martha? She brought with her a large supply, and Miz Mary, knowin' I love colors, give me some in a jar. I dyed some ribbons and wool for socks an' some things for Maggie. It is pretty, but it fades somethin' fierce. At least you don't have to boil no stinky snails, like you do with the old-fashioned purple."

"You were lucky. It's hard to get it," Belle said.

"Yes, Miss. The lady chemist said her young friend found it by accident when he was trying to make quinine in the lab. He didn't make quinine. He made a sticky black goo, instead. Then he put some alcohol in it, to clean it out. And instead of 'clean,' he got this amazing purple dye stuff."

Martha said, "Yes. Yes. His announcement made a big splash among artists in Cuba. I remember it, because I made a pair of purple leather shoes with it. That was nine years ago. His name is William Henry Perkins, and he was only 18 years old. That artificial purple was quite a happy accident for him."

Polly said, "I dyed belts and hair bows for some of my friends, who help with Maggie."

"How is your daughter, Polly?" Belle said.

The cook set down her bowl and clapped her big capable hands over her equally big ears, finishing with them on her rosy cheeks. "Land sakes. She's growin' like a weed," she said with a chuckle.

"Have you thought any more about marriage?" Belle said.

"Yes. I think I have to tell him, like you said. I'm just biding my time."

"Don't wait too long, lest you lose his attention," Martha said.

"Mmm," said the girl, evasively.

"We actually need your help," Belle said. "Are the workers still superstitious about the old barn?"

"No, Miss, not since master Charles said Miz Deleila is happy."

"Do you think they'd be willing to demolish the old barn now?" Belle said.

"What is 'demolish?'"

"Tear down."

"Yes. Matter of fac', we been talkin' amongst ourselves about what an eyesore that thing is. I s'pect we'd rather have a new better building."

"Great. Will you pass the news that tearing it down will begin tomorrow morning? Everyone who comes to work will receive a bonus."

"... 'a bonus,' Miss?"

"That's when you get extra pay."

"Oh, my friends will like that. They are near done clearin' the log jams out of the river. Most ever'body will come if'n they know tha're gettin' paid extra."

"I hope so. Tell everybody you see."

CHAPTER THIRTY-FIVE

June 4, Grapevine at Cypress Pointe Plantation

Terra and Celeste sat in the large comfortable parlor, heads together, deep in conversation at teatime, while other voices swirled around them. "Mama is saying that now the war is over I can be presented to society in a coming out party. The trouble is, I do not care much for society."

Celeste said, "You don't want to be a debutante?"

"No," said Terra. "I would feel like a prize mare being examined by bidders at an auction."

"But how are you to find a suitable husband?"

"I'm not sure I want a husband."

"You would miss out on the joys of marriage?"

"As a bride I would lose my freedom to choose my own path -- I love research. I would lose access to my own money and property. I would lose my ability to be myself, and I'd become just an extension of someone else."

Celeste said, "I don't think it's as bad as all that."

Flora approached with a tray. "Coffee or tea?"

"Yes. Coffee, please," said Celeste.

Terra said, "Tea, thank you. One lump."

Belle and Martha appeared and sank onto a comfortable sofa. When offered refreshment, Belle said, "Tea for me, thanks Flora, and a small sandwich."

"Yes, tea, by all means and a slice," Martha said.

"Where is Aunt Mary?" Celeste said.

"Mary is sitting with Albert to give Jane a break," Belle said.

"Please ask Zack to take them a tray -- tea, I think, and plenty of cake. That boy has an appetite like an elephant. He must have hollow legs," Martha said.

"Yes, ma'am. And excuse me for asking, but is it true what they're saying? That the old barn will be torn down tomorrow, and the workers get paid extra?"

Martha said, "It's true, but how did you know?"

"I heard the footmen talking about it. They say everyone knows, and they all want to be there to see it come down... and to get paid extra," she said, with a chuckle.

"Good. I'll be glad to see the end of it. Excuse me please. I need to find John and show him where to dig. We'll have a short service for Philippe after dinner."

CHAPTER THIRTY-SIX

June 4, Dinner, Burial at Cypress Pointe Plantation

"That's a right pretty place you chose for Philippe, Martha," said John. "The oaks spread a big canopy of shade over the spot, and the magnolias are blooming -- they give it a lemony smell."

At the head of the table, Martha said, "Yes, I've always enjoyed the peacefulness there. Let's all walk over to the site together for a short service after dinner. Everybody, wear sturdy shoes. It's still a little marshy in places."

After several agreeable nods, dinner conversation lagged. One could hear the faint rumbling purr of Fredrika, who once again had made her way onto Terra's lap.

John said, "The big news is that our crew has finally cleared the river. Logs, branches, and boulders are all gone. And the cart path is clear for carriages. We can finally turn our attention to tearing down that old barn of yours. I guess tomorrow will be a big day for you ladies," he said to his hostesses. "All available hands will be at the old barn to commence demolition."

"And none too soon," said Mary.

Virginia said "I'll say this for you Merritts. News in these parts gets around faster than a hummingbird. You mentioned this at teatime, and already the whole plantation is talking about your barn." She laughed.

Ben said, "The road and river are clear? Then I'm ready to go home."

Eyebrows raised around the table, but all were quiet.

Phoebe said, "Don't worry about a thing, Ben. I'll pack our things, as soon as we get back from the funeral."

Martha said, "If we're almost finished here, I'll go get a lantern in case it gets dark before we get back. I'll meet you all back here after you change."

It was a golden-green twilight, with the sky fading from blazing pink and purple, when they all headed to the small graveyard. Belle could hear a pair of owls conversing.

Whoo-who-wu-whooo!

Whoo-Who-who-whooo-to- you-too!

The bourbon rose that Mary pressed into Belle's hand smelled spicy sweet. But its leathery stem felt rough under her fingers, and the thorns pricked.

A whippoorwill announced approaching bedtime. "Whip-poor-will."

. A warm breeze lifted Belle's hair as they crossed a glade. *Mmmm.The sweet lemony smell of magnolias. We are almost there.*

Then they gathered around the new grave, and Martha read John 3:16. "For God so loved the world, that he gave his only Son, that whosoever believes in him should not perish, but have everlasting life."

Belle said, "Please join me in the hymn, 'Shall We Gather at the River.' Shall we gather at the river? Where bright Angel feet have trod, With its crystal tide forever, Flowing by the throne of God." The voices trailed off.

"We welcome comments from friends at this time," Martha said.

The only sound was that of the crickets and owls.

"Thank you for coming to show respect for Philippe. We haven't known him much in recent days. But we lovingly lay to rest our brother," Mary said. She laid a bouquet of sweet-smelling gardenias on the grave.

Belle added the rose.

"Rest in peace," Ben said in a strong tenor voice.

"Rest in peace," murmured the others. And it was finished.

As they started back to the plantation house in the growing dark, Belle thought, *I hope my friends and relatives will have something good to say about me after I die.*

Swinging the cold lantern in one hand, Martha walked up next to her and said, "Hold back with me." Twilight was closing in. The first lightning bugs twinkled in the bushes, and the crickets increased their volume.

Belle said, "They are all ahead of us."

"I didn't want to be overheard. Voices carry on this breeze. Dodge into that shed. It has the best view of the barn door," said Martha.

"Did you bring the gun we found in Philippe's bedroom?"

"No. I am not much of a shot in the daylight, let alone in the dark. I was afraid I'd harm someone accidentally."

When Martha opened the shed door, Belle could just make out two small cabinet beds with feather beds on top. "We have two more beds behind these. Paul brought them this afternoon. We boxed them like they were going into normal storage during spring cleaning. We also have a jug of tea, a bag of lemon sugar cookies with icing, and a lidded chamber pot," Martha said.

"Good thinking, Martha." She laughed softly. "It wouldn't do for us to be seen stumbling around outside in the middle of the night. And I don't like the idea of squatting behind a convenient tree."

"We can prop this door open partway for a clear view of the big front doors, as well as the smaller side door. That is, unless you object to breathing the night air?"

"I quite like night air."

"We'll have to sleep in our clothes. I hope you aren't wearing your corset."

"I gave up corsets for Lent...some time ago, but before the evening is out, I might wish to trade this cumbersome skirt for some trousers, like Dr. Mary Walker's." Belle saw Martha grin in the pale moonlight.

The actress investigator stepped inside and leaned over a bed, fingering the linen. *Mmm. There's that lovely smell of lavender again. And smooth sheets. I'll bet the Merritt sisters don't have any rough sheets.*

Mary and Jane came skulking around the side of the building. "We just told the others, 'It's been a long day' and 'I'm for bed. Goodnight,' when we got back. I hid the cricket bat and a length of rope from the scullery under my skirt, but nobody was watching when we slipped out," Jane said.

"Right. Who wants to take the first watch with me?" Martha said.

CHAPTER THIRTY-SEVEN

June 4, Late Night Stakeout at Cypress Pointe Plantation

"I can take the first watch," said Belle.

Jane fumbled around under her skirts and retrieved the cord and solid willow bat. "I'll leave these here, leaning against the door."

Belle said, "This may be a wild goose chase, and nothing at all will happen."

"On the other hand, we might catch that wild goose, and we better stay alert," Jane said.

Belle said, "Yes, it could be a crazy wild night. And it might be dangerous. You don't have to do this, you know. There's safety in numbers, but if you are having second thoughts, go back to your room, and we will tell you all about it in the morning."

Only a bullfrog spoke into the silence.

Bullyrum, bullyrum.

Martha said, "Good enough. Cookies and tea on that table in the back, along with our dark lantern and matches. Chamber pot behind the curtain. Everybody go now, or you'll be investigating with crossed legs. If you are not on watch, you will sleep in one of the back two bunks. When on watch, we will sit or lounge on the front beds while we look at those barn doors. And we'll wake you for your shift in four hours. Questions? Good. Silently, now. And let's pray we catch this killer."

And pray he doesn't get us, Belle thought.

Belle lay on the mattress and propped up her head so she could see out the door. *No talking*, she reminded herself.

She tensed as a scary bone-chilling growl sounded from a distance. A shudder ran through her.

Ohhh. It's all right. Relax. That's a gator staking out his territory with that awful bellowing. My friend Gator back in Enterprise said they grunt and vibrate their larynx -- must be like an opera singer's vibrato. He's a big guy — for me to hear him calling "here-I-am-girls" this far from the river. I suppose their mating was interrupted by all the activity on the river.

Martha mimed an alligator and pointed, indicating a long distance away. She signaled 'be calm.' The older lady sat on the edge of her bed and peered out into the dark. A light breeze swirled the leaves.

Surprising how well I can see in the dark, once my eyes get used to it. Mmm. The air smells woodsy. A welcome scent in this cramped shed. Feels like it might rain, thought Belle.

Whoo-who-hu-hoooooo.

Now the orchestra of crickets, gators, and owls was joined by the faint counterpoint of bullfrogs. *Just imagine what those critters would look like doing a contra-dance. Can't stop picturing them as a cartoons – dancing. Mmm, the dance at Palatka was nice, and the feel of Noah's arms around me...was what?*

A warm flush ran through her body. *He actually cares enough to send me a letter on the back of a pigeon. And he has a surprise. What can it be?*

Belle listened to the distant music of the insect orchestra and thought of various scenarios for her future. *Do I really have to choose between Noah and being a Pinkerton agent?*

Is Noah even a choice? He's on a boat most of the time. I could live on a boat with him. What would I do? I could be a singer again. Would I be satisfied with that? What do I really want?

Belle breathed in the lavender scent from her linens, until it was almost time to change the watch. *Too bad Dan went home already.* Everything went quiet, except for a gentle snoring from Jane.

The wind freshened and whistled through the cracks of the clapboard shed. *A storm coming?* Belle mimed to Martha, "Do you want something to eat or drink?"

"Yes," she nodded back and clutched her throat.

"You go. I'll keep watch," Belle signaled.

Her hostess went to the back of the shed, leaving Belle to peer out into the night.

After a few minutes, during which Belle heard Martha drinking tea and eating lemon cookies, her friend returned to the front of the shed. *Good. It's my turn. Then we wake the others.*

She started to turn away, but a tiny glimmer of light from the barn caught her attention. *Was that my imagination, or was that a flash of light?*

She stopped still, then motioned for Martha to look. All was dark. A raindrop plopped down. Another splatted in the open doorway in front of them. *Was I dreaming?*

Flash!

They both saw it. Martha reached for the bat. Belle picked up the rope, wrapped it around her waist, and tied it.

They looked at each other. *It's really happening,* thought Belle.

Belle lit their dark lantern and shuttered the light. The rain was a light sprinkle. Martha said quietly, "Mary. Jane. Wake up. It's time to go to the barn."

Mary said, "What? Mmpf. Why are you whispering?"

"Shh. Get up, dear. We have to go."

Jane immediately sat up and reached for the back curtain.

As soon as all the ladies were up and functioning, Belle took command.

She said, "Look. A light. Coming from the barn. The culprit must've gone in the side door with a dark lantern. Now he needs more light. For what? Stay together. Be very quiet. Watch where you step, lest you crack a stick or trip and cry out, alerting our prey. Ready?"

Martha, with her cricket bat over her shoulder, led the posse as they crept across the yard in the swirling mist.

"This light shower feels cold," said Mary, almost inaudibly. "I hope we don't all catch pneumonia."

Once at the barn, they noticed the side door ajar. They tiptoed through quietly, and Belle exaggerated stealthy movements. She pointed in the faint lamplight at her feet moving barely inches at a time.

Then came loud noises.

Whack. Crunch!

Whack. Rrriiip. Clang!

They aren't bothering to be quiet. What is that crashing noise? And how many are in there? Two? Three? More?

Like four stalking cats they crept, hearts pounding, toward the light and the bashing sounds at the back of the barn. Over the rising noise from the building storm, a steady beat of heavy rain and moaning wind in the cracks, came metallic sounds.

Hammer hitting a nail?

Clink. Thud.

Against the side of a stall with a door hanging askew from a broken hinge, showed the elongated black shadow of a crouching figure.

What is that? Weeping?

Belle signaled 'hold back.'

Rain beat down outside.

Grunts, groans, thrashing inside.

They watched the shadows.

An anguished wail sliced through the night air, almost indistinguishable from the howling wind outside.

The silhouette straightened.

Raised a long shadow weapon...

and hurled it at the back wall.

Crash.!

Creak. Crack!

Wood splintering, Belle thought.

Do I attract crazy people? First John Booth. Now this.

Hardly daring to look, she peeked around the door.

I've led these valiant ladies into danger.

In the stall at the back of the barn, just visible in the circle of yellow light from his lamp on the ground, a dark figure was wielding a crowbar amidst a pile of rubble.

Long hand-forged nails stuck out crazily from the wall.

He's pulling boards from the back wall... to expose...

Martha stepped in front of her. Between the uprights for the mostly-disassembled wall hung a skeleton with elaborately braided black hair and grinning teeth.

He has exposed a skeleton! Belle opened the shutter on their lamp for more light. He looked up in surprise.

"Tom!" Martha said explosively.

A look of amazement crossed his face. "What are you doing here? This is private." He raised his crowbar menacingly.

Belle stepped from behind Martha and said, "Oh, no you don't."

Martha challenged him with her cricket bat.

He hesitated.

"I should say not," Mary said, as she pushed in between her sister and Belle.

Jane moved forward and said, "Tie him up, Belle."

Tom saw the four staring faces in the circle of lamplight. Outnumbered, he swung his crowbar in wild arcs. He scrambled to get away.

"Look out."

"His lantern..."

"He broke the lantern."

"Fire!"

"Get back."

Lamp oil ignited the last vestiges of hay that burst into bright orange flames.

Tom pulled up and hauled himself over the partition.

"He's getting away."

The burly man ran toward the doors.

"Oh, no you don't," said Belle. Again she tied her skirts between her knees. She sprinted after the rogue.

"I'm coming, too," Martha said, following Belle's lead with cricket bat at the ready.

Out the side door they ran. Belle thought, *It's hard to see him in this pelting rain. There he is. Go.*

She stumbled over the uneven wet ground, but caught herself and kept going.

Right behind her, Martha shouted, "Tom. Stop."

Bright white lightning struck in the distance, lighting the landscape momentarily.

Belle could see the docks in the distance.

"He's headed for the boats," Martha said, panting.

"Only a lunatic would try to escape on a sailboat in this weather," Belle hurled over her shoulder.

The wind increased intensity and blew frigid rain sideways into Belle's face.

Tom reached the wharf. He jumped into a red boat, the largest of the Merritts' fleet of shallow-draft cat boats. By the time Belle got there, he had the sail partially up. *Oh, no. He's pulling away. The swirling winds of this thunderstorm are whipping him around. Will he capsize?*

CHAPTER THIRTY-EIGHT

June 45 Night Chase at Cypress Pointe Plantation

B elle leaned over, hands on knees and panting. Then she stood. She headed for another of the cat boat fleet.

Martha ran up. Over the noise of the storm she shouted, "Can you sail?"

"I know the general principles. I watched you on our way here. That should be good enough." She reached to the cleat and untied the bowline. The determined actress waited until an upswing of the bucking boat, then grabbed the gunwale and jumped in.

"Not in a monsoon. Move over," Martha said. She untied the other line of the cat boat, which was gyrating wildly up and down in the water at the dock. "He's not getting away from us."

She hopped in. Martha said, "We're lucky. Someone left it reefed."

Belle looked up at the very small flat triangle of sail. *The whole bottom of the sail is rolled up and tied, so it's not exposed to this beastly wind anymore.*

The two sailed south, away from the wharf.

"Where is he going?" Belle said, her question nearly blown away by the gale force winds.

"If he can get away up one of the feeder streams, he will ditch the boat and disappear into the bush," Martha shouted. She deftly maneuvered the boat through choppy water and foam.

"He has a head start."

"Yes. Tom is stronger than we are. He knows the area. Knows the boat. And he's desperate. But we'll catch him."

Hollering over the howl of rain and wind, Belle said, "How? Is this boat faster?"

"No. Slower." Wind-whipped waves tossed them like a cork. "But I'm a better sailor."

Thank God for Martha at the helm. Cold rain stung Belle's face and pelted over her cold drenched clothing.

Martha said, "Hold on. The water will be shallow in the estuary, and we're going to run into breakers, not swells." She gripped the sheet in one hand and the tiller in the other. The seasoned sailor leaned as far windward as possible.

She's leaning into the wind. Belle copied her.

"Good. Brace with your feet. And watch his red boat. I'm pretty busy here. I have to tail this line. The sheet, that's the line that controls the sail, is on a cleat. But I only wrapped it around once."

"Couldn't it slip? And get loose?"

"No. I've got it. The cleat takes pressure off my arms. With just one wrap I can watch the water and adjust the angle of the sail fast... adjusting to these swirling winds."

Belle could barely see Tom's boat through curtains of rain. *It's coming down like pitchforks with the tines downward.*

"Look, Martha. The end of our sail is dipping down into the water," Belle said in alarm.

"Yes. We are in a rough sea. Wind is trying to push the bow down. Don't worry. It'll just slow us down a little."

Belle said, "He's turning left."

"So are we. Hang on. We're taking a swooping turn to the east. We'll be going down wind, which means running with the wind directly behind us."

She let the sheet slip through her fingers until it came to the knot at the end, which she held.

The boom swung out, and she pulled on the tiller, to swing them around.

The reefed sail, still on their left, filled with air instantly. They shot forward.

I can smell that distinct tang of salt water, Belle thought, as brackish bay water sprayed over the bow.

"Get as far to the stern as you can." Martha pointed to the back of the boat. "We want to plane to make more speed."

Belle moved aft, and the 22-footer slid across the tops of the waves fast.

Martha said, "I'll bet he's heading for Rice Creek. He's probably been hunting and fishing there before. If he can get up in there with the 25-footer, he can slip away and just disappear. I've heard of hunting blinds in there that he could use for temporary shelter. But he's going to have to thread the needle."

"It's narrow?"

"Very! And oyster bars surround the mouth with thousands of razor-sharp shells sticking up. Lord help him if his center board rams into that bar."

"What happens then?"

"He pitchpoles over into those sharp oysters, as if hurled by a slingshot onto a bed of knives."

Lightning lit up the nighttime sky. "Crash."

Belle leaned around and squinted into the swirling wind, trying to spot Tom's boat. "You're right. He's turning. He went left again," said Belle.

"We're gaining on him," Martha said. "And we will turn, too. It's going to happen fast. Watch out for the boom. It's going over our heads — to the right side of the boat. It sounds crazy to turn right in order to go left, but we're going around three quarters of a circle. It's safer."

"Do we grab the boom or just duck under?"

"The sail's going to flap around wildly, and that boom will pitch up and down and bang around. Just duck and follow me to the upwind side of the boat again."

"Duck and move into the wind?"

"Right. As soon as Tom turns to port, left, we'll get ready. When we turn, I need your weight on the windward side of the boat." She pointed. "Get out there as far as you can. DON'T fall in."

Belle said, "He's turning."

"Get ready. Soon. Almost. Ready? Now!" She pulled on the taut sheet-line to take up slack as she turned the rudder, wrapped the sheet around the cleat, and jumped windward. The sail filled explosively.

Belle said, "It felt like the hand of God just pushed us forward."

"More Belle. Lean. The wind is trying to push us over."

Soon they were flying along close behind Tom's 25 footer. Martha said, "It looks like he is trying for that little creek, but..."

Lightning struck near them.

Flash! Belle thought, *it's as if a giant hand flipped a light switch on for a few seconds, then plunged us once again into darkness.*

"I can see a light streak in the water near shore. That can mean only one thing -- water's being pushed away from the shore. It's a lot shallower than Tom will remember."

"Is that a line of foamy SURF?" Belle yelled.

"Yes. I've never seen surf there before. Wind has pushed the water out of the bay. With his center board down, he'll never make it across that bar."

Just then, Tom's center board slammed into the reef at speed.

CRUNCH!

"His stern went up."

Above the gale came his cry, "Aaaraaaagh."

"Pray to God that he's alive," said Martha. "He flew nearly 20 feet up in the air."

"He'll be sliced to bits. Can we get him off the razor-shells? "

CHAPTER THIRTY-NINE

June 5, Wee Hours of Morning in the Barn

Jane and Mary stood at the barn door looking out at sideways blasts of rain.

Jane said, "Quick. Find something to carry water. We have to see about that FIRE."

Mary's feet stayed rooted to the spot. "I'm worried about them. Shouldn't we help them?" Mary said.

"I think they can handle themselves. I don't see what we can do out there in the rain. And a fire's blazing at the back of the barn. Come on."

They turned and began to search.

Mary said, "I found a bucket. But there's no water. Now what?"

"Here's another bucket. And I think I saw a rain barrel," Jane said.

She scrambled to the side door, edged outside, and made her way under the eaves to the corner of the barn. "Bring your bucket outside," she said, over the storm's noise and the splash of water filling her bucket.

Mary stuck her head out the side door and met Jane carrying water.

"That barrel may be leaking, but it's raining so fast that the thing is full to overflowing." She rushed past Mary and headed for the fire.

When she reached the back stall, the fire had started up the partially dismantled wall. She threw her bucket of water at the skeleton.

Mary struggled up with her sloshing burden. Jane said, "Wet down the wall below the bones." They rushed back for more.

Two trips later, Mary said, "We're gaining on it."

"Right. Glad Martha suggested we wear boots for the walk to the graveyard. We're making a muddy mess in here."

Many trips to the water barrel later, Mary said, "This barrel is still overflowing."

"Our repeated bucket-filling might have emptied it, had it not been replenished at such a fast rate. Thank God the fire's out."

"It did its best to erase the evidence of murder," Mary said. "But we won. Did we get all the little pockets of flames? Is it completely out?"

"Yes, but all it takes is one little spark to start it up again inside that wall. Let's douse the skeleton and the surrounding area one last time."

Two bucketfuls later, Mary said, "I think we've earned a rest. But let's watch it for a while in case it starts again."

Jane groaned. "Are you sure? The bed sounds really good right now."

Mary said, "Just a little while, to make sure. Go on to bed. I'll watch it." She turned her bucket over and sat, looking away from their unshuttered dark lantern, and casting a short shadow on the derelict door.

"I'll stay," Jane said. She followed suit. "Who do you think it is? The skeleton, I mean."

"There is no question about it. I'd recognize that hairstyle anywhere."

The two exhausted and sleep-deprived women sat staring at the skull, covered with loops and coils of jet black.

"Her hair was beautiful and glossy. She considered it her crowning glory. Our bucketfuls of water washed the dust of 15 years from her intricate chignon. Seeing her lodged in this wall tells me that the old rumors were true."

Jane leaned forward to rest one side of her ample bottom from the hard tin bucket. "Who is it? What happened?"

"It's a story of great love, jealousy, and betrayal."

"Ending in murder?"

"Evidently. Tom and Phillippe were half brothers. Their mother Deleila was said to have died in a fit in front of this barn. Hers was the ghost that all the workers feared."

"Belle said something about her having epilepsy?"

"Yes. Her seizures struck fear into people. Some said she disapproved of Philippe's friendship with Tom's wife."

"It was perhaps more than friendship?"

"Whispers hinted at that. About the time that Deleila died, Tom's wife is said to have run off with a visiting salesman. And Philippe was sent to school abroad."

"Don't tell me that's Tom's wife! Walled up in the barn?" Jane visibly shuddered.

"Yes. That is undoubtedly Crozbi."

"It looks like Tom is our killer. If Philippe did have an affair with Crozbi, Tom must have been incredibly jealous. Yet he couldn't take any action against the son and heir. So maybe he lashed out at his wife."

"I can see how he could have been so jealous that he killed her, maybe accidentally, and spread the story that she ran off."

"Imagine how he felt when Philippe returned after all that time."

"We rewarded the prodigal with the position of manager. Tom must have resented Philippe bitterly."

"And he's been harboring this resentment against his wife's lover for 15 years."

Mary said, "It's no wonder he wanted to kill Philippe. But how could he have done it? He wasn't even there until after we found Philippe dead."

"Belle has some thoughts about that. And shouldn't they be back by now? He had a head start. Who knows where he went? He wouldn't hurt them, would he? What could he gain from it?"

"No. I don't think he would. He's probably planning to run up a little creek that feeds Indian River and head off into wild country."

"Well, where are they? I'm worried. We can't just sit here. We need to do something."

"When the storm blows over, we can go to the dock and check the boats."

"The rain is slacking off. Let's go now."

CHAPTER FORTY

June 5 Early Morning Rescue, Near Indian River

B elle and Martha were a few yards behind Tom, when he pitchpoled, also endangering their craft. Martha ran a little east downwind. The winds calmed a bit.

"Hold on. When we come into the wind, grab that anchor up there," Martha said. She pointed forward. "Can you tie a bowline?"

"Yes."

"Good. Secure the free end of the anchor line to that cleat."

Then she came up shortly into the wind, bouncing and bucking alongside the oyster bar. "Now throw it away from the oyster bar, over there. Use the boat hook to push us off the bar if we swing too close."

"Help. Oh, help."

Martha said, "I'm not really sure I want to help him get off that oyster bar."

"I know. But it's the right thing to do. Maybe there's an innocent explanation for why he was removing a skeleton from your barn."

"No time to think about that. I'm worried about our safety. With rough seas tossing us up and down we could end up right on top of him. If we lean out too far to reach him, we might fall in and get crushed between the boat and the bar. Or our boat could be swamped or pounded repeatedly up onto the bar, smashing it into splinters."

"Oh, joy! There must be some way we can get him off safely. We can't just leave him there."

"We'd need something between him and those oysters. Perhaps he can climb onto something and we can drag him across. He would have to help."

"How could he help? He was thrown in the air and hurled onto that reef like a ragdoll. He must have cuts all over and broken bones."

"And from the sound of his groans, I think he's in a bad way."

"Help," came Tom's faint call, as if on cue..

"Folly, fudge, and flummediddle. We have to at least try."

"All right. Go forward and get the heaving line -- a rope with a monkey's fist knot tied at the end to make it easier to throw."

Martha cupped her hands beside her mouth and yelled, "Tom. Is there any boat debris near you? Anything flat you can climb onto?"

Belle said, "Pieces of his boat are strewn all over the bar. Can you see him?"

They stared intently. The rain let up for a moment. "There." Belle pointed. "He's on a beam. It isn't moving. Is it stuck on the oysters?"

"Yes. The water is too shallow to float it. Can you throw the line that far? I'm afraid my throwing arm got traded for white hair."

Belle, sitting with the line coiled at her feet, said, "I'll give it my best."

Martha tied one end of the line to a cleat. She shouted to Tom, "We are throwing you a line."

Martha said to Belle, "All right. Heave away."

The boat bucked up and down. Belle planted her feet, picked up the bulk of the line, held it beside her, twirled the end several times in an ever-widening circle, and then let it fly.

Kersplash.

It missed.

The rope landed atop the oyster bar, halfway to Tom.

"Try again."

Where is a catapult when you really need one, thought Belle.

She brought the line aboard with difficulty, snaking it up and down and pulling repeatedly to disentangle it.

"Whew."

With wind pelting her face, she tried again.

Kusplush. She lost sight of the monkey fist as it disappeared in the trough of a huge swell.

It went farther, but didn't reached Tom. Once again, she worked to retrieve the line.

"Tom. Can you come any closer?" Martha shouted over the wailing of the squall.

They watched the injured man grab hold of a nearby stick of wood.

"Yay. Tom, push down. Dislodge that beam."

Tom jabbed down, but the storm worked against him.

He and his beam wobbled up and down in the shallow water above the razor-sharp shells.

The catboat slewed sideways, climbed the mountainous waves, and then pounded down into the troughs. But inch by painful inch the women moved Tom toward their boat.

"We'll throw you the line again," Martha said loudly.

Belle said, "Your arm may not be as strong as mine, but I think it would help if you throw the bottom half of the line."

"You mean pitch it out right after you throw the knot and the top half of the coil?"

"Yes. Let's try it."

Martha and Belle looped the line around neatly again, each holding half. Belle said, "On the count of three. One. Two. Three."

Belle heaved. Martha heaved. The wind tried to blow the line away.

Finally, the monkey's fist splashed- *kesplosh* – next to Tom. He scooped it onto his 'craft.'

"It worked," shouted Belle. "Tie it around your waist, Tom. Bounce the beam."

"Tug on the rope when you are ready for us to pull, Tom," Martha shouted.

Splayed flat on his piece of debris, Tom held on for dear life and repeatedly poled his makeshift craft up off the shells. When they timed their rope-pull accurately, he slid toward them.

Slowly, in spite of their craft behaving like a bucking bronco in the rodeo, Martha and Belle floated Tom on his piece of wood toward the outer edge of the oyster bar.

"Keep pulling. If I don't bail, we are going to be swimming," Martha said. She reached for a bucket and scooped water from the cockpit.

"We are swinging dangerously close to the bar," Belle said.

Martha picked up the boat hook. "I'll push us off."

She shoved against the hard encrustation of treacherous shells once, twice, three times. "That should do it," she said.

Belle said, "Looks like the storm is letting up."

"Good. Florida weather is unpredictable. If you don't like it, wait a minute."

"He's closer," said Belle.

"When we get him into deeper water, we'll pull him to the gunwale, where he can grab hold," Martha said.

Belle kept exerting pressure on her rope. Martha, boathook ready, kept watch of their position.

Suddenly Tom floated free. "He's off," said Martha. Belle pulled steadily, hand over hand.

"I am ready to grab the loop of line around his waist."

It's like reeling in a whale. He's smashing through roiling waves, thought Belle. *I hope he doesn't drown.*

The wind and waves now combined to make the cat boat move like a crazy corkscrew.

"That's as close as we can get him with the line. Help me pull him aboard," Martha said, as the boat pitched up and then dove into a trough.

She can't keep the sharp hook steady. "Turn it around and use the knob?"

Without sticking him, Martha maneuvered the knob under the rope, which was lodged under his armpits. She tugged.

Belle hauled and pulled on the big man.

"Let's lever him up. Push down on the handle while I yank up," Belle said.

The lady plantation owner wrenched him higher. "Tom. Help us," she said.

Finally, he flopped over face down close to the centerboard, like a giant fish.

His legs lay at impossible angles.

Red blood seeped from hundreds of cuts, turning the water in the cockpit pink.

He groaned.

"Stay with us, Tom. We'll get you home as soon as we can," said Martha.

The rain lessened to a light drizzle, and the wind velocity decreased.

"It's going to take us a lot longer to get back. We've had the wind behind us. But going back we can't sail into the wind. That means zigzagging most of the way home."

"So, I'm about to get practice moving the sail around?"

"Yes. By the time we get back you'll be a champion at tacking... and bailing."

Belle and Martha lowered the sail, untied the reefing ties, unrolled the sail to expose another set of ties, retied it into a slightly larger triangle, and hoisted it back up.

"That should do it. Let's go home," Martha said.

"I hope Mary and Jane are all right. We left them in quite a fix."

CHAPTER FORTY-ONE

June 5, Magnolia at Cypress Pointe Plantation

Polly tied on her white ruffled apron at daybreak. "Hello, Fredrika. Looking for an early morning handout?" She scratched behind the ears of the friendly feline and gave her a bit of smoked bacon. Then she opened the door and said, "Shoo, now. Go and bother the lizards. Out. Out of my kitchen." She looked up.

Abe Miller stood at the door with a basket of fresh vegetables in one hand and a bouquet of three sweet-smelling white and gold lilies in the other. "Oh. Abe. Good morning. What brings you here so early?"

He handed her the fragrant blossoms. "I thought you'd like these, and I heard that many hands are needed to tear down your old barn. I thought I could be neighborly and help."

She took the flowers and stepped back, tripping over her other foot. "Oops." Abe reached out a rough hand to steady her.

"I've got ya," he said gently.

Polly burst into tears and splayed her not-so-dainty long fingers over her face.

"Dear Polly, whatever is the matter?"

"I'm so clumsy. You don't want to court me. I'm not the girl you think I am," she said, as fat tears rolled down her cheeks and plopped onto her fresh apron.

"I think you are the girl I want to marry. You are the kind, generous, funny, clever, and unpredictable girl with a head full of melodies, who dances jigs while she stirs hearty victuals."

"I have big ears and a big nose."

"That's more of you to love, dear Polly."

"Folks say I'm odd."

"I like that you are yourself, quirky -- a little superstitious. You know, when we can't explain things, we make things up. We could figure out and explain things together."

"Oh, Abe. That's not all. I promised Belle and Martha that I'd tell you. I'm not proud of it, but I'm not ashamed, either." She watched his face for signs of rejection. So far, all she saw was patience and persistence.

"It was near two years ago when a fast-talking peddler paddled a canoe, with his shiny-silk hair ribbons and fancy soaps, plumb around them blockades."

She gained courage as she told him all about Maggie.

"... and Nanny takes care of her in Lulu's house in the cane workers' quarters, where I go every evening. Her name is Magnolia. But I call her Maggie, and I'll never give her up as long as she needs me."

"Oh, sweet Polly. A one-year-old, blonde, blue-eyed version of you? How wonderful! When can I meet her?"

CHAPTER FORTY-TWO

June 5, Excitement on the Katie Asbell

"Great Jehoshaphat. There she goes. I hope this leash holds," Noah said, stepping to the railing.

He squatted down and carefully pulled the struggling puppy up, hand over hand on the long sturdy strap he had braided. He brought her over the lip of the deck combing and cuddled the frightened animal in his arms. "Oh, you scamp. Now I'm sopping wet," he said in a slightly scolding tone. "No more of that." *Note to self: shorten the leash by coiling it in your hand.*

When he felt her heartbeat return to normal, he set her on the deck and said, "Let's run some of that energy off of you." They ran two laps before he stopped and talked Abel, Adam, and Joe into taking it in turn to jog Pepper around the decks.

"I'm going to go relieve Shorty now. Thanks, fellas, and please don't do it on your watch. Somebody has to keep this steamboat off the shoals."

"Aye, Cap'n," they chorused.

"Keep towels handy for drool. She can shake her head and sling drool a good distance."

Pepper yodelled, *Wow Wooo Wooo*, and nearly tugged the leash out of Adam's hand, as if to say, "I smell something great over there. Let's go."

"And keep her leash short. Scents take her on tangents."

"We need to start training that nose of hers," Abel said.

"When she's tired, we will take her to my cabin and play hide and seek. Hide a smelly sock or something," Joe said.

Abel said, "We'll let her smell my sock, then hide it. If she finds it, then we hide it in a different place with socks from Joe and Adam, too. We'll see if she can tell the difference."

Joe said, "I know. We'll do it in the salon. It's bigger and would be more of a challenge."

Noah said, "All right, but do that when you're off duty. And don't you dare leave any dirty socks in the salon. Heaven forbid that any of our more delicate guests should pull a stinky sock from under their seat."

CHAPTER FORTY-THREE

June 5, Dawn at the Dock

Mary was lying flat on one end of the bench and Jane was lying on the other end. As her eyelashes fluttered open, the plantation owner wondered aloud, "Where in the world am I?" She felt the rough wood of a formerly-damp bench under her. The landing was bathed in shards of sunlight, splintering through nearby trees. The rays warmed her dew-moistened, but sooty, face and dress. Across the clear blue sky, orange and purple ribbons floated. *I have to get up.*

She struggled up as sweet trilling songs of finches filled the fresh air. *I smell grass.*

She groaned. "Oh, my aching back."

And everything else.

Jane stirred and sat up on her end of the bench. "Oh. Look at you -- all covered in black soot."

Mary laughed and said, "You are, too. But I'm too tired to care."

Jane said, "I am stiff and sore all over."

Mary said, "Why did we decide to sleep on this dratted hard bench? I am 1000 years old this morning."

"Ha, ha. I don't think it was a matter of deciding. We just ran out of steam. One minute we were talking and the next we slumped over, unable to go anywhere else."

"I remember now. We were waiting, sure that Martha and Belle would be along soon." The sun came from behind a cloud. Mary said, "If this weather doesn't beat all. Now we have sunshine, with blue skies and fluffy white clouds."

Somewhere downstream something flapped in the breeze. "What is that? A flock of egrets? Sounds like... it is. A sail luffing! Somebody's coming around the curve."

Pop. A sail filled with air, putting an end to the flapping.

They heard a distant voice, around the bend, say, "I'll bring her up to the dock, and you take the painter and step over."

"It's Martha! They're back," Mary said, all tiredness gone from her voice.

"Hallelujah," said Jane.

The flapping sound started again and got louder as they came up into the wind. Jane and Mary roused and rushed to greed the sailors.

Martha slid the boat expertly up next to the dock.

"Oh. There's Tom, with water washing all over him," Mary said. "What did you do to him? He looks terrible."

Jane said, "Ahoy, there. Welcome back. What happened?"

"Jane, alert the house and bring the footmen with a plank," Belle said, as she jumped ashore and tied the painter to a dock cleat.

Martha said, "I'm tying off the stern, and then I'll drop the sail. Hang on, Tom."

"Let me help," said Belle, as she stepped back aboard.

"I always struggle to time the swing of the boat," Mary said, as she stepped aboard and hugged her sister and the intrepid Belle.

Paul and Zach came charging across the lawn with a flat board. Jane followed in their wake.

"What happened?" Zach said.

"Tom's hurt. We need to take him to the house and attend to him. Hurry. Step over and be careful lifting him," Martha said.

Other plantation guests, in their dressing gowns, rushed up and crowded the dock. They watched mutely as Paul and Zach carried the plank onto the catboat. Jane steadied the vessel, then jumped aboard.

Celeste leaned forward, a twinkle in her eye, and said quietly, "Belle! You poor thing. You must've had a terrible fright -- and it has turned your hair a ghastly bright red."

"Hush, Celeste," Mary said. "Here, Belle. Take my scarf."

Belle ran her fingers through her wind-tangled hair, and quickly put on the large silky square. *Oh folly, fudge, and flummediddle. I've lost my brown wig. Maybe none of the guests noticed me in the shadows. I guess I'll be wearing a hat or a scarf until I leave here.*

Zach touched Tom, then drew back as the injured man cried out.

"Aaaaae. No!"

The footman eyed Tom with dismay. His look said, "It's hopeless," and he shook his head at Paul. They stood watching as Martha gripped Tom's hand in a soothing gesture.

The battered overseer fluttered his eyelids and strained to speak. "I, I, didn't mean to kill her. Crozbi," he said weakly. "I didn't mean to kill Crozbi. Accident. Phillippe's fault. I loved her."

"Did you come in through the window during the séance, Tom?" said Belle. Jane's eyebrows flew up with surprise, but she remained mute.

His lips moved into a small smile and he rallied. "Yes. He wanted Martha and Mary dead. He thought if they were out of the way, he could take over. He offered to pay me to handle it. I agreed. "

"You agreed to kill Mary and Martha for money?"

"Yes. Especially Martha."

"Why would you want to kill Martha?"

"She is a strong voice for modernization...Couldn't let you find Crozbi in the wall."

"How was he to pay you?"

"He had silver from selling Merritt rum. Said it was his. You owed him." He coughed weakly. "Ha. I tricked him. He would blow out the candle and let me in the window. I would ring the bell." Tom stopped. "I would be the ghost... say 'keep the old barn.' That was to keep my secret safe. The medium beat me to it. But she said, 'Modernize.'" His words trailed off. "I locked the window back. Nice touch. He won't bed... a married woman... again."

"Do you mean *you* killed Philippe?" Martha said.

He seemed to gather strength. "Yes," he said softly. "I've hated him for 15 years. I swore I'd kill him if he came back -- and I did — with his own cussed knife."

"Thank you for telling us. You rest now, Tom. We'll take you in out of the weather," Belle said.

The footmen looked at her questioningly. She nodded. They moved forward to lift him onto the plank, but before they reached him, he turned his head to the side and moaned.

Gurggle...

Gasp! He then lay completely still.

The footmen moved back.

Everyone stood silently for some minutes, watching. Water, the color of tea, swirled past the dock, carrying twigs and iridescent, black-winged damselflies toward the Indian

River and the Atlantic Ocean. In the top of a tree overlooking the stream, a mockingbird sang a medley of trills, whistles, and calls copied from finches, blue jays, doves, and catbirds.

Finally, Martha, still holding his hand, said, "He isn't breathing. He's gone. His body was just too broken. At least he made it home and told his story. But you had already figured out most of it, hadn't you, Belle?"

"Yes, but I had no proof." Belle looked up to the dock and said, "John, will you organize a grave for him? I'm sure Martha will show you where to dig."

John said, "Yes. Of course. Right after breakfast."

"That won't be for hours yet. The sun and song birds just rose, and here we are in our dressing gowns. I'm going back to bed," said Virginia, grabbing his hand and turning to go back to the plantation house.

"What a splendid idea," and "Yes," chorused Belle, Martha, Jane and Mary, clearly exhausted from their overnight adventures. "Right after a steamy bath," said Mary, wrinkling her nose at her blackened hands and clothes.

Guests started peppering them with questions -- "What happened to Tom?" "Why were you out in the middle of the night?" "What are you doing on a boat at dawn?" "Why are Mary and Jane covered with black?" "Are we going ahead with the barn demolition?"

Belle held up her hand. "We are so tired we cannot wiggle. Let us get clean, get some rest and food. Then I'll tell you all about it. Breakfast would be a fine time."

CHAPTER FORTY-FOUR

June 5, Aboard the Katie Asbell, Balance

Noah, at the helm of the *Katie Asbell,* looked down at Pepper, the little red scenthound. She lay curled at his feet, and her leash was tied around the leg of his chair.

Preoccupied, he thought, *Aristotle was right about balance. He believed you create inner balance and peace as long as you have, "Something to do, someone to love, and something to hope for."*

He would probably think me very lopsided. Where is my balance? I'm all "Something-to-do." My life is 100 percent business.

How can I get balance in this world of extremes? I am an extreme businessman.

And I need my business. Just not all the time.

I want love and a family.

Don't let Sadie go.

Tell her. Show her, too.

He remembered an earlier conversation with Sadie.

She had said, "Just because Jane bought chickens and needs a coop, that doesn't mean you have to make one."

"I know, but I want to. I used to be a fair carpenter. All I need are some lumber and tools."

Famous last words, Noah thought. *But it's true, and I want to take care of that for her.*

Sadie had replied, "In that case, I think the south side of the garden would be a good place for it. Not too far from the back door."

"How many nesting boxes do you want?"

"Hmm. Maybe four. If Jane is as good at raising chickens as she is at everything else, we'll have a flock before you can blink."

Noah caught sight of Palatka, his anchorage for that evening. The boat captain docked his steamer and roused his little sidekick. Pepper had been running around the decks for hours and now was perfectly happy at his feet. They went down and greeted the passengers who disembarked to explore the tiny, but growing, town. Pepper was puppy-polite, with cheerful and energetic tail wagging, except to the lady in the purple hat. She offered the pup a kiss and received an ebullient, wet, doggy, goodbye kiss in exchange.

After they toured the decks to assure Captain Noah that everything was shipshape, they strode down the gangplank, with only a slight misstep from Pepper, and headed for the mercantile store.

"Hi, Curly," he said to the owner. "Do you have any of that lumber left from the old sawmill?"

"Sure do. How much do you need?"

"Enough to make a chicken coop for Sadie. I need some chicken wire and hinges, too."

"Lumber's scarce, since the war."

"You'd think, with all the sawmills we had around these parts, that there would be some excess lying around," Noah said.

"AyeYup. Follow me around back. I'm sure we can find everything yeh need. And as it's for Sadie, I'll give yah a discount."

Pepper helped them search. Stacks of pine heartwood came to light, along with two sawhorses and the required hardware. Curly helped Noah carry his purchases onto the freight deck of the *Katie Asbell.*

Excellent. We're in business. Those were some tall pine trees. The boards look to be about 16 feet long. I'll make it eight feet by eight feet.

Soon sawdust was flying. He had plenty of time to think as he sawed his boards. Captain Asbell measured, cut, and completed four nesting boxes before losing the light.

Lamplight twinkled above the door of the Mercantile. The lilting melodies of Happy Dan's fiddle brought dancing couples onto the square in front of the store. *Sadie's letter said Dan was in Eau Gallie. Maybe she will be home soon.*

Noah joined the fun.

"Dan just came paddling up with Gator and started playing. He may rent a room from us for a while. Fiona says he's good for business. His music certainly improves our steamboat evenings," Curly said.

"Yes. Everybody seems to be enjoying themselves," Noah said. *It's just not the same without Sadie.*

CHAPTER FORTY-FIVE

June 5, Final Gathering at Cypress Pointe Plantation

Breakfast was served late at Martha's request, and they all gathered in the dining room. The four adventurers had enjoyed a wash and a bit of rest.

Belle said, "I have a special surprise for everyone." She beckoned to Martha, who stood with someone else in the doorway. Albert, leaning a little on Martha for support, entered the dining room and sat quietly at the nearest place setting. Cheers went up all around. The boy smiled.

"He's not strong," said Martha.

Albert said, "I had to get out of bed, Aunt Martha. I'll just eat and listen."

"It's good to have you back, Albert. I scrubbed off the soot in honor of your return," Mary said jokingly.

"Me, too," said Jane, to those around the table. "I feel so much better since I am clean."

Mary said, "And I'm famished."

Flora and the footmen loaded the table with heaping platters, and Albert helped himself.

"We are taking Ben home today," said Virginia. "He seemed perfectly normal this morning when I went to his room to see him."

"Good," Belle said. She applied knife and fork to a piece of smoked ham.

Celeste said, "Tell us what happened last night."

"You asked if we are going on with the barn demolition," Martha said. "The answer is yes. Absolutely. We've given young Joshua the job of manager, and that building will be history as soon as they remove the bones."

"Bones??" said several guests at once.

"Yes. We found Tom removing Crozbi's bones from the barn wall, where he placed them after he killed her 15 years ago. He was in a rage after she told him about her affair with Philippe. That's why he spread rumors to keep everyone away from the barn and couldn't let Martha and Mary tear it down," Belle said.

"Oh, Aunt Mary. Then the rumors about Philippe and Crozbi were true!" Celeste said.

"They were."

Belle said, "And Tom used Philippe's jealousy over not inheriting Cypress Point Plantation to make him think the two of them would play a trick on us by secretly letting Tom in through the dining room window during the séance."

"How did he do that with us all sitting there?" said Phoebe.

"Philippe himself blew out the candle and let Tom in. Tom carried out his own agenda of killing the hated Philippe. Then Tom re-locked the window. But before he could say 'keep the old barn,' we had already heard the voice of Charles saying, 'tear down the old barn.'"

Celeste said, "... and with Belle striking matches to light the candle, all he could do was pretend to come in the door!"

"That explains the other water on the floor," Terra said.

Belle said, "Yes, I soon realized that the heavy water trail on the west side of the room was really from the window to the door. And that tallies with the mysterious blood path on that side of the room."

"It was Tom who attacked Martha in the middle of the night?" Virginia said.

"Yes. She was the strongest voice for modernizing, and that meant tearing down the old barn. He couldn't let that happen," Belle said.

"I had my suspicions and was worried about our personal safety. Thank God for Belle. Everyone needed to be more alert, so I thought since she has been training to be a Pinkerton agent, she would teach us all how to protect ourselves."

"It worked, clever neighbor. I learned lessons that I'll use all my life," Virginia said, with a smile.

Terra said, "Me, too. Thanks, Belle. We women were practicing how to be safe, but poor Albert was left on his own."

Belle said, "And to Tom, Albert was a threat, because he's a nosy boy and was curious about the barn and the boats."

Jane said, "When I checked on him this morning, he remembered that he saw Tom coming at him with a brick the morning he fell into the vat of molasses."

"And I saw my father stealing the plantation's rum," Albert said, in a quiet voice.

"Lord have mercy. Why didn't you tell us this yesterday and save all the kerfuffle?" Mary said.

Phoebe suddenly sang a bright happy song. "The last to arrive was Big Black Bug, Uh, huh. Ho, ho. He drowned in the molasses jug. Uh, huh. Ho, ho."

They all looked at her in surprise.

"Oh, sorry. Nursery song. It just bubbled out. Sorry. Nothing's childish or funny about attempted murder."

"Indeed," Martha said.

Ignoring the odd interruption, Celeste said, "Why were you and Jane so dirty this morning, Aunt Mary?"

Mary said, "Oh didn't we say? Tom set the barn on fire as he was trying to get away from us. Jane and I put it out."

"Lord, have mercy," said Virginia.

Terra said, "He was a menace, but why would Tom attack Lucky? The man I pounded and scratched was tall and lanky, not like your husky Tom."

Belle said, "That wasn't Tom. Some over-corned lad, stimulated by the liquor and the dance, was just trying it on."

"Ah. And you and Aunt Martha were in the catboat with Tom this morning because..." said Celeste.

Belle said, "Tom tried to get away from us in the 25 footer, but he forgot about the oyster bars. The wind blew most of the water off the sharp oysters, clumped and grown together. He slammed into a bar, capsized, and was thrown onto the reef. Both his legs were broken, he had cuts from stem to stern, and the boat was reduced to splinters. We rescued him and brought him home in the dark and drizzle, fighting a gale and torrential rain most of the way."

"Belle tried to stop his bleeding."

"But all I could do was protect him from the cold rain with a portion of my long skirt — the only good use for all that fabric."

"If it hadn't been for the near - constant lightning, we might never have caught him," said Martha.

"I'm glad it's all over, and we can finally go home. I'll begin the task of burying the poor fellow, if you'll point me to your preferred spot, Martha," John said.

"Of course, John. Thank you. Excuse us, please," Martha said. She stood and nodded politely to her guests ranged around the table. "Oh, Belle," Martha said. "Let me take you and Jane up the coast to Jacksonville tomorrow. It's the least I can do, and it will be much faster and less expensive than going on a steamer."

Jane said, "How kind of you. That would be delightful." She looked at Belle for confirmation. "Provided it's all right with Belle."

"Think about it. I'll be back directly, and we'll talk," Martha said, as she departed with John.

Phoebe took this as her cue. She rose and said, "Come on, Terra. Let's go pack. We must get ready for the trip home. I hope Ben will be in a good mood."

Belle said, "Phoebe, I've seen cases like Ben's before. Doctors are calling it "soldiers heart.""

Phoebe looked at her hard and said, "He used to be cheerful and outgoing. But now he's nervous and has headaches and heart palpitations all the time. He just wants to be left alone."

"Doctor DeCosta in Philadelphia is studying soldiers like Ben, who saw horrors during the war. A reclined position and forced bed rest is most beneficial. Don't give up on him. Keep loving him."

Phoebe looked at Belle speculatively, then turned and hurried away.

"You know a great deal about medicine for a séance medium... or a Pinkerton agent. Who are you, really?" Celeste said.

Mary was quick to defend Belle and said, "Celeste, she's a friend. We invited her here to help us. And she has done so, brilliantly. Let's leave it at that."

Jane said quietly to Belle, "At last we can go home. Snow Bird Cottage will be very peaceful compared to this."

Belle said, "I am ready, but we must bury Tom. Then, home sweet home. Both steamers will be in Palatka tonight. We can't get there today. Tomorrow Noah will be headed down to Enterprise.

The budding sleuth did a rapid calculation. *From here it's 130 miles sail up to Saint Augustine. Then we must choose: we could spend three hours of tomorrow in a rough ride over land to Piccolata and catch the only steamer, which is Darlington going to...Jacksonville! Or -- save some bruises and the price of two coach or steamer tickets by riding with Martha to Jacksonville.*

"Jane, I think we should ride with Martha to Jacksonville tomorrow and catch the Darlington tomorrow evening. We would be in Palatka the next day." *And see Noah.*

CHAPTER FORTY-SIX

June 6 News in the Kitchen at Cypress Pointe Plantation

Belle put a neatly folded white linen blouse into the suitcase laid open on her bed. *I'll be glad to get home to my wardrobe of greens, blues, reds, purples, — mauveine. All this black and gray is killing me.*

"Knock, knock."

She opened the door to Martha, who said, "Belle. Good news. You'll never guess. Well, maybe you can. Come see for yourself," as she grabbed the sleuth and pulled her out the door.

Belle laughed and said, "My goodness. Where are we going?"

"You'll see." She propelled her out to the kitchen. There, amidst pots, pans, and bowls, Polly danced, twirling around the room with a song and a bowl of batter.

Standing just inside the door was a tall, muscular young man in his mid 20s, dressed in clean denim overalls and a red shirt. His curly brown shoulder-length hair was neatly tied back, and intelligence shone from his brown eyes, which crinkled at the corners. He gazed adoringly at Polly.

Polly pulled him into her dance, twirled once, and then pulled Belle and Martha in, adding to her whirling circle. They were a child's toy top -- spinning, spinning.

"What is all this?" said Belle, though, now that she recognized Abe Miller from the dance, she was pretty sure she knew.

"Please stop now. I'm getting dizzy," Martha said.

Polly relented. "Oh, Miss Belle, you was right. Thank you, thank you. And you, too, Miz Martha. I should'a told him a long time ago."

Martha said, "Belle, this is Abe Miller, who brings us beautiful vegetables and fruits. Abe, meet our intrepid investigator Belle."

Belle said, "Pleased to meet you Abe. I understand you have property nearby, where you grow produce for markets up north."

"Yes, ma'am," he said, shyly.

"He went with me yesterday down to Miss Lulu's to play with Maggie," Polly said.

"Magnolia is beautiful and smart, and full of fun, just like her momma," Abe said. "I can't believe my good fortune." He grinned from ear to ear

Belle said, "Then...?"

"She finally said yes. Polly said yes. She will be my bride as soon as we can arrange it," said the joyous young man.

"Congratulations," said Belle and Martha together.

"And don't you worry about your Polly. I have just purchased more property adjoining my present acreage, and I've hired a farmhand. We'll get along just fine. And she can come visit you whenever she wants."

Polly said, "You can come see us, too. And I'll cook some of Miss Jane's mouth-watering recipes."

June 6, Hen House Puzzle

"**K**eeping up with this pup is going to improve the wind and the stamina in all of us. That's five laps of the freight deck for me," Abel said, as he stopped to catch his breath and let Pepper lick his face.

"You know you love it," Noah said, with a laugh. "I'll take over. Go make doubly sure that every last passenger has disembarked. It looks like they're all on the hotel's wide veranda."

Minutes later Abel jogged up. "They are all gone, sir."

The captain put Pepper in her crate, which she seemed to enjoy. It was placed so she had a view of all the scenery as they traversed the river. "Good. Let's go."

The *Katie Asbell* steamed directly to the shoreline opposite Snow Bird Cottage. The gangplank went down.

Noah swung a bag of tools over his shoulder and picked up a nesting box with the other hand. "Everyone, grab a piece of the henhouse puzzle and follow me," said Noah.

"Tell me again why we're building a chicken coop," Adam said.

"I'm hoping to get invited for more of Jane's home-cooked meals during my future overnights in Enterprise," he said, with a smug look.

"You better get us an invite, too, as we are helping you," Joe said.

"This looks like a henhouse *kit*," Adam said.

"Yep. That's what all my hammering was today. I think we can get it all put together before we lose the light," Noah said, leading the way to the Snow Bird Cottage backyard.

Roo, roo, arooooo!

"Joe, please go get our helper," Noah said, "while I sort these components. She sounds lonely," he said with a laugh.

Joe returned with the puppy, on her leash.

Noah said, "Look, Pepper. Your new home. Just wait until your mistress sees you." He gave her treats and installed her on the back porch with water, where she could see them work. He made another trip to the steamer and then assigned jobs. Everyone went to work.

Mmmm. A breeze and warm sunshine. Song birds keeping us company. And a view of ducks and ducklings swimming among the little wavelets lapping the shore of Lake Monroe.

Noah chiseled out areas for his door hinges.

"Where does this piece go, Noah?" said Abel.

He sorted all of the difficulties associated with putting together his 'kit.' And he thought about 'balance.'

Aristotle was big on temperance. Today, he probably would be a member of the American Temperance Union.

Temperance and balance in all things, he said, are necessary for happiness.

With the smell of sawdust still in his nose, he said with a flourish, "Tah-dah. A new deluxe floored henhouse with a hinged door -- which squeaks -- but only a little."

"That's some highfalutin' building, just for chickens," Abel said.

"Isn't it? I can't wait till she sees it. It's fully outfitted with four cozy nesting boxes. And because chickens need balance between being indoors and being outdoors, I have provided the portable fenced run."

"So that's what that contraption is," Joe said.

"You can move it to a fresh bit of grass every so often. That should keep them happy and healthy."

Joe, Adam, and Abel all burst into laughter and punched Noah's arm.

"She'll be amazed that you are concerned with *balance* in the life of *chickens*," Abel said.

"Yes, that'll really impress her."

Noah said, "Come on you sorry crew. There's a surprise for you around front." He untied Pepper and led her along.

"Joe, hitch Pepper to the front porch railing, please, while I make a quick trip to the lake."

"Our surprise is in the lake?" said Abel.

"You and your surprises," said Adam.

"Just have a seat." Noah strode to the lake's edge, rolled up his pants legs, and waded in. He reached into the water and pulled up a box.

"Curious," said Abel, as Noah lugged the box to the front porch.

As he deposited it on the floor, he said, "Your surprise is in that box. They came all the way from Australia, and they are called 'Kirks Surprises.' You can pick from three flavors -- Strawberries and Cream, Summer Sorbet is mango and peach, and Fizzy Flamingo is peach and raspberry. Have a bottle."

"Soda! Out here in the middle of nowhere. Thanks, boss," Joe said.

The four sat on the front porch with their drinks. They leaned against the house and watched the sun dip down into Lake Monroe. The sky was ablaze with purple, blue, and gold mirrored on the lake.

Joe said, "This is a great surprise. And they are nice and cold."

"I put them in the cold spring-fed lake before we started work," said Noah. "Have another."

He patted Pepper. In his imagination, Sadie was there with him. *Sadie, you are going to love Pepper.*

Sadie, Jane, and Martha watched the same sky 140 miles away as the tired sailors docked in Jacksonville. Sadie thought, *Tomorrow Palatka and Noah.*

CHAPTER FORTY-EIGHT

June 7, Reunion Evening, Palatka, Florida

He *Darlington* had docked, and Dan's lively music floated across the serene St. John's River to the *Katie Asbell* as she chug, chug, chugged up to the dock. Couples from the *Darlington* were already lining up for dances.

"Come on, Pepper. Let's go down to the passenger deck and mingle, before they all leave," Noah said. *I don't think I want to dance without Sadie.*

Soon they were alone at the rail, watching the dancing. "Just listen to that happy music, Pepper." *I wish Sadie could be here now.*

He looked down and saw flaming red hair. *Sadie? It can't be. It's someone else with red hair.*

He said to Pepper, "I guess I might as well go down and say 'Hi' to Curly and Fiona. But you're not ready for such a melee. Will you be happy in your box? No? All right. Let's go put you in my cabin."

Pepper trotted along beside him on deck. "The stairs are still too tall for a youngster like you. Up you come," he said, as he carried her up the companionway.

In his cabin he washed and dressed in a clean crisp shirt and his good trousers. Pepper climbed on the foot of his bunk. "Oh, ho. You look mighty comfortable there. All right. Just until I get back and then you have to start getting used to sleeping in your crate. Stay out of trouble."

He headed down the gangplank, absently watching for Sadie. Then he saw her.

Can it be? "Sadie?" He shouted across the heads of a sea of dancers. "It is…Sadie!"

The moment their eyes meet, electricity zinged through the air. Time stood still. Then Sadie ran through the throng of dancers. "Excuse me. Coming through."

Noah met her in the middle. For a full minute they hugged, while the dancers carried on around them.

"How can you be here?" Noah said, looking down at her radiant face.

"I'll tell you later. Let's dance."

The big silvery moon was up and stars twinkled in the heavens. For two hours they twirled in each other's arms, politely declining, with the exception of Sadie's dance with Curly, to dance with others.

As the energy of dancers began to wane, and the dance wound down, a scary howl rent the air. *Roo, ouroo, roo-roooo!*

The music stopped.

Roo, roo, roo-roooooo!

Dancers startled. Some shuddered.

"What *is* that?" said many, as they looked around them.

Sadie said, "Oh, a shiver just went down my back."

"Uh-oh. Great Caesars ghost," said Noah. He grabbed her hand. "Come with me."

"Where are we going?"

He dashed with her up the *Katie Asbell* gangplank, up the companionway stairs, and to his cabin. They stopped, out of breath, in front of the door. *WooRoo, roo, roo-roooo!* came the mournful yowling.

"Pepper. Pepper, hush," said Noah.

Silence.

"Noah. What have you got in there?"

"This isn't the way I imagined your introduction."

"Introduction?" She looked at the closed door.

"Yes, to Pepper. I just wanted you to love her as much as I do. She'll be really useful to you in your work. Close your eyes. Here is your surprise."

Sadie's heart beat faster than it ever had.

Noah opened the door. "Oh, no. Not the stuffing out of my bunk." Pepper stood happily on the bunk with a giant wad of white mattress stuffing hanging from her mouth. "You were supposed to make a good impression, not show your new mistress that you are a champion chewer."

"My surprise is...You got me...?" She leaned forward for a better look in the dim room.

"...a scenthound! Sadie, meet Pepper. She can smell 300 times better than we can."

Sadie gulped. "A dog? Not flowers? Not chocolates? A dog is a, a great deal of..."

Pepper reached up with an affectionate wiggle and licked Sadie's cheek and neck.

"...of work." She giggled. Pepper tried to give her a hug and ended up in Sadie's arms, happily licking her arm and hand.

"I'm jealous," Noah said.

"...of her or me?" Sadie said, with a laugh.

"I've got her leash. Bring her outside for a moment or two.

They stood at the rail looking up at the big romantic moon, high up in the midnight blue sky with millions of pinpoints of light. Noah put his arm around Sadie, who cuddled Pepper in her arms. "She smells of new puppy," Sadie said.

"Yes. She had a bath with Jacksonville Mercantile's best lavender soap today," Noah said.

They began to sway in time with Happy Dan's final waltz. Then the two, no, three of them waltzed around the *Katie Asbell* deck, making up silly lyrics to the tune and chuckling as they swirled with wild abandon.

Noah thought, *I never tire of watching Sadie. She presents quite a beautiful picture, with the breeze tousling her hair, lit with silver moonlight. I'll be glad when she comes home to Enterprise.*

"Are you looking forward to being home? You have new Yale locks, a new hen house with four nesting boxes, and a fancy new portable fenced chicken run."

"Thank you, Noah. I'm looking forward to seeing your handiwork."

"Oh, and I almost forgot. There's a letter there for you from the Pinkerton agency."

THE END,

until Sadie's next adventure.

Thank You!

Thank you for reading one of my books! This is the ninth book I've published since 2018. Don't misunderstand. My computer is full of stories that I've written throughout a lifetime of writing stories for friends and family as a gift for special occasions. But until then I had not published any.

When I visited my nephew in Colorado, a family member read stories from my computer to entertain three children. I sat watching and listening to their enthusiastic reactions. It was then that I began to think about what it would take to publish. *I'm no artist.* I thought, *How am I going to get pictures that will suit my work?* I also knew nothing about publishing. But I didn't let that stop me.

Learning how to publish a book was a lot of work. And many evenings when others were curled up happily watching a movie, I was learning and implementing new technical skills.

I collaborated with an artist friend and, one very large learning curve later, I created all the digital color work for the images and published <u>Chloe and Orangina,</u> a short story I wrote for my granddaughter on her sixth birthday.

When asked what kind of story she wanted for her birthday, another family member said," I want a novel, a murder mystery." The result of the next couple of giant learning curves was <u>Control Game,</u> my first full-length mystery novel.

I'm working on a new Chloe book about how trees communicate through fungi on their roots. And the next Sadie Snow book is halfway plotted. But I can't say it gets any easier. The ideas for my books spend a long time in the mulch pile inside my head. It's always a challenge to face that blank page at the beginning of turning an idea into a book.

I am pleased to offer you the result of many months of research, plotting, and writing — Book 2 in the Sadie Snow series of historical cozy mysteries. The research for this series has been a lot of fun, so far.

If you enjoyed <u>Death by Séance</u>, please leave a review to HELP me make the next book better and to HELP others find this book. People have told me, "I don't know how to leave a review." It's easy. **Simply tell people what you liked about the book. Did you like the characters? Was the plot interesting? Did you like learning about life in 1865? Did you like the cat?** Just tell 'em.

About those stars: five stars gives me an A, which tells people you liked the book. Four stars gives me a C and tells people, "Meh! Marsha's book was just average. Nothing special here." And three stars or less is an F and says, "Marsha has failed and the book has little or no redeeming qualities."

I promise I will read every word of your review. Now ust mosey on over to Amazon and Goodreads to review

PLEASE REVIEW DEATH BY SÉANCE

Goodreads:

https://www.goodreads.com/book/show/206158469-death-by-alligator

Amazon

https://www.amazon.com/review/create-review/?ie=UTF8&channel=glance-detail&asin=B0DCPZPPPC

Fictitious Characters in Sadie Snow Series, Books 1, 2.

Bows and Curtain Calls (Play my game: Imagine the following characters taking their bows under stage lights. Anything distinctive about their dress or manner of bowing?)

Protagonist:

Sadie Snow, actress and budding sleuth. (I imagine her in short navy blue skirt over matching trousers, white blouse, and thigh-length navy jacket. She strides to center-stage, with red, curly, shoulder-length hair flying behind her, and bows frpm the waist.)

Evangeline Bright, Sadie's stage name when she worked at Ford's Theater in Washington, D.C. (I imagine her in a cobalt blue full-skirted "Our Cousin" costume and holding an enormous beribboned wide-brim hat. She glides before the spotlights and gives a deep graceful bow, like a Royal Lippizanner horse.)

Charles Snow, the alias chosen by Sadie Snow, when she traveled as a man. (I imagine him, elbow out at nose-height, with forefinger pressing on his mustache, and waggling his fake bushy eyebrows)

'**Belle**' the alias chosen by Sadie Snow, when she played the role of séance medium. (I imagine her sedately walking centerstage, holding her large black wide-brim hat, arms outstretched, nodding and munificently acknowledging audience applause.)

I gave Sadie characteristics of various real-life residents of a **real** West Florida plantation, called Chinsegut Hill.

The last name "Snow" came from a plantation family who lived there just after the Civil War. Elizabeth Robins, actress and author, who, with her brother, owned the plantation in the early 1900's, was my inspiration for Sadie. You can visit the sumptuous antebellum plantation house, which is located five and a half miles north of Brooksville, Florida.

Interesting real-life history of Chinsegut Hill: In 1842 Colonel Bird Pearson acquired the original land grant for 160 acres. He had a ship's carpenter build a log cabin, which was framed with hand-hewn 12-inch cypress, and encircled by a defensive fence.

In the 1850s, new owner Francis Ederington, a planter from South Carolina, built a two-story home southwest of the original building. He and his wife, Precious Ann, raised ten children there.

Their eldest daughter, Charlotte Ederington, married dentist Joseph Russell Snow, after the Civil War. They renamed the plantation "Snow Hill." Joseph served in the Florida House of Representatives, and the 1885 census states the family grew corn and sweet potatoes.

In 1904, world traveler and adventurer Colonel Raymond Robins and his sister, Elizabeth Robins, who was an acclaimed actress and author, purchased the property and renamed it "Chinsegut Hill." Robins had been an advisor to five different presidents, and he, as well as his sister and his wife, had a wide range of national and international political and social connections. They entertained many famous people at their home. Robins, in his will, deeded 2000 acres to the US government for education. Upon his death, Chinsegut Hill became the property of the University of Florida.

More Fictitious Main Characters:

Noah Asbell, owner and captain of the fictitious stern-wheeler steamboat, *Katie Asbell.* Katie Asbell was the real-life name of my wonderful maternal grandmother. (OKAY. Your turn. How does he bow?)

Jane Marsh, former slave. Sadie's friend and housemate. She is the daughter of a rageaholic Spanish plantation owner in Cuba.

Martha Merritt Stone, along with **sister Mary,** is heiress to a plantation in Eau Gallie, near Saint Augustine, Florida. Previously she was a journalist with the *New York World.*

Mary Merritt Menendez, widow of regional physician, with her sister Martha, is heiress to the Eau Gallie plantation.

Guests at fictitious Cypress Pointe Plantation in Eau Gallie, Florida:

Celeste Menendez, New York journalist and Mary's niece visiting the Merritts in Eau Gallie.

John Crews III, owner of fictitious plantation *The Landing*, near the Merritts' Cypress Pointe Plantation in Eau Gallie.

Virginia Crews, John's wife.

Ben Crews, son of John and Virginia, was a blockade runner captured and held prisoner in the North until the end of the war.

Phoebe Graves Crews, wife of Ben.

Terra Graves, botanist and Phoebe's younger sister, who is visiting the Crews.

Cypress Pointe Plantation workers, their families, and neighbors:

Philippe Cooper, half brother of Martha and Mary, worked as plantation manager.

Albert Cooper, 14 years old Philippe's son.

Tom Cooper, overseer at Cypress Pointe Plantation, half brother of Philippe.

Polly Butters, quirky cook at Cypress Pointe Plantation in Eau Gallie.

Abe Miller, Polly's suitor. Nearby farmer, who grows vegetables and fruits for the northern markets.

Winston, Butler and buck dancer.

Petunia, Mary Merritt's maid, who loves hats.

Lucky, Merritts' upstairs maid.

Flora, Merritts' parlor maid.

Bertha, Merritts' housekeeper.

Paul, Merritts' footman.

Zack, Merritts' footman.

Pablo, Merritts' pigeon master.

Jaz, young boy, Pablo's helper

Happy Dan, itinerant fiddler

Fictitious characters living, working, or visiting in real-life Enterprise, Florida and Palatka, Florida:

Michael MacNally (Mac), former Pinkerton detective and Sadie's mentor. He stands for justice, integrity, compassion, and wisdom. Respect for others and for their different practices and beliefs are important to him.

Aunt Cora Bird, Sadie's aunt and owner of Snow Bird Cottage. Author of popular women's fiction and tracts on women's suffrage and abolition of slavery (written under pseudonym), activist.

Curly and Fiona Hunter, Proprietors of the Palatka mercantile store.

Colonel Brown, provost marshal, stationed in Jacksonville.

Guillaume Lavigne, Brock House manager.

Daisy Miller, Brock House head housekeeper.

Mrs Flowers, Brock House head cook.

Percy, The Brock House negro dishwasher and serving boy with tight blond curls.

Fictitious Guests at Real-Life Brock House Hotel:

Helen Jones, Martha's planter friend from Savannah, Georgia, who suffered under Order 15 --redistribution of land. *Guest at Brock house.*

Christine Sheldon, Helen Jones' sister from Griswoldville, Georgia, whose property was burned. *Guest at Brock house.*

Luther Greim, compulsive gambler aboard the steamer, *Katie Asbell Guest at Brock house.*

Buck Stotts, salesman and ladies' man. *Guest at Brock house.*

Neville Beaumont, plantation owner and aspiring politician. *Guest at Brock house.*

Ava Maas, owner and operator of a large family mercantile store in New York City and wife of Bram Maas *Guest at Brock house.*

Bram Maas, wealthy Dutch merchant, from northern New York. *Guest at Brock house.*

Kat Ashley, governess for the fictitious family of Doctor Alvarez, south of Saint Augustine. *Guest at Brock house.*

Crew of Fictitious steamer *Katie Asbell:*

Shorty, 6'0", first mate
> **Christian, cabin boy.**
> **Jim, stoker**
> **Bill, engineer**
> **Abel, deckhand**
> **Adam, Abel's brother, deckhand**
> **Joe, deckhand/Shooter**
> **Pete, deckhand/Shooter**
> **John 'Cookie' Lane, Cook with circus experience.**
> **Jan, server**

Steamers:

E.W. Hall, **ocean-going sidewheeler.** I named this steamer in honor of my dad.
> *Katie Asbell,* river steamer named after my maternal grandmother.

Real-Life Characters, Places, and Things in 1865

These characters, places, and things were a real part of history in 1865. In keeping with their personalities, I ascribed to them fictitious interactions with my fictitious characters in the Sadie Snow Series, Books 1 and 2. Here they are in alphabetical order.

Argand **lamp** is a type of oil lamp invented in 1780 by Aime Argand. Its output is 6 to 10 candelas, brighter than that of earlier lamps.

Edwin Booth, (November 13, 1833-June 7, 1893) John's brother. He owned the acting company putting on the play at Ford's Theatre and was a well-known actor.

John Wilkes Booth, (May 10, 1838-April 26,1865) famous actor, who assassinated President Lincoln. In 1865, he was the highest paid actor in the world. He was considered the foremost *Hamlet* of his day.

The Bowery Boys and the Dead Rabbits were fierce rival New York gangs. **Bill "The butcher" Poole** was a feared Bowery Boys leader.

Jacob Brock, (July 5,1810-September 22, 1876) prominent steamboat captain and a pioneer in the early establishment of Enterprise, Florida.

Jennie Brock and Hattie Brock, daughters of Jacob Brock.

Captain Louis Coxetter, very successful privateersman and block-ade runner in the British-built runner, *Herald.* The North put a price on his head for being a "pirate." After the war he returned to the Charleston-Palatka run until 1873,

The *Darlington* Side-Wheel Steamer was owned by Captain Jacob Brock of Enterprise, Florida. It was captured by the Union Navy during the American Civil War and christened the USS Darlington. It was re-purchased by Brock after the war and used commercially between Jacksonville and Enterprise, Florida.

Enterprise, Florida is a flourishing city in Central Florida.

Everhard Faber traveled from Germany to New York **1830-1834** hunting for splinter-free wood for pencils. He found abundant red cedar in Florida's Gulf Hammock area. He bought land and timber, floated logs to the Keys, and shipped logs to the family factory in Germany.

Sam Felton, president of the Philadelphia, Wilmington, and Baltimore Railroad.

Will Ferguson, call boy at Ford's Theatre April 15, 1865.

Ford's Theatre, 511 10th St., Northwest in Washington DC was the site of President Lincoln's assassination.

Robert Gamble Plantation, originally 3,500 acres of sugarcane south of Tampa on the Little Manatee River. Robert Gamble House in Ellenton, Florida off US 301, is a Florida State Park.

Helen Getty, a 130-foot sidewheeler steamer with cabin space for 80 passengers.

Harry Hawk, (April 28, 1837-May 28, 1916) sole actor on the stage at Ford's Theatre, when Abraham Lincoln was shot. He was arrested on $1000 bond.

John Carroll Houston, (April 3, 1842-February 22, 1918) one of first permanent settlers and mayor of Eau Galli, Florida.

Laura Keene, (July 20, 1826-November 4, 1873) actress, entrepreneur, playwright, director, and theater manager. She starred in *Our American Cousin* the night President Lincoln was assassinated.

Kirk's Surprises, Kirks is a soft drink manufacturer founded in Queensland, Australia in 1865, producing a selection of soft drink flavours.

LeMat gun, .42 or .36 caliber 9-shot cap and ball black powder revolver, which also had a secondary 20 gauge smooth- bore barrel, capable of shooting buckshot. Built by Jean Alexandre LeMat of France, US patent 1856. LeMat was a resident of New Orleans, Louisiana.

Abraham Lincoln, (February 12, 1809-April 15, 1865) President of the United States. He was carried to Petersen's Boarding House after the fatal shooting and died the next day.

Mary Todd Lincoln, (December 13, 1818-July 16, 1882) President Lincoln's wife.

Lycée **Pape Clément** in french wine country, still in existence today and was supported by a very rich cleric.

Marshall House Hotel, prominent Savannah, Georgia hotel.

Petersen's Boarding House on 10th St. in Washington D.C. Is across the street from Ford's Theatre and is available for tours. Many visiting actors and actresses stayed there because it was convenient to the theater.

Pigeon Post, No established **pigeon post** existed during the Civil War, but individual hobbyists joined together unofficially. Technology progressed quickly and advances in photography made the use of pigeons practical in the **First and the Second World Wars**. By 1878 to 1957 the US military used what they called '**war pigeons**.'

Mary Surratt, boarding house owner was convicted, with three others, of conspiracy to assassinate Lincoln. She was arrested April 17, 1865 and jailed until the trial ended June 28. This was informing the actions of my Fiction heroine Sadie Snow. Mary was hanged July 7, 1865 -- the first woman to be executed by the United States government.

William Tecumseh Sherman, (February 8, 1820-February 14, 1891) former commanding general of the United States Army. Captured Atlanta and lay waste to Georgia and South Carolina. Nickname 'Cump.'

Edwin Stanton, (December 19, 1814-December 24, 1869) Pittsburgh lawyer who served as Secretary of War, questioned witnesses in the back parlor of Petersen's Boarding House.

Harriet Beecher Stowe, (June 14, 1811-July 1, 1896) Author of best-selling book, "Uncle Tom's Cabin," and her husband Reverend

Calvin Ellis Stowe, professor of Biblical Literature at Bowdoin College," traveled on the St. John's after the Civil War and purchased property at Mandarin, Florida, on the river.

Cornelius Taylor, (1785- 1849) in 1841 built a boardinghouse on top of the shell mound near the spot where Jacob Brock later built his Brock House Hotel in Enterprise, Florida.

Doctor Mary Walker, (November 26, 1832-1919) American abolitionist, prohibitionist, prisoner of war, and surgeon. In 1855, she earned her medical degree at Syracuse Medical College in New York, married, and set up a medical practice. In September 1863, Dr. Walker became the first female U.S. Army surgeon, served in the Civil War, received the medal of honor, and wore pants. Her unconventional dress, knee-length skirt over long pants, caused raised eyebrows and the occasional coarse comment.

Kate Warne, (1833 -January 28, 1868) American law enforcement officer known as the first female detective in 1856 in the Pinkerton detective agency. She discovered a plot to assassinate Abraham Lincoln before his inauguration. She created and implemented a plan that averted the assassination attempt.

Walt Whitman, (May 31, 1819-March 26, 1892) U.S. poet, journalist, and essayist. During the Civil War, his brother became ill and the poet went to Washington to nurse him. After his brother recovered, Whitman continued nursing in various Washington hospitals.

Linus Yale Jr. (1821-1868), New York locksmith, patented a new Yale lock with cylinders and pin-tumblers in June, 1865.

Jane's Deer Steaks with Bacon and Gravy

-EIGHT SERVINGS

Ingredients:

2 pounds tender deer meat

1-pound slab of bacon, sliced thin and diced

Bacon drippings from cooking the bacon

1 or 2 coffee cups of beef gravy

3/4 coffee cup of flour

1 teaspoon salt

1/4 teaspoon pepper

1 egg, beaten a little

2 tablespoons milk

1 cup finally chopped dry bread crumbs

1/2 cup crushed rice cracker crumbs (stale is fine)

2 tablespoons orange or lemon juice

Directions:

1. On a large plate, mix together flour, salt and pepper. In a shallow bowl beat together egg and milk. And in another shallow dish mix bread crumbs and cracker crumbs.

2. Cut all the fat and gristle off the deer meat, then cut it into half-inch steaks. Slice each steak again -- into a butterfly shape by cutting them horizontally, from the small part towards the large. Leave some of the large side to connect the two 'wings.' Use a wooden hammer to flatten each steak a little more and make a few small cuts around the edges of each steak, so they don't curl up when you fry them.

3. Flatten them more with the hammer until they are thinner than a baby's little finger. Dip the steaks in the flour mixture. Dip those steaks in the egg mixture, then press crumbs onto both sides.

4. Fry the cut-up bacon in your biggest iron skillet over medium heat, while you stir it. Take out the crispy bacon pieces and set aside in a dish. Carefully put all the steaks in a single layer in the pan and fry them two or three minutes on each side until golden brown. Remove from the skillet to plate and let drain. To serve: sprinkle each with orange/ lemon juice, drizzle with beef gravy, and top with crispy bacon bits.

Jane's Buttermilk Chocolate Dish Cake Recipe

Ingredients for the cake:

1/2 pound butter (1 cup)

1/3 coffee cup of unsweetened cocoa powder

1 cup water

1/2 cup thick buttermilk

Two eggs, beaten

1 teaspoon baking soda

1 1/2 teaspoons extract of vanilla

1 pound of sugar (2 cups)

1/2 pound flour (2 cups all purpose) fluffed with a fork

1/4 teaspoon salt

Ingredients for the buttermilk frosting:

1/2 pound butter (1 cup)

1/4 coffee cup of unsweetened cocoa

1/3 cup thick buttermilk

1 1/4 pounds sugar ground fine (2 1/2 cups powdered)

1 1/2 teaspoons extract of vanilla

How to Make the cake:

Heat oven to moderate temperature (350 degrees)

Slice butter and add to a saucepan on medium heat.

Add unsweetened cocoa and water. Mix well.

Stir until smooth and mingled. Remove from heat. Let cool.

In a large bowl add the eggs, buttermilk, baking soda, and vanilla. Beat together.

Slowly pour chocolate combination into the buttermilk mixture.

Mix together sugar, flour, and salt and fluff with a fork. Add to chocolate buttermilk mixture.

Pour into a greased copper or tin pie pan (9 x 13 cake pan)

Bake 30 to 35 minutes or until a knife tip comes out clean.

Cool cake for at least 30 minutes.

How to make the Frosting

Melt butter in saucepan over medium heat.

Add the buttermilk and unsweetened cocoa. Stir well.

Pour ground (powdered) sugar and vanilla extract into saucepan. Mix well with a wire whip until all of the lumps are gone

Allow to cool for a few minutes

Pour onto the cake. Cool the cake for a few minutes more. Cut into wedges or squares for your serving plate.

Jane's Zippy Carrots

2 tablespoons butter

1/4 cup brown sugar, Firmly packed

2 tablespoons prepared mustard

1/4 teaspoon salt

3 cups sliced carrots, cooked and drained

1 tablespoon snipped parsley

What to do:

Melt butter in skillet. Stir in brown sugar, mustard, and salt. Add cooked carrots, heat, stirring constantly until carrots or nicely glazed, about five minutes. Sprinkle with parsley. Makes four servings.

Books By Marsha

 **<u>Control Game : a Murder Mystery</u> Type in Browser** https://myboo
k.to/0cAL or Scan

Maria wants it. Can Liz find a banned computer game, which has power to topple governments and disrupt drug cartels, before it's used to steal free will from millions?

 **<u>Death by Alligator</u> Scan or Type in Browser** https://mybook.to/pRn
4AB

Escape to the tranquil setting of the Saint John's River in Florida with Evangeline Bright, a talented actress and amateur herbalist on the run.

 **<u>Death by Alligator LARGE PRINT</u> Scan here or Type in Browser**
https://mybook.to/3Tg7EsF

<u>Death by Séance: a Sadie Snow Historical Cozy Mystery Book 2</u>   Scan below or Type in Browser As the storm rages outside, Sadie leads a séance to calm her friends' superstitious workers. But when a family member is murdered, she becomes entangled in a dangerous investigation. With the killer still on the loose and time running out, will Sadie be able to stop them before it's too late?

FOR CHILDREN

<u>Chloe and Orangina</u> blends magic, singing, and friendship in a gentle tale set in a beautiful woodland. Chloe sings and POOF! There's a baby elephant who 's orange. They want lunch, but trouble could end their new friendship. Bonus: have fun finding an ABC of hidden animals. **Scan here or Type in Browser https://mybook.to/fYE0pPI**

<u>Chloe et Orangina – French Edition</u> Scan here or Type in Browser https://mybook.to/OAaBbK9

<u>Chloe y Orangina – Spanish Edition</u> Scan here or Type in Browser https://mybook.to/HPsyr

 **<u>You and Orangina</u> – Adult Coloring Book**. What color is singing for you? Relax. Reduce stress. Create personal color schemes. Add your name or the name of someone special. Read the completed book with Friends or make it as a Gift for that special person. You are the HERO. **Buy it Here** https://mybook.to/LwXbBY

<u>Jaeval Handles It!</u> Jaeval enjoyed his drawing class, until his teacher ERASED most of Jaeval's work and replaced it with a picture of his own! The boy wants to learn to draw, but he's angry with his teacher. Will he find the courage and words to speak out, or will he quit Art forever? **Buy it Here** https://mybook.to/p79ON

Control Game
https://www.amazon.com/dp/0999898000

Death by Alligator paperback
https://www.amazon.com/dp/0999898086

DbA LARGE PRINT
https://www.amazon.com/dp/B0CTXJMNW3

Death by Séance

Chloe and Orangina

https://www.amazon.com/dp/0999898043

Chloe et Orangina

https://www.amazon.com/dp/099989806X

Chloe Y Orangina

https://www.amazon.com/dp/0999898078

You and Orangina

https://www.amazon.com/dp/0999898051

Jaeval

https://www.amazon.com/dp/0999898035

Website & Social Media Information

Contact me for a FREE SHORT STORY and information here: Marsha@MarshaWhitneyBooks.com

And FOLLOW me for updates on new releases and promotions on FACEBOOK HERE: MarshaWhitneyBooks

and on INSTAGRAM and THREADS HERE: Tales4aDifference